Forced Union

TWISTED ARRANGEMENTS
BOOK TWO

CASSIA QUINN

Wednesday Ink

Forced Union

*To those who love a
dirty-talking bad boy. xx*

Content Information

Dear reader, before you turn the page, please know that this is a romance with dark themes and potentially difficult situations.

Content includes, but is not limited to kidnapping, stalking, needles, captivity, violence, death, spanking, dark themes, possessive/jealous hero, attempted sexual assault, gun violence, dubious consent, mention of possible infant death, age gap, mentions of sex trafficking and trauma, mention of underage rape, homosexuality, PTSD, torture, and more.

Please read the entire list here: http://cassiaquinn.com/twisted-arrangements/

XX
Cassia

Forced Union Playlist

You Put A Spell On Me - Austin Giorgio
Obsessed - Mariah Carey
Boyfriend - Dove Cameron
Power Over Me - Dermot Kennedy
Dangerous Hands - Austin Giorgio
Middle Of The Night - Elley Duhe
Dangerous Woman - Ariana Grande
Shameless - Camila Cabello
Don't Give Up On Me - Andy Grammar
I'm Yours - Isabel LaRosa
Dandelions - Ruth B.
Infinity - Jaymes Young
Listen on Spotify

Contents

CHAPTER 1

Arianna

My phone pings with the arrival of a new text message while I'm going over the final- ized plans for my sister Sophia's wedding in Italy next week. Everything is already in place and set in motion. I just like to quadruple check every single detail. Just to be sure.

Dread crawls up my spine and settles into my gut as I catch a glimpse of my phone's screen. A notification pops up, showing the sender as Unknown Caller. The chill races back down my spine and I shiver.

I wish I could save that number to my contacts and name it *Creep*. But since it's unknown, I can't do anything with it. I can't even block it.

The back of my neck breaks out in a cold sweat despite the humid, warm June weather we're having in New York City. Reaching for my phone, my thumb hovers over the screen for a couple of seconds before I swipe to open the text message.

The cold sweat turns into a full-body shiver and my

mouth goes dry.

The picture that appears was taken earlier this morning when I was meeting with Mrs. De Luca to finalize my sister's wedding plans. We were at her favorite brunch spot in Manhattan, and the photo is a closeup of me sipping from my tea cup.

My phone pings again, and I nearly drop it on my desk in surprise. It's another message from him. At least, I assume it's a *him*.

UNKNOWN

Kisa, I love the way you look in the mornings.

I shudder, set my cell on the desk and shove it away. As if that can possibly distance me from my stalker.

With a sigh, I bury my face in my hands. I can't believe I have a stalker. *Me.*

The worst part is, I have no clue who he is, or how he found me. It's not like I'm a celebrity or anything. And if he's stalking me because of my family's business, then why not target my parents, or someone who's deeper into the business?

I'm a nobody.

I want out of the mafia world I was raised in. In fact, I'm already on my way out. Mrs. De Luca has opened up a whole new world of event planning for me, and I believe I've found my calling. Something I'm actually good at doing. This potential career is my one-way ticket out of this place, far away, where this dangerous world and the people in it can't touch me ever again.

I've made myself some promises over the past few weeks. As soon as we're back from Italy, I'm going to find a job. I'm also only going to date nice, sophisticated men, who have no ties to the criminal underworld. Then I'll find a suitable husband, work my dream job, and settle into a *normal* life.

God, how I crave a normal life. A quiet existence away from all of the violence and danger this reality holds. I don't want my own children growing up like I did. I don't want them to have a mafia *don* for a father or be subjected to arranged marriages to form alliances with our enemies.

My eyes turn skyward and I run my thumb across the pearls around my throat as if they're rosary beads. Maybe, someday, God will answer my prayers.

But for the time being, God helps those who help themselves.

So I'm helping myself. I'm taking charge of the direction of my life. Starting now.

The south of Italy in summer is stunningly gorgeous. A blazing sun overhead beams down on shimmering blue waters as far as the eye can see, and the green and golden brown landscape is picturesque. The wedding venue is a sprawling villa, and adds yet another layer of exotic beauty to the scene.

Best of all is my sister Sophia's happiness. She hasn't stopped smiling since the priest pronounced her and Roman De Luca to be husband and wife. I'll admit I had my doubts about their relationship. Rightfully so, since

Roman literally kidnapped Sophia from her engagement party to another man, after forcing Papa to agree to the new arrangement. Though that all seems like ancient history now.

They're happy together. Truly happy and in love.

Which I get an ear full of, from where I sit beside my newly wedded sister, as they discuss their honeymoon plans.

Roman whispers to Sophia, loud enough that I overhear him say, "I'm keeping you in bed for two full weeks. We're going to turn off our phones, order room service for every meal, and I'm going to worship every inch of your body—again."

Sophia's cheeks redden.

"Ahh, I heard that." I purse my lips, side-eyeing them. I should have sat across the table with my other sister and cousins. "Don't you want to do something more productive, like tour Italy or England?"

"Obviously," Roman levels his yellow-hazel gaze on me, "you've never been attracted to another person. Much less in love."

He's right, I've never been in love. As far as attraction goes... again, not really. It's never been high on my priority list.

I push my food around the gold-rimmed plate. "Love is an emotion. You can be in love with someone without jumping into bed with them every chance you get. That's lust, not love."

"It's a package deal." Roman sips his wine.

There's no use arguing with him, especially today. But I firmly believe that love and lust are two separate states of being. Love is with the heart, and you can love someone without being physically attracted to them. Alternatively, you can lust after someone who you don't love—maybe even someone you hate.

One day, I want to marry for love. A kind, sophisticated, and loyal man who's a good husband and father. That's what I want. I don't need passion or lust, those emotions only seem to cloud people's minds and make them act irrationally.

Beside me, Sophia sharply inhales.

I glance over at her. "Are you okay?"

"Fine. Just fine," she squeaks.

I try not to look too closely at my sister and new brother-in-law because I have the feeling that he's doing something naughty to her under the table. In front of the entire family. I really don't want to know about it.

My phone vibrates and I pull it from the hidden pocket in my dress. Distracted by my sister's muffled moans, I mindlessly swipe to open the screen and immediately gasp. I freeze, feeling everyone's eyes on me.

"What's wrong?" Sophia asks, concern coating her voice.

"Nothing," I say, feeling the blood drain from my face. This is not good. Not good at all. I shouldn't have opened this text in front of them. "It's nothing. Please excuse me."

In a daze, my heart hammering against my ribcage, I flee inside the villa, as if that will somehow protect me from my stalker. Usually, I read his text messages when I'm alone and have some privacy. I can't believe I opened his latest one in front of my entire family. What if someone saw my screen? How would I explain it to them?

My sisters, Sophia and Ginevra, catch up with me in the hallway. I guess I'm about to figure out how to explain this, because now I have no choice. I've never been terribly good at lying.

"What is it?" Sophia asks, drawing my attention away from my phone's screen.

I lick my suddenly dry lips, and pocket my cell, wishing I could hide it away. "Really, it's nothing. My stomach just doesn't feel so well all of a sudden." I'm not usually one to try to be deceptive, but desperate times...

Sophia places her hands on her hips and eyes me. "Liar."

"Something's up," Ginevra pipes in. "You've been checking your phone all day. That's not like you. Oh! Is it a boy?" Her brown eyes brighten with misplaced excitement.

Have I been checking my phone all day? Maybe. Honestly, I'm always on edge these days—correction, the past several weeks. When will my stalker text me again? Will he include a photo of me? Sometimes I feel like I can track his movements by when and where he sees me. But I doubt he sends me a photo of myself every time he's stalking me. He could be anywhere, at any time.

Fear splashes over me like icy water.

I have to remind myself that here, in Italy, I'm safe. He can't reach me. He can't touch me while I'm thousands of miles away from him.

"No," I snap at Ginevra. "It's not a boy." At least not in the way she thinks.

Suddenly my eyes sting and my throat feels like it's closing. I choke on a sob, and turn away from my sisters.

"Oh my god, Arianna, what's going on? Are you in trouble?" Sophia comes in closer, hovering near me.

"I-I don't know. Maybe." I'm so tired of bearing this burden alone, but I also don't want to trouble either of them with it. We've always been close, but I haven't been able to find the right time or words to tell them I have a stalker. Not to mention, I don't want them to get hurt.

"Come on, just tell us." Gin rubs my shoulder. "Together we'll figure it out. Whatever it is."

I chew on my bottom lip, debating about how much to tell them. My shoulders slump as I give in to the inevitable. A half-truth won't get us anywhere. If there is a way to find out who this man is and put an end to his harassment, then I need to come clean about everything.

"Okay. Th-these started about two weeks ago." Pulling out my phone, I flip through several photos of myself, candid shots, taken around the city by my stalker.

"Someone's taking pictures of you?" Ginevra asks. "Why?"

With shaking hands, I reveal the next piece of the puzzle. "They're sent with these messages."

Sophia takes my phone and scrolls through the text thread. I visualize what she'll find in there, how he always compliments me in the photos, my demands for him to stop texting me, and his threat to kill anyone I tell about him. He insists this has to remain a secret between us or there will be consequences.

Which is another reason I've kept quiet. I don't know if he has the ability to hurt my family, but I'm not willing to risk finding out.

Sophia glances up at me. "*Kisa?* What's that?"

"I looked it up, and it means like, *kitty* or *kitten* in

Russian. I think he's Russian." That's as far as I've gotten in identifying him. It's the only real clue he's given me. Not that I can trust it, because he could be pretending to be Russian when he's not, just to throw me off.

"It looks like you have a stalker. Why didn't you tell Papa?" Sophia asks me. Gin glances back and forth between us, her golden curls bouncing, as she follows our conversation.

"You saw what he wrote. He'll kill anyone if I tell them. I shouldn't even be talking to you two about this, but hopefully he hasn't followed me here." What he doesn't know, that I've confided in my sisters, can't hurt me or them.

I rake my fingers through my hair, then immediately regret messing up the styling. "What am I going to do? I'm terrified to go back home."

My sisters exchange a worried glance.

"Are you sure you don't know who it is?" Sophia asks. "You haven't met anyone recently who seems a little... off?"

"No, no one." I've been too busy planning this wedding to have much time for social interactions.

Ginevra clutches our hands. "I've got it! What if you don't come back with us? You could stay here with cousin Elena for a while. Maybe the creep will get bored and go away, then you can come home."

"I don't know..." I take a moment to think about Gin's suggestion. I do feel safer here than in New York. At least, a little. "I guess I could stay."

Though that puts all of my plans on hold. When I decided I want to be far away from New York and the mafia world, I wasn't thinking Italy. I have way too much extended family in this country. Family that would be more than happy to marry me off to a real Italian don.

What a nightmare that would be.

Sophia nods. "I think it's a good idea. We don't have to tell Papa and Mama what's going on, though, I think we should just in case this escalates."

I sigh. My choices are either stay in Italy or go home. My stalker's been asking where I am recently. So, I guess that's really not a choice at all.

"I guess you're right. I just wish I knew who this guy is, you know?" I tell them.

If I stay in Italy with my cousin for the rest of the summer, there's no guarantee my stalker won't be waiting for me when I return home. I want to figure out his identity. Only then can he be dealt with, gotten rid of, and erased from my life.

"Well, we think he's Russian, so..." Sophia starts. Her brow creases and I know she's trying to follow the meager clues. Though I've tried to do the same a hundred times and I'm no closer to an answer now than when he sent that first creepy message.

Gin nudges Sophia. "You just had an epiphany. What are you thinking?"

"Has Papa mentioned anything about the Kozlovs since we broke our agreement with them and I married Roman?" she asks us.

"I don't think so." Ginevra looks to me for confirmation.

The Kozlovs. Russian mafia. How can I be so blind?

Any blood that was left in my face drains away and I momentarily feel faint.

"Oh my god," I whisper in horror, clutching the pearl

necklace at my throat. "Could it be Dimitri Kozlov? He's second in command and he was the backup groom if anything were to happen to Nikolai. Now that Nik's dead... And I'm the backup bride if anything happened to you, Sophia. But now you're married and I'm—" I cut myself off as the full weight of this situation sinks in.

But... why would Dimitri Kozlov anonymously stalk me? From what Papa told us, the agreement—that we broke—clearly states that if Sophia and Nikolai are unable to marry, then that responsibility falls to me and Dimitri. Except, our family hasn't made any attempts to hold up our end of the bargain. And the Kozlovs haven't made any demands of us.

I don't understand what's going on.

As far as I know, Papa has called the whole thing off. But that doesn't mean that Dimitri Kozlov is satisfied with that outcome. In fact, he's probably furious. Is he trying to punish me and my family by harassing me? What does he want? What does he think he'll gain?

My phone pings with an incoming text. All three of us lean in to read it.

UNKNOWN

See you soon, kisa.

The attached picture shows a plane ticket from New York City to Catania, Italy.

Dimitri's coming for me. Right now. This is a nightmare. I need to leave, to run and hide, before it's too late. Because I will *never* marry a man like Dimitri Kozlov.

He stands for everything that I am desperate to get away from. He's pure violence, a Russian brute. I'd rather die than become his wife.

CHAPTER 2

Arianna

Three months later

Silence. That's what I've received from my stalker since my sister's wedding day in Italy. A day that ended in chaos and fear as Papa called in favors to triple the number of guards around the villa. All of it in vain when neither Dimitri, nor anyone else, showed up for the rest of our vacation.

Eventually, Sophia and Roman went off on their honeymoon and the rest of our family returned to New York City. The abrupt drop in contact from my stalker has left me with an eerie feeling, and I'm constantly looking over my shoulder. These days I don't go anywhere without a security detail.

Now that my secret is out, will my stalker retaliate? Will he make good on his threats? Will he even resurface?

Is he Dimitri Kozlov, or was that just a guess?

I may never know. That not *knowing* is worse than

my stalker's constant harassment. At least then, I knew what he was up to, to some extent. Now? Nothing. I'm left in the dark.

My driver stops in front of Leonidas Gentleman's Club, and I crane my neck to gaze up at the towering Greek columns that support the covered entrance. Anxiety clashes with anticipation as I climb out of the vehicle and set foot on the marble stairs. I've never been inside this exclusive member's only club, but I have heard the rumors.

Rumors of... illicit affairs, a playground for the ultra wealthy where the law can't touch them and nothing is off-limits. Though wealth isn't a ticket into this club, oh no, you have to be invited. You have to know someone on the inside to even have a shot at getting an invitation from the nefarious owner, Grayson Hyde.

Luckily, Roman is a member, and through Sophia I've been invited to interview for my dream job. Joining the event planning team at Leonidas would open up a whole new world to me. If I get this job, and work here for a year or two, I'm guaranteed a spot at any event planning company across the nation.

This is my ticket out of New York. It's the opportunity I need to launch my career in this industry. With those credentials leading me into that normal life I desperately crave.

My fingers flutter over my pearls, then smooth down my Valentino dress, as my heels click on the glossy entry floor. Making my way to the reception desk, I give my name. The attendant picks up the phone to let the lead event planner, and hopefully my future boss, know I've arrived.

While I wait, I glance around the expansive foyer that's from another era, an older era. The ceiling is at least twenty feet high, with gold-painted crown molding. High windows let in an abundance of light that makes the interior glow. It's practically ethereal.

This is just the entry, I can only imagine what the rest of this palatial building must look like. While it's a little old and lavish for my tastes, there's no doubt about the power and wealth within these walls. It exudes decadence.

If these walls could talk... I can only guess at what they've seen since this club opened in the late seventeen hundreds, after the American Revolution, but well before the Civil War. Yes, I did my research on the place.

All at once, I see why Sophia is obsessed with art history. It's all about the stories.

"Arianna Pontrelli?" a voice rings out, and I spin around, toward the mention of my name.

"Yes." I come face-to-face with a woman in her late twenties. Her hair is pulled back into a bun, except for the few escaped blond ringlets that frame her heart-shaped face. Her blue-grey eyes are warm but appraising.

Finally she reaches out a hand. "I'm Tarina Ives, and I'll be interviewing you today."

I give her hand a firm shake, and offer a smile. "It's nice to meet you. Thank you for seeing me."

Her answering grin is guarded. We both know I wouldn't be here if it weren't for Sophia and Roman. While they got me in the door, it's now on me to impress this woman enough that she'll give me the job I'm after.

No pressure.

"Follow me."

Straightening my spine, I trail her further into the club. We climb a spiraling staircase to the second floor and turn down several wide, wood-paneled corridors that lead to an area that houses the offices. She walks so briskly that I barely get more than a glimpse into the rooms we pass until we're seated on either side of her desk. Two large windows overlook the sprawling side lawn.

Tarina opens her laptop and quietly reads whatever is on her screen before glancing across at me. "To be perfectly blunt, you're young and inexperienced. I don't think you're the right candidate for this job."

My heart pounds against my ribcage, but I try not to show how nervous I really am.

I lick my lips, taking in her honest assessment. "I've been working with Mrs. De Luca for the past five months. If you'd like a list of the events—"

"Mrs. De Luca is a socialite, not a professional event planner. Granted, she throws exquisite parties, but there's always someone else doing all the legwork to organize the details of those events."

"Yes, I know. And that's been me." I fold my sweaty palms in my lap.

Tarina studies me as if she doesn't believe it.

I lean forward. Chances are good that Tarina runs in the same circles as the rest of us since she's the lead planner at Leonidas. "Did you attend her summer soirée in July?"

She nods.

"What did you think of it?" I'm really putting myself out there with that question. What if she hated the event? Then this will be a very short interview.

I mentally shake away that thought. I'm damn good at what I do. I am and I know it. Now I have to prove that's true to this woman.

"Honestly..." Tarina considers her response. "It was the best one she's hosted in years. The flow was better than usual, the formality of it was edged down just enough to make the event feel more welcoming, and the catering was a pleasant surprise."

"The caterers are new in town. I took a chance on them to change it up a bit and I would certainly hire them again. As for the rest, I made some suggestions and Mrs. De Luca took them to heart. She let me take the lead on that soirée and I planned it down to the finest detail."

Tarina sits back in her chair, her gaze reassessing me after receiving this new information.

"What about the Kennedy wedding last month? Mrs. De Luca had a hand in that, if I'm not mistaken."

"Yes. She found the venue and I planned the rest. Were you there?"

"I was. The groom is a friend of a friend. Plus, it was the wedding of the season, no one wanted to miss it."

True. Manhattan Wedding Magazine had named it the wedding of the year. They even did a full piece on it for their next issue, including an interview with me. With that kind of publicity, I could make a name for myself as a wedding planner, but I have loftier goals.

Leonidas Gentleman's Club kind of goals. If I get a job at a club that's this exclusive, I can literally work anywhere in the world and for anyone.

Tarina crosses her arms. "Planning a wedding, even a massive wedding like the Kennedy's, is an entirely different beast to the New Year's Eve celebration at Leonidas."

"Oh, I'm very aware of that. But that's why I'd be part of a team here, instead of on my own. That is correct, isn't it, you have a team of planners?"

"That's right. I'm the lead event planner and normally I have five assistant planners working under my direction."

"Normally?" I ask, curious.

She sighs, dropping her arms. "I have less than four months to put on this year's grandest event at Leonidas, and one of my planners is on maternity leave, and another was fired last week. That leaves me with three, two of which seem to only be able to do one person's job. So..."

"So you're short staffed." I look her in the eye, summing up every shred of confidence. "If you give me this chance, I won't let you down. I promise. I'm a hard worker, smart, and resourceful. Just tell me what you need and I'll get it done. And not just get it done, it will be stellar."

A more genuine smile graces her lips. "You seem quite sure of yourself and your abilities, Miss Pontrelli."

"Problem solving is in my nature. I'm also very detail-oriented, and have a good aesthetic sense." I'm trying desperately to win her over, while not coming on too strong and seeming desperate. It's a tricky balance. But, in truth, I know what I'm good at, and this job is where I excel.

Tarina types on her keyboard. "I will be following up with Mrs. De Luca and the Kennedys to verify your experience. Do you have any other references?"

My stomach dives, then floats up into my throat. She's taking a chance on me, isn't she? Is this really happening right now?

I nod. "Yes, my first event was Mrs. Tiller's spring ball. I will send you her number."

"Good." Tarina stands up. "Know that this is a trial run, an internship, if you will. You'll get paid, but you're not a club employee. Impress me, make it so I can't do without you, and your employment status will change. Fail and you'll be let go of in an instant. Do you understand?"

"Perfectly." I can't keep the grin off my face. "Thank you so much."

She shakes my hand. "Don't thank me. This job is a nightmare. You'll see soon enough."

As if on cue, a booming roar sounds in the hallway outside of her office. "Miss Ives!"

Unperturbed, she smoothes her skirt. "Please excuse me for a moment. I'll be right back with your paperwork."

Curious at what the commotion is all about, I tiptoe to the door after she leaves and open it enough to peer into the hallway. The clip of her heels fades away to the double doors at the end of the corridor and she disappears inside. I catch a glimpse of an imposing masculine form before the door closes behind her. Is that Grayson Hyde's office? Must be.

Trying to mind my own business, I sit back down and text Sophia the good news. I'm still reeling, I can't believe I got the job. Even getting it on a trial basis is more than I truly expected. A place like this must have a deluge of applicants for any position that becomes available.

While my phone's in hand, a new text pops up.

CONNOR BANE

Hello Beautiful, I'll pick you up at six tomorrow. We have a reservation at Spades. I hope that's agreeable to you.

A cage full of butterflies is released in my stomach, and I allow myself a moment to mentally swoon. Connor Bane is a gorgeous, intelligent, billionaire who plays in the stock market, but is most known for his modeling career. He's one of the notorious Bane brothers and most eligible bachelors in the city. Correction, most eligible bachelors in the entire country. And he asked *me* on a date.

We met at a house party last week and spent the evening chatting about absolutely anything and everything. He's the kind of man I want to eventually settle down with, and if tomorrow goes well, we might just continue dating and see where it takes us.

I message him back, saying that Spades is an excellent choice and I'll be ready at six sharp.

Dream job today, dream date tomorrow night. Life is almost perfect. Everything I desire is moving closer and closer, almost within reach.

I tuck my phone away when Tarina comes back into her office. She sets a stack of papers in front of me, then sits in her chair and leans on the desk.

"One last word of advice," she says, visually flustered. "If you want to make it here, steer clear of the owner, Mr. Hyde. He's an ogre on the best of days. Don't say I didn't warn you."

The livid expression in her grey eyes gives me pause.

Great, so my boss's boss is a complete asshole. Noted. Tarina seems pretty level-headed so I can only guess at what he did to rile her up this much.

Even with that warning, I fill in the paperwork, sign the Non-Disclosure Agreement, and honestly would sign away my soul for this opportunity. Once it's all finished, she collects up the papers and offers me a genuine smile.

"Welcome to the lion's den."

CHAPTER 3
Dimitri

"Sweet, *kisa*." My fingers trail through her silky, deep chestnut hair as she sleeps. Her room is dark except for the faint glow of street lights through a gap in the curtains. That sliver of light illuminates her beautiful face. She looks like an angel.

My angel.

Getting past the security system, and the perimeter guard wasn't easy, but totally worth it. I haven't seen my gorgeous *kisa* in far too long. Twelve weeks, six days, and thirteen hours to be exact. I know because I've been counting the days, annoyed at each one that's passed without catching a glimpse of her, without scratching the itch of my obsession.

It's *not* an obsession.

It's revenge. It's payback for making the Kozlov Bratva look weak in the eyes of our enemies. For abandoning us when we needed the Italians the most. They broke their word and shit on us. We became the laughingstock of New York. Seemingly overnight other alliances turned their backs on us, debts owed became overdue, and people mistakenly started to think they could walk all over us.

What did all of that lead to? My uncle's murder.

Someone had the balls to eliminate him, the Kozlov Bratva's *Pakhan*, execution style, right in our backyard, on our turf. Now, more than ever, I want the Pontrelli's to pay. If they had followed through on their promise to wed their daughter to my cousin Nikolai, none of this would have happened. No one would have dared to cross my family and my uncle would still be alive. The Bratva would still have its leader.

My fingers curl into a fist in her long hair. Now I must do what I should have done months ago—take this woman as my wife. Use her as the leverage I need to control her father and his men. Then show my enemies that no one breaks a deal with the Kozlovs without penalty.

In truth, I should have insisted on our marriage as soon as her sister wed that Italian, Roman De Luca. I could have saved my uncle's life. If it wasn't too little, too late by then.

But now there will be repercussions. The man who murdered my uncle is going to find that out soon. Once I find him. And I will find him. The powerful Don Pontrelli, with all of his *capos* and soldiers, is going to help me hunt the bastard down.

I'm going to steal from him what he holds most dear, his daughter Arianna. The fool actually let his eldest daughter, Sophia, marry for love. He broke our agreement first because of blackmail then for the love of his children.

His daughters are his weakness. A weak spot that I plan to exploit.

The man's a fool for letting his daughters have so much power over him. He should have stuck with the arranged marriages he had planned out for each of them.

My *kisa* murmurs something in her sleep, drawing my full attention. I can't wait to have her in my house, in my bed, belonging to me and only me.

"Soon," I whisper to her slumbering form. "Soon you'll be all mine."

I snap a picture of her before I leave. A keepsake of this moment.

I steer my motorcycle into the underground parking garage beneath my club, the four glowing golden letters of the night club's name always sets me at ease. They blaze across the front of the building. *RIOT*.

From the garage, I take the elevator up to the top floor and it opens into the penthouse where I've lived for the past decade. The foyer leads to the living room and a breath-taking view of the bay. Floor-to-ceiling windows create an unobstructed panorama.

"Hey, *Pakhan*." Maks, my best friend and occasional bodyguard, is sprawled on the sofa, watching TV, the sound muted. "Where have you been? It's late."

I pour myself a splash of vodka from the dry bar before turning toward him. "I was out. Had some personal business to attend to."

FORCED UNION · 23

Maks grunts, and goes back to watching his silent show.

If he were anyone else, I wouldn't have humored him with an explanation, even one as vague as I just gave. But he's my oldest friend, and right now, the only man I completely trust.

Making my way through the darkened penthouse, I enter my office. The windows offer a city skyline view on this side of the building.

I drop into my leather chair, and swallow down the vodka while I wait for my computer to wake up. The glowing screen partially illuminates the sleek wood paneling around me.

A couple of mouse clicks pulls up a file containing the gruesome photos of my uncle's murder. I've been studying them ever since the funeral concluded. No way will the local police look too far into Vadim Kozlov's death—not unless I pay them to do it.

To them he's just another crime lord that met an untimely end, and they say *good riddance* to men like him. While the media latches onto all kinds of theories on who wanted Uncle Vadim dead. Some sources say it was the Irish, others the Italians. Most of those theories are wrong, while some hit closer to home. But my gut feeling says this was an inside job.

I think the Brotherhood murdered their leader. But why?

He ruled over us for the last thirty years, his men respect him, and there's never been unrest among them. All signs that the Kozlov Bratva is thriving. Except I can't shake the feeling that there's a snake among us. A viper that struck and has now vanished back among the troops.

When I volunteered to go through with the backup arranged marriage that would bind me and Arianna Pontrelli, my uncle refused. He said the Pontrellis had broken their word and there'd be no union between our families. But he also avoided punishing them for their transgression, and I don't know why.

I should have gone against his wishes and taken Arianna Pontrelli as my wife.

Did his refusal to condemn her family make him weak? I trusted that he had a plan, a reason for his decisions, but I never found out what they were before he was executed.

I wish I could blame my uncle's murder on the Irish, Italians, or even the Mexicans. That's what my brothers want me to do. As soon as I name a group, they're prepared to take them out, to seek vengeance.

If only I could shake this gut instinct that's driving me to look deeper into those closest to me. Those who had been close to Uncle Vadim. But I can't. Now I need my enemy's help to investigate my own brotherhood.

My phone pings with a new text message. I take it from my jean's pocket and swipe my thumb across the screen.

BORIS

When are we doing the ceremony? It's been almost three months since you took over and I should officially be made your second in command. It's what your uncle wanted.

Muttering a curse, I set my phone down. Boris has been on my ass about his position as my second since before the funeral. Technically, he's right. When Uncle

Vadim was our leader, our *Pakhan*, I was his second, with my cousin in the place of his third.

I was always a little uncomfortable with outranking Uncle Vadim's own son, but my father was Vadim's older brother and had run the Bratva when he was alive. Vadim always acted as if I should have stepped into my father's position instead of him. But of course I wasn't old enough to be our leader when I came to live with Uncle Vadim and my cousin Nikolai.

Instead, he made me his second, treated me like a son, knowing I'd inherit everything along with my cousin Nik. That all changed with Nik's betrayal and then death. Boris rose to fill my cousin's position as third, and now I'm stuck with him, unless I want to rock the boat and choose someone to replace him.

Which I don't want to do. Not yet. Not until I get to the bottom of my uncle's murder. The Bratva has undergone too much change already.

I'm torn between which track to pursue first—flush out Vadim's murderer or strengthen my standing by marrying Arianna Pontrelli. In truth, I need to do one in order to do the other. I need leverage.

Arianna is first. My *kisa* is the key to the larger plan I will set in motion. As much as I hate to admit it, I need the Italians, outside allies, to find my uncle's murderer.

Though I can't deny that I'm going to thoroughly enjoy taking her as my wife. I've wanted to sink my cock into that gorgeous body of hers since I first laid eyes on her. She's going to be a good wife, my very own perfect mafia princess. And best of all, she's going to be all *mine*.

CHAPTER 4
Arianna

Tarina wasted no time adding me to the event planning team. I woke up to a flurry of emails this morning, containing information on the venue, task lists, vendors to hire, and so much more. I dove in with a sense of excitement I haven't felt in a very long time—if ever.

Some time later, Ginevra pokes her head inside my room, her blond curls swaying. "Is your new boss really making you work on a Friday night? What happened to that whole nine to five idea?"

"I'm just getting caught up on everything, I don't officially start until Monday. However, I doubt I'll only be working nine to five."

"Well to celebrate your new job, Papa suggested we all go out to dinner tonight."

I rub my bleary eyes and glance at the clock, surprised that it's already after five in the evening. "Actually, I have a date tonight."

"Oh my god, you do?" Gin fully steps into my room.

"Who's it with? Is he handsome? Is this your first date? Tell me everything."

I shake my head at her excitement, and blush. "Yes, it's a first date. His name is Connor Bane."

Her jaw nearly drops to the floor. "Bane as in the Bane billionaires?"

"Yes." Heat spreads from my cheeks to my chest. "Now if you don't mind, I need to start getting ready. Give my apologies to Papa."

"Do you know what you're wearing? Can I help?" She's a frenzy of energy as she heads straight into my walk-in closet and begins pulling out potential outfits.

I groan. "Gin, can we take it down a notch?"

"Absolutely not. This is not just your first date with Connor Bane, but the first time you've even been on a date, isn't it?" She doesn't wait for an answer before she starts gathering heels to go with each dress. "You're finally taking advantage of the freedom Papa promised us. This is huge. Can't you see that?"

Hesitantly, I nod. Really, I do see what she's so excited about. After everything that our eldest sister Sophia went through with her arranged betrothals, Papa had a change of heart. He decided to break tradition and allow us to choose our own husbands.

No more arranged marriages for the Pontrelli family. We're free to date whomever we want.

Suddenly, I'm nervous. Gin's right, I haven't done this before. What if I make an idiot of myself in front of Connor? Are there certain rituals to follow, or rules to know? I really should have researched this instead of going in blind. I've just been so busy with finding a job.

Too late now. He's picking me up in less than an hour.

"I know I've already told you this, but you look absolutely stunning tonight." Connor's brilliant blue eyes sweep over my face before briefly dropping to my cleavage.

I straighten in my chair, enjoying his appreciative glance. Ultimately, Gin and I decided this dark green silk dress looked best on me. She said it brings out the green in my hazel eyes.

"You look amazing too," I tell him as I sip champagne. He's a sight to behold in that tailored suit that emphasizes his broad shoulders. His deep cerulean shirt matches his eyes so perfectly that the choice seems intentional.

I keep getting lost in his stunning blues. They're so vivid, if I didn't know any better I'd think they were colored contacts. But the *Big Apple Buzz* did an article a few weeks back that included childhood photos of Connor and his eyes were the same color then as they are now.

I'm sure that's partly why he's such a successful model. Those eyes paired with his short, dark brown hair is a stunning contrast. He's difficult to look away from.

"So, tell me more about your new job. I'm actually a member of Leonidas, so it sounds like I might see you around the club." He's so relaxed, at ease, that my nerves begin to settle.

"I officially start next week, and I know it will be hard work, but I can't wait. I'm so excited. And it would be nice to see you at the club, but as an employee I'm only supposed to interact with members in an official capacity." I offer him an apologetic smile.

"Ah, I see. Well then, I guess we'll have to keep our dates a secret from your boss."

Our *dates*? Plural? Does that mean he wants to see me again? Warmth expands in my chest.

Connor Bane is everything I want in a man. He's kind, attentive, sophisticated, and easy on the eyes. His attention is focused on me and I feel that his interest is genuine. Plus, he's not part of any organized crime family. The Banes are powerful, but by entirely legal means, as far as I know.

It's refreshing. He embodies the future that I crave.

I give him what I hope is a dazzling smile. "I am agreeable to that. I'm glad we met at that house party."

He tops up both our champagne glasses, then says, "I have a confession to make, last week wasn't the first time I saw you."

"Oh?" I quirk a brow, my heart hammering against my ribs. When did he see me? I don't remember our paths crossing before.

"The first time I laid eyes on you was during Halloween at a club. It was about two years ago." He reaches across the table and takes my hand. "Which means you must have had a fake I.D. Such a naughty girl," he says teasingly.

I swallow hard, but my tone is light. "I'll admit, I'm not always a good girl."

"I bet." He shoots me a wolfish grin, his thumb drawing circles on the back of my hand.

I barely feel his touch as my mind reels with his confession. He saw me that night, the night of the... incident that led to the first encounter with my dark knight. That's what I call the man who intervened and rescued me that Halloween. The alley was so dark, I never saw his face.

Could Connor Bane be the man who saved me? Is he my faceless dark knight who makes an appearance in my naughtiest daydreams?

I open my mouth to ask him a question, when our food arrives. I'm starving but my stomach is so full of butterflies that I can't imagine trying to eat this salmon salad. Patiently, I wait for the server to leave our table and give us privacy.

"*Bon appetit*," Connor says, giving my hand a squeeze before releasing it.

I study him for a moment, allowing him a chance to reveal his secret identity to me. When he doesn't, I press forward. "Did we also cross paths in Times Square on—"

My phone chimes, once, twice, three times, drawing my attention. It could be work, or my family.

"I'm sorry, I need to check this." I fish my phone from my clutch as Connor politely nods. Such a gentleman.

"No worries. My phone is usually blowing up at all hours, so I understand."

I glance down at my screen, and freeze.

UNKNOWN

Are you on a fucking date, kisa???

UNKNOWN

I don't like his hands on you.

UNKNOWN

Make an excuse to leave. Right now. Or
I swear I'll end his life.

Fear prickles my skin, followed by a wave of fury. How dare my stalker threaten my date. Did he choose this moment to resurface just to ruin tonight? I hate him.

I swipe out of his messages and text my security detail to give them a heads up. We're leaving. I can't risk putting Connor's life in danger more than I already have.

Anger and fear mix in my gut, causing my hands to shake. I stare at my screen waiting for the go ahead from my bodyguards.

And wait... and wait. Where are they?

"What's wrong?" Connor's serious tone brings my attention to him.

"I-I'm sorry, but I need to leave. Right now."

His brow pinches. "What's wrong? Did something happen?"

I shake my head. "I can't— I shouldn't—" I blow out a heavy breath. "Something has come up and my security team isn't responding. I can't leave without them."

"Is it something I said, or did?" He sounds genuinely concerned.

"No! Not at all. I wish I could stay, but I can't." Not without being harassed via text and putting my date's life at risk. "I'm so sorry."

"There's no need to apologize. I wish you could stay, too." Connor glances around the restaurant. "I remember them coming in with us, but now they're gone. Could someone have gotten to them? Are you in danger?"

Dread makes me momentarily light-headed. Could my stalker have taken out my bodyguards? How is that possible? He'd have to be really big, and skilled, or working with his own team.

Dimitri Kozlov is the head of the Russian mob. I found that out a while ago. He's recently taken over as their leader. If it's him, then of course he could take out two trained bodyguards. He has the resources to do anything he wants.

Panic makes my mind race. How am I going to get out of here and away from him? Without my guards, I'm a sitting duck. I'll never make it home on my own. *Think, Arianna.*

My sisters. I can call my family and they'll come pick me up.

"Come with me." Connor stands, his easy-going nature replaced with a stern countenance. "I can tell you're in some sort of danger. I'll get you out of here. Stay close to me."

"No, it's okay, I'll call my family and they'll come get me." I don't want to take advantage of his kindness, or get him involved.

He shakes his head. "The longer you sit here, the more you're exposed. Anything could happen. Let me get you out of here. Please."

"But... But you don't have any bodyguards." I point out.

Connor smirks. "I'm a Bane. No one would dare lay

a finger on me because they know my brothers have my back. My family will ruin them. You're safe with me. I promise." He holds out his palm. "Come."

I don't risk putting my hand in his, for fear that my stalker is watching. Instead, I rise to my feet and we head toward the exit. Connor tells the host to put our bill on his account as we walk out.

Outside the air is cool and crisp, tinged with the promise of autumn. Connor drapes his suit jacket over my shoulders as we wait for the valet to bring his car. A moment later, his flashy sports car idles in front of us. Connor opens the passenger door, allowing me to climb in before going around the front of the vehicle to the driver's side.

The car rumbles with a low purr, and he eases into traffic. I glance in the mirrors to see if anyone's following us. A shiver runs down my spine when I spot a black SUV on our tail.

"Do you want to tell me what's going on?" Connor asks.

"I think we're being followed." I twist in my seat to get a better view of our pursuer, but it's too dark to get a good look at them.

"I see them. Just sit back, I'll lose them." He speeds through traffic.

"You will?" I glance at him in surprise.

He grins, breaking his serious expression. "I haven't always been a good boy. I spent part of my youth drag racing with my brother Heath before cleaning up my act."

"Oh." I never would have guessed. "So you can lose them?"

"You bet I can." He blows through a yellow light and alters our course, making one sharp turn after another until I've lost all sense of direction. "Who is he?"

I hold on for dear life as Connor speeds through the city. "I don't actually know. He's been stalking me for several months."

"Hmm. My brother Niall has a security company that's okay with... bending the rules, if you need someone to track down this stalker and get him away from you."

Drag racing, rule bending... maybe the Banes aren't the upstanding citizens everyone thinks. Even so, their hands are cleaner than any mafia family member's are.

"Thanks for the offer. I just want to make it home alive." My knuckles are white from gripping the sides of my seat.

"Have a little faith. I've got this. We're going to be— *Shit!*" He slams on the brakes, I brace against the dashboard, the tires screech as he avoids plowing into the SUV that's appeared out of nowhere to block the otherwise deserted street.

Behind us, another SUV boxes us in. We're trapped. My pulse spikes with terror.

Connor turns to me, his features hard. *"Run."*

CHAPTER 5
Dimitri

As I exit the SUV my fingers ball into fists, fury has me seeing red. My *kisa* went on a date with another man. She'll regret that. She let him touch her, gaze at her exquisite body, make her blush for him. I'm done playing games with her, tonight I'm going to make her mine. *Permanently.*

I stride toward the sports car that almost gave my men the slip. To my surprise, the driver's door opens and out steps Connor fucking Bane, the man must have balls the size of Jupiter to confront me head on like this. His features are stern, the expression in his eyes unreadable. What I don't see is the one emotion that I wish was present: *Fear.*

This fucker isn't afraid of me. That's about to change. Because looking at him now, all I see is his hand on Arianna's, his lips smiling at her, his body too close to hers.

I walk right up to him and jab. My punch is so

powerful that it knocks him out cold. His body crumples onto the asphalt.

A startled cry comes from inside the vehicle. The passenger door flies open, and my *kisa* makes a run for it.

Begi, kotyonok, begi. Run, little kitten, run.

With a wolfish grin, anticipation rushing through my tense muscles, I dart after her.

She kicks off her heels, running barefoot along the filthy sidewalk. With every few steps, she glances over her shoulder, watching as I gain on her. Her eyes widen.

That's right. I'm going to get you.

My much longer stride eats up the distance between us. I catch up to her beneath a street light, and reach out, ready to grab her, to touch her body for the first time.

She spins around, facing me. For a moment, I think she's going to give up, give in and come quietly with me like a good girl. I should know by now that my *kotenok* has claws.

She lifts her arm and pepper sprays the shit out of me.

I cover my eyes with both hands, grunting at the red-hot pain in my lungs and nose. I can't breathe or see. Even so, I lunge for her, catching her by surprise. With one hand, I disarm her and lift her over my shoulder. She struggles and screams, pounding her small fists against my back. In this deserted industrial area there's no one to hear her cries for help.

Eyes, nose, and throat burning, I carry her to one of the SUVs and toss her in the back seat. She claws at me when I follow her inside. A fresh tickle of pain slashes across my face. I touch the wound, my fingers coming away bloody.

Damn, she's feisty.

"Maks, subdue her." I hold her as steady as I can while Maks injects a sedative into her arm. Then I release this fierce creature and watch as her attempts to fight back become slower, lethargic. Finally she quiets down.

"We're all good here, Boris. Tell the men they can go home," I order.

Boris shoots me one hard glance before he exits the driver's seat and marches off to fulfill my command. He's still pissed at me for not putting a firm date to his acceptance as my second, but I don't have time for that shit right now. My other plans come first.

"Maks, take us to the church. Get the fucking priest out of bed and tell him we're coming."

"You got it, *Pakhan*." He takes over as our driver.

I relax into my seat, wiping at my burning eyes, as anticipation has my knee bouncing. In less than an hour this woman will be my legally—mostly—wedded wife.

She looks so peaceful sleeping on the seat next to me. I pull her body against my side and loop my arm around her, nestling her against me, and sigh.

Maks shoots me a concerned frown in the rearview mirror, but I ignore him. He won't actually ask questions or voice his concerns—not tonight. Not while we're in the middle of this. Which is why I'm having him, and only him, as my witness for what I'm about to do.

Boris would have a fucking fit if he knew I wasn't only going to kidnap Arianna Pontrelli but actually marry her too. He'd have all kinds of questions that I'm not yet ready to answer. The only explanation I can give my men is that she's part of an unsettled debt, and I've called it due.

I can't tell them I need her father's help, or that I don't trust a single one of them other than Maks, or that my *kisa* is so much more than a debt collected.

That last part, I barely want to admit to myself.

This is pure business.

No, it's obsession.

I hate that judgmental voice in my head. It needs to shut the fuck up. I'm not obsessed with her, it's simple lust. Once she's my wife, I'll fuck her out of my system and then I'll stop thinking about her all the time. She'll stop crowding my thoughts and I'll be able to focus on work better.

Even in the past few months having to deal with my uncle's funeral, and taking over the Bratva, and investigating his death, thoughts of her have intruded as soon as I let my guard down.

One moment, I'd be gazing at the flowers during the funeral service and the next I'm thinking of the first time I saw her in that white dress with little blue flowers all over it. How if Arianna were a flower, she'd be a primrose because she's so prim and proper all the time. Then I wonder, what is her favorite flower? I know she likes fresh flowers, but I haven't been able to figure out her favorite yet.

What kinds of thoughts are those? *Absurd.* That's what they are, absolutely absurd. I'm losing my goddamn mind because of this woman.

I mentally shake my head at myself and stare out the window.

Arianna begins to stir by the time we reach the church. She'll be loopy for some hours still, and probably sleep well tonight, but I need her awake for a while. Pliable, but conscious.

Maks parks and I hand him my briefcase to carry while I lift Arianna into my arms. We enter through the front, and the sight before me is pleasing. The priest is ready, candles burning, everything set up for the ceremony. I didn't have time to purchase Arianna a wedding gown, but I do have the papers to legalize our union.

"Good evening, Mr. Kozlov," Father Misha greets us. "Did you bring the marriage license?"

"I have it here." I nod to Maks, who retrieves it from the briefcase. Sure, I could bribe the priest like I did the clerk to get this license in the first place, but I want everything from here on out to be as above board as possible. As legit as possible.

"Very good. I will sign this after the ceremony is complete." The priest briefly eyes Arianna. "Is she okay?"

I level a stern look at him. "Just do your fucking job, Father."

"Yes, sir."

With Arianna propped up beside me, Father Misha performs the ceremony. We keep it simple. The priest rambles on about marriage and oaths and such for a while before getting to the good part.

"Do you, Dimitri Kozlov, take this woman to be your lawfully wedded wife?"

"I do." My chest warms as I gaze down at her gorgeous face.

"And do you, Arianna Pontrelli, take this man to be your husband?"

She frowns in confusion. "I don't—" she slurs.

I place my palm over her mouth and force her to nod in response. "Obviously, she does."

The priest swallows hard, but this isn't the first questionable marriage he's performed, so he continues, "By the power vested in me, I pronounce you husband and wife. You may kiss the bride."

I angle my *wife's* face up to mine and stare into her unfocused eyes. Cupping her cheek, I brush a chaste kiss to her lips. Her memories of this will most likely be vague, and I want her to fully remember the first time I kiss her for real. This peck is a promise to be fulfilled at a future time.

"What's happening?" she murmurs, her body swaying into mine.

I catch her before she falls and lift her bridal style in my arms. "Father, sign that marriage license so we can get this over and done with."

"Yes, sir." He does as he's told. "Congratulations."

I grunt in response, carrying Arianna back to the car. Maks grabs my briefcase, then runs ahead to open the door.

Once we're inside, I glance at Maks, "You know where to next."

"Sure do, *Pakhan.*"

Arianna pushes away from me, wedging herself against the far door. Her eyelids droop, then spring open, as if she's struggling to stay awake. I snap a photo of her as she gazes at me.

"What..." she trails off.

She's my *wife*. I let that realization settle over me for a moment before I proceed onto the next part of my plan. My chest feels so full that it's tight. I've bound her to me before man and God, now I need to play the rest of this game carefully.

I send the photo to her father.

My phone immediately rings.

"Mr. Pontrelli," I answer his call.

"You son of a bitch, where is she? What do you want?" He's livid, his tone already laced with desperation. His daughters truly are his weakness. How fucking pathetic is that?

"I want you to fulfill your end of the deal. Arianna *Kozlov* is now my wife. We're family. I'll send my demands to you soon. Until then, don't do anything stupid. If you retaliate in any way, she's dead. Got it?"

"I understand. Please don't hurt my daughter." His anger is tempered with defeat. He won't do anything that will put her life in danger. I have no clue how he's still the head of his family. Some day, someone is going to come along and knock him off his throne.

Except... now we're joined, so if anyone tries to dethrone him, I'll have to kill them. Isn't that a funny twist?

"I won't hurt her as long as you cooperate." I hang up on him. That's now settled.

With his daughter as my wife, Pontrelli will help me hunt down my uncle's murderer. He wouldn't dare double-cross me.

When his oldest daughter, Sophia, was engaged to

my cousin I watched the whole situation unravel from afar. What I figured out by all that happened is that Pontrelli will literally do anything to protect his family— even destroy his reputation as a man of his word.

As long as Arianna belongs to me, so does her father. He'll be good and do as he's told. Just like she will.

CHAPTER 6
Dimitri

B y the time we arrive at Riot, Arianna is out cold, so I carry her up to my penthouse. I leave Maks to close the door behind us and take her into my bedroom. There I gently undress her, brush her long brunette hair, then tuck her under the covers. Her breathing is steady and even throughout. She looks like a sleeping angel.

Anger curls through me when I realize that she wore that pretty green dress for Connor Bane without any underwear on underneath. That thin piece of silk is all that lay between her body and his prying eyes.

I watch her sleep, the cave man inside me calms knowing that I've laid my claim on her. We need to consummate our marriage, but not tonight. When I plunge my cock into her sweet body for the first time, I want her eyes on me. I want her begging for it as I make her come over and over.

For now, I leave her be. We'll have a lot to talk about

in the morning. I make my way to where Maks is seated in front of the television in the living room.

"I'm going down to the club tonight. You're officially my wife's bodyguard and driver. Just don't let her out of here until I say so."

He nods. "Understood, *Pakhan*." He folds his arms and lifts a brow at me. "Do you really think this is smart? The Italians, and her family especially, are going to be pissed." I read the worry in his eyes. He's concerned about my reckless actions.

"This was the original fallback plan when her sister didn't marry my cousin. I'm simply seeing it through." I shrug.

Maks eyes me. He's known me too long to fall for my crap.

"I call bullshit. You're up to something else, but I can't quite sniff it out. What's up? And don't tell me it's about Vadim's murder. This is about *her*, why her?"

I'm not ready to answer that question. Not yet. "It's a long and complicated story. I don't want to get into it right now." I rake my fingers through my short hair. "Just keep an eye on her for me."

"You know I will." He leans slightly forward on the couch, elbows resting on his knees. "I know you're the *Pakhan* now and all, but you can still trust me to keep your secrets, Dimitri. I won't let you down."

"I know. In fact, you're the only one I trust at the moment. The others don't even know about my marriage, not yet."

"Why keep it a secret?" he asks, his expression concerned. "Why not tell them about your plans?"

I shrug. I'm not sure why I don't want them involved,

other than this gut feeling of unease and distrust for my own men. Soon enough they'll learn the truth. I can't keep Arianna hidden away, all to myself, forever. As much as I'd like to do just that.

"Just trust me," I tell Maks. "Everything will be sorted out."

I hope. One way or another. Either I'll find my uncle's murderer and avenge his death, or I'll end up dead. I just wish I knew where the threat lay hidden. I hope I'm on the right track.

But that's what I'm going to fucking find out. And soon.

Maks nods. "I trust you, *Pakhan*. See you later. I'll keep an eye on your girl."

My girl. My *wife*. I like her described as both of those things.

With one last lingering glance at my bedroom door in the hallway, I take the elevator down to Riot, to the underground club. There's a fight going on tonight between a local favorite and an out of towner.

As soon as the elevator doors open, I'm hit with the scent of sweat and blood. The mix of smells immediately sets me at ease. This is where I'm in my element, where my mind is clear and I can actually think straight. Ironic, given my past in the fighting cage. But down here neither the outside world nor my own chaotic thoughts can touch me.

Lingering near the back, I watch the rest of the match. The crowd goes wild with every punch and kick that lands, some of them rooting for one opponent over the other, but mostly they're here for the blood.

And that's what I serve them, brutality. The air is

thick with testosterone, and they eat it up. These fights are ruthless. They bring in good money.

I watch the local favorite, Ireland, as his body language alters and I can picture the glint in his eye from back here. He's done playing with his food. He's given the crowd the show they came for, now he's going in for the kill.

Sure enough, the other guy doesn't stand a chance as Ireland comes at him mercilessly, landing hit after hit. His opponent goes down and stays down. The crowd cheers and shouts as he raises his hands in victory. He smirks, showing bloody teeth.

I make my way to the ring and congratulate him on his win. "I'll try to find a more challenging opponent for you next time." I glance at the guy who's groaning on the floor.

Ireland slaps me on the back. "You can try. Either way, I'll be back next month."

"You keep drawing in the crowds like this and we'll keep that arrangement," I tell him. He makes good money for the club.

"Will do. Maybe someday you'll get in this cage with me and we can see who's the better man."

It's my turn to smirk. "I'd take you up on that offer, but I don't want to wound your fragile ego, Ireland. We both know you can't stand losing."

"Which is why I never do."

"And neither do I." I lift his hand into the air for one last round of praise from the audience before he exits the ring.

I'd enjoy a match with Ireland, he'd be an equal, and I'm honestly not sure which one of us would win. But if he lost, that would damage his reputation. And if I lost, I'd have no choice but to kill him. So, it's best we avoid fighting each other.

I stand in the center of the cage and nod to the announcer. He knows what's on my mind tonight, because I only take this stance if I'm after one thing. Blood.

His voice booms through the room. "We have a surprise fight tonight! Twenty thousand dollars goes to any man brave enough to face Dimitri "Knockout" Kozlov in the cage. Do we have any takers?"

Of course we have takers. This crowd is so full of bloodlust, at least one of them will want to get their hands dirty. Ireland knows I won't fight him, so he doesn't bother volunteering, instead he folds his arms and watches the audience.

However, the man who steps into the cage, and claims that spot for himself catches me by surprise. Boris, my second-in-command. I carefully eye him. Not only is he one of my men, he's also in his late-forties, though solidly built. I know he was a boxer in his day, so I don't dare underestimate him.

"Boris, what the fuck are you doing?" We both know that I can't let him beat me, or the rest of my men will begin to question my place as their leader.

Or is that what he wants?

"I'm doing what I need to do." He seems to deliberately leave off the word *Pakhan*. His lack of respect doesn't go unnoticed, but I also don't point it out.

"Is it the money you need?" I ask.

He shakes his head. "No. What I need is your attention."

"Well, you fucking have it." I spread my arms wide. "You want to do this, publicly? Fine, we'll do it." Apparently my second needs to be shown his place.

His grin doesn't reach his calculating eyes. "Let's do this."

The MC announces our fight. "Place your bets now, we'll start in ten minutes."

I head to a private locker room to change, as does Boris. That fucker really wants to meet me in the ring? What am I missing? How is beating the shit out of him going to make him happier to serve under me?

Ever since Uncle Vadim's death, Boris has been questioning my decisions and overstepping. If this is what he needs in order to know that I belong in charge, then so be it. I'll happily cover myself in his blood.

By the time I step into the ring, I'm both furious and looking forward to this fight.

I can't lose. If I do, then I'm not fit to lead the Bratva.

Boris wears a smug expression on his face, knowing exactly what kind of predicament he's put me in. I'm going to wipe that grin off with my fist.

For the first round we dance around each other, each of us landing a few blows. I want to learn what kind of man he is, how he fights one-on-one, before I hand him his ass. He has good technique, but it's from formal training, not from fighting for his life on the streets.

In round two Boris's meaty fists bruise my ribs, and he lands a vicious right hook across my jaw, making my ears ring. The calculated excitement in his beady eyes tells me he's assessing my skills as much as I'm judging his. He knows exactly what he's doing and what's at stake here.

This motherfucker is going down.

The crowd's roar dims as my focus narrows in on Boris. He comes in close, moving faster than I expect, and suddenly I'm on my back with him throwing punches at my face, chest, and ribs.

My raised arms protect my head as he pummels me. I taste blood in my mouth, and I grunt from the impact of each jab.

He's relentless, going for one soft spot after another. And for a second that feels like an eternity, I wonder if I underestimated him. When I feel a crack, that I know is one of my ribs, the bitter taste of defeat sours my tongue.

I can't let him win, or else I lose everything.

I'm as good as dead if I don't get up, don't get him off me before it's too late.

I drop my guard, going on the offense. My legs wrap around his hips and we roll until I'm on top.

My head swims, my vision blurring as I try to focus on him, and I jam a fist into his face. His head jerks to the side, blood spurting from his lips. I grin, satisfied to wipe that cocky expression right off.

The brutality that I normally keep on a short leash, I release on Boris. This *ublyudok* thought he could publicly humiliate me, take my place as *Pakhan*, and try to kill me in my own fucking club?

Not tonight, you piece of shit.

Only when I'm being pulled off of him by the referee do I realize that Boris is lying limp on the floor. Blood flows from his nose and mouth. I can't tell if he's dead or alive, and right now I don't fucking care either.

The audience is chanting, "Finish him! Finish him!"

That's it. This is done.

I turn to the ref. "If he's still alive, put him in storage and let me know when he wakes up."

"Yes, sir."

Shit, my second in command now needs to be replaced. As I watch him being carried out of the cage by two big guys, I wonder if he's the man I've been searching for, the snake who killed my uncle.

I'll find out soon enough when I question him, one way or another.

CHAPTER 7
Arianna

Groggy, I roll over only to find out I'm not in my own bedroom. I sit up and gasp, taking in the unfamiliar, masculine space. My mind races to reconstruct the events of last night. I went on a date with Connor Bane—the man who might be my mysterious rescuer from two years ago—but something tells me this isn't his room. No, this bedroom doesn't fit his personality at all.

The colors are too stark and cold. It lacks personality with its bare minimalist furnishings. This is the room of a man who has no heart, no warmth, and doesn't want to showcase who he is at all. A man with no soul.

I can't quite put my finger on what... That's it, the place looks staged. Like a property listing photo. Too clean and perfect.

I think back to last night's blurry details and confusion furrows my brow. Connor walked me to his car, after my stalker texted me—

Wait, where's my phone?

I reach beneath the blanket at the same time as I glance around for my clutch, only to find that I'm wearing nothing. My green dress is gone. Underwear and a bra would have shown lines beneath the dress so I'd gone without them. Last night, someone took my clothes off. Horror makes my chest clench and my pulse pounds in my ears.

More details surface. There was a car chase, and then I ran when I saw *him*.

Oh my god.

Dimitri Kozlov. I tried to fight him off when I couldn't outrun him, but he caught me anyway. Then someone drugged me. Vague images of his face swim in my mind's eye, then the inside of a church, and a... tattoo parlor.

A chill runs down my spine as I stare at my hands. On the ring finger of my left hand is a tattoo, something written in script.

Shakily, I lift my hand to read it. On two distinct lines, it reads: *Property of Dimitri Kozlov.*

Cold dread washes through me, only to be replaced by hot fury a few seconds later. At that exact moment the devil himself walks out of the ensuite bathroom. He's dripping wet, a towel wrapped low on his hips.

My furious gaze sweeps over him, taking in the swollen eye, busted lip, and myriad bruises peppering his muscular torso. Black ink tattoos cover both his arms, his chest, and run up his neck. Briefly, I drop my eyes to the deep V that disappears beneath his towel.

"Like what you see, *kisa?*" he asks, his voice grates on my frayed nerves.

"No," I snap, and the smug grin on his lips vanishes. "I don't know what game you're playing at, but you will return me to my home. *Promptly*."

"This is your home now." He steps into the closet and lets his towel drop to the floor.

My lips part in outrage. Does he have no decency?

That's a stupid question to even consider. Of course he has no decency, he's a psychopath. He's... the leader of the Russian mafia, a cold-hearted killer, and the man who's been stalking me. He kidnapped me last night.

His chuckle draws my attention to his face, and I realize I've been staring as his firm glutes. My face heats with humiliation and I glance away.

What did he just say? My mind was elsewhere.

I pin him with a glare, ignoring his half-nude body as he gets dressed. "This is *not* my home. You will release me or my father will—"

"He'll do nothing." Dimitri walks out of the closet as he tugs a T-shirt over his head. "I spoke with your father last night, after our wedding ceremony, and he understands that the deal between the Kozlovs and Pontrellis is now done. You're mine."

Wedding ceremony?

"What wedding ceremony?" I murmur.

"Don't you remember the church? Father Misha married us before witnesses and God. He's filing the paperwork today."

I shake my head, more snippets of memory from the church coming back to me. "I didn't sign any paperwork. We are absolutely *not* married."

He steps closer and some of the fear that had been

drowned out by my anger rises to the surface. His olive green eyes bore into me.

"Whether you signed or not doesn't matter. What matters is that there's a wedding license with your signature on it filed with the state. It's a done deal, *wife*."

I gape at him. He drugged and dragged me to a church, forged my signature, then tattooed his name on my finger.

What an absolute *stronzo*.

Reaching for the nightstand, I grab the vase of blue delphiniums and hurl it at his head. Unfortunately, he ducks just in time to avoid the projectile and the glass vase shatters against the far wall.

With a curse, he glances at the mess then back at me. "Those were for you by the way."

"I don't want flowers!" I seethe up at him. "I want my damn clothes back, then I want to get out of here. You cannot do this to people and get away with it." I point at my tattooed ring finger.

His expression darkens. "Actually, I can. And you're not going anywhere. I, on the other hand, have some urgent business to attend to this morning. Be a good girl while I'm away."

"Fuck you!" I say to his retreating back. I rarely curse, but this man is infuriating.

In the doorway he glances over his shoulder. "Don't worry. I promise we'll consummate our marriage soon." The door closes behind him.

Heat crawls up my neck, all the way to my hairline. My entire body trembles with fury, outrage, and horror. We will absolutely *not* be consummating anything. Ever.

What am I going to do? He took my phone, so I can't

call anyone. I'm somehow legally bound to him against my will. This is a living nightmare.

My only hope rests with Connor Bane, if he is in fact the man I think he is, the one who I call my dark knight. Will he save me this time, too? Or did Dimitri Kozlov and his men kill Connor? I have no way of knowing.

When a sob lodges in my throat, I swallow it down and straighten my back. I just got my dream job, I'll have enough money to move out of my parents house by the end of the year, and my future will be what I've envisioned for it. No way in hell am I going to let Dimitri Kozlov take everything away from me. Not without a fight.

My sister Sophia was kidnapped by a man who thought he could own her, and she ended up falling for him. That is *not* how this is going to end. My freedom is more important to me than anything.

I have to get away. Even if I have to do it on my own.

I need to find some clothes, then get out of this house. I know my family won't turn me away if I go to them, but that's what Dimitri will expect me to do. Plus, I won't be able to stay long at my parents house because of the agreement between my family and the Kozlov Bratva. I don't think the original deal still stands, but I have no doubt Dimitri Kozlov will demand that it does. My father won't rescue me, he *can't*, not without further risking his already damaged reputation.

I wanted out of this life, and this situation has only expedited my plans.

I'm leaving New York. Getting as far away from this city, and Dimitri Kozlov, as possible.

Glancing down at my tattooed finger, I let my rage

boil over, giving me courage for what I need to do. I'm practically vibrating with fury.

Climbing out of bed, I dart across the room and relieve myself in the spacious, marble bathroom. Then I enter his closet to find something to wear, and stop short.

Half the closet is full of his clothing, a few suits mixed in with T-shirts, jeans, and jackets. The other half makes my stomach drop. It's filled with women's clothing, all in my size, and my preferred colors. The shoes are my size as well, and when I open a drawer, I find bra and panty sets that are a perfect fit.

The sight leaves me with a feeling of trepidation. How long has he been planning my abduction?

It doesn't matter, I'm getting out of here.

I quickly dress, then search the room for anything of value. In one of his drawers, I find a wad of hundred dollar bills and don't hesitate stealing all of it. How much does it cost to have a tattoo removed? Plus, starting fresh under a new identity? I'm going to need all of this cash and more.

My fingers brush against the pearl necklace I always wear and I consider how much I can get from selling it. Probably a good chunk. But I'll only part with it as a last resort. My parents gave it to me for my twenty-first birthday and I love it. Some day, it may be the only thing I have left to remember them by.

Slipping into a pair of sensible heels and a jacket to ward off the autumn chill, I head for the bedroom door. Twisting the knob, I pull, but it doesn't budge. I try again. And again.

Did he seriously lock me in his bedroom?

I pound against the door. "Let me out of here, *stronzo!*"

Crossing the room, I open the drapes and discover that I'm in a penthouse, high above the street. From this room there's no fire escape access. Surely, that's a safety violation.

Sighing, I consider the situation. I'm trapped.

The door unlocks and swings open. I grab a figurine from a nearby table, arming myself. Except the man standing in the doorway is not Dimitri Kozlov. I frown, confused.

"Good morning, Mrs. Kozlov, I'm Maks, your body-guard." *Mrs. Kozlov.* That name makes me shudder. "Would you like some breakfast?"

My stomach growls at his offer, but I ignore it.

"No, I don't want breakfast. And my name is Arianna Pontrelli. You may call me Miss Pontrelli." I edge toward the open door and side-step the massive wall of muscle standing in my way. He's supposed to be my bodyguard, courtesy of Dimitri, but I don't feel safe in his presence at all. If anything, he's more likely my jailor than my protector.

Darting past him, I head along the hallway to an open floor plan kitchen, dining, and living room. To the right is a short hall that leads to the door.

Hope blossoms in my chest as I sprint for the exit, and my freedom.

I grip the handle and wrench. It won't open. What's wrong with the doors in this place? Seriously.

My gaze settles on the keypad and biometric scanner on the *inside* of the door. Who locks the front door from the inside, preventing someone from leaving? Then it dawns on me. A prison. This place is a prison.

The bodyguard, Maks, eyes me from the end of the hall. "Had those installed just last week. There's no way out of here."

He confirms my worst fears, sending me spiraling. If I can't escape, then I have to face my stalker, my abductor. I'm going to have to find an opportunity to get away, but who knows how long that will take. And in the meantime...

I shake my head to clear away those dark and distressing thoughts before they can take root. Sinking into despair is not an option.

Maks inclines his head to where I'm still holding the figurine as a makeshift weapon. "You should put that down, Mrs–." At my glare he corrects himself. "*Miss* Pontrelli. The *Pakhan* isn't an easy or forgiving man and you don't want to upset him if you can help it." He speaks with a noticeable Russian accent.

"*Pakhan?*" I ask, only somewhat familiar with the word.

"Boss."

Well, he's certainly not the boss of me.

I gaze back at Maks, placing the figurine on the entry table. Neither of these men know me at all. If they did, they'd realize that I'm neither easy or forgiving. I have my deep-seated reasons for needing out of their world, out of the life I grew up in. I'll stop at nothing to get what I want.

I've lived my entire life surrounded by men like Dimitri. Big, scary men who think they rule the universe.

In reality, they are men with huge egos and small minds. I'm not afraid of him.

If Dimitri Kozlov wants to back me into a corner, then he'll get what's coming to him. I'll make his every moment a living hell until he serves me with divorce papers. Then I'll get far away from here.

CHAPTER 8
Arianna

I'm stuck here, for now. So after breakfast, I settle in front of the television and click through the available channels. I've poked and prodded around every room in this apartment, and Maks was right, there's no getting out of here. Now all there is to do is pass the time and wait for an opportunity to escape.

"You can watch whatever you want, just mute the volume," Maks says from where he's perched at the kitchen island.

"Why?" What's the point of watching TV without hearing it?

"Because I need to be vigilant at all times, and I can't hear shit with all that white noise. Just turn the caption settings on."

I do as he requests, making note that the bodyguard can't hear over white noise. I'm sure I can use that to my advantage at some point. Besides that, Maks doesn't seem to have any weaknesses. He has to be almost six and half feet tall, just like his employer, and equally as muscular. They're both huge Russians. Their difference lies in their coloring. Dimitri has brown hair with green eyes, while Maks is blond with very pretty baby blues.

"I misspoke earlier," Maks says, his gaze glued to his phone. "The *Pakhan* is not that bad once you get to know him. He's just rough around the edges, and those edges run deep. You should give him a chance, since you're stuck with him and all."

I release a very unladylike snort. "I have no intention of getting to know him."

"He's a good man underneath. Loyal, kind-hearted, and fiercely protective."

"Are you sure we're talking about the same man? The one that kidnapped and then forced me to marry him?" I cross my arms, slouching on the sofa. "You know what, I don't want to talk about him. Tell me something about yourself."

His gaze flicks up to mine, and some emotion quickly flits through his baby blue eyes. Panic? Fear? Uncertainty, maybe? I can't quite place it, but it strikes me as peculiar.

"What about me?" He pockets his phone, shifting in his seat.

I shrug. "Anything. Tell me about yourself, Maks, it seems we'll be spending plenty of time together."

"I really shouldn't..." He frowns.

"Please?" I bat my eyelashes at him, which makes his brow furrow. "You tell me something about you, then I'll answer any question you have about me."

"I don't want to know anything about you," he says in a rush.

I arch a brow. "Oh really?"

"No offense, Miss." A faint crimson climbs up his neck. "But we shouldn't get too friendly. Dima's a really possessive man, in case you haven't already figured that out."

"Dima?" I question.

His face flushes bright red as his eyes widen. "That's — Forget I called him that. Please?"

I cock my head to one side, letting that nickname roll off my tongue. "Dima. Is that short for Dimitri?"

He nods. "But don't you dare use it, or tell him I let that slip." He sounds downright panicked. His boss really must be a tyrant.

"I won't. You have my word." I eye him, curious. "You two are close, aren't you? Did you grow up together? Are you related?" Why else would he call his boss by a nickname?

Maks quickly glances at the front door, as if to make sure Dimitri isn't standing there listening to our conversation. When he sees the coast is clear, he says, "Yeah, we grew up together."

I wait, but he doesn't elaborate. Tight-lipped, this one. Not that it matters, I won't be around here for too much longer.

That night I pretend to be asleep in the guest room when Dimitri comes in. Maks warned me that Dimitri would hate finding me in any bed but his, and

FORCED UNION · 63

that only fueled my desire to get under my captor's skin. If he hates it, good. I'm not sleeping in the same room as the man who wants to call himself my husband.

"*Kisa?*" he whispers in the dark. "Are you awake? You can't sleep in here."

He doesn't sound especially irritated. Luckily, sleeping in a different room isn't the extent of my plan tonight. When he reaches for me, I twist around in the bed and stab at him with the kitchen knife I stole earlier.

He hisses in pain, momentarily retreating. In the dark, I can't tell where I stabbed him. I was hoping to aim for his heart.

Then his hands are on mine, squeezing my wrist until I'm forced to let go of the knife. He snatches it away and flicks on the bedside lamp. I immediately spot the blood soaking through the side of his dark T-shirt. Damn, it's only a graze.

Though I didn't mortally wound his body, his gaze sparks with icy anger. I sit up straighter and glower at him.

"Is this how you greet your husband when he comes home at night?" He gestures toward his bleeding side.

I scoff. "You're not my husband. You're nothing to me."

His olive green eyes flicker with hurt. Probably because I wounded his fragile ego. What does he expect me to do, welcome him home with open arms and ask him about his day? That's ridiculous.

"I am your husband," he says, crawling onto the bed and forcing me to retreat to the other side. "And I have rules."

"Of course you do," I snap at him as I scoot away.

He advances on me. "One, we will share a bed every night. Two, you will join me for dinner. Three, you will be loyal and faithful to me until death do us part. I don't care how many men you've slept with before, but you're mine now."

I scurry away from him, but he follows until I'm about to fall off the bed. Even as my heart hammers against my ribcage at his close proximity, I see another opportunity to strike and take it.

"You don't care how many men I've given myself to before you?" I goad him. Arrogant bastards like him hate being reminded of other men, and of a woman's past with those men. Their frail egos can't handle the mere idea of competition.

His jaw ticks, irritation radiating from him. "On second thought, you'll give me their names so that I can destroy them."

I tap my chin thoughtfully. "Hmm, it's going to take me a while to get those to you. There are so many."

He clenches his teeth, his anger prickling my skin. He's a dangerous man, I know that, and I shouldn't be punching his buttons like this, but I can't help myself. I'm so... *furious*. And when I'm angry, I say and do stupid things. Apparently.

He raises his hand, the movement sudden, and I flinch, recoiling against the headboard.

"*Kisa*," he says, his tone soft, as his fingers caress my cheek. "I would never raise my hand in violence to you."

I swallow hard, having fully expected him to hit me for angering him. How far can I push him before he does strike me? That's what men with overinflated egos do, they hurt those who damage their pride. I've seen it before, in dark corners of crowded rooms, in an empty hallway when a couple thinks they're alone. Those men always lash out in private, too cowardly to show the world how pathetic they really are.

His thumb brushes over my lips, and vindictively I open my mouth and bite down—hard. The tangy, metallic taste of blood coats my tongue.

I realize my mistake when lust flashes in his eyes. My gaze widens with surprise. He doesn't see this as a punishment, but as a turn on. That was not my intention at all.

He presses his thumb further into my mouth, then part way out, then back in. His gaze flicks between my mouth and my eyes. I remain frozen in place, unsure of how to handle this situation, and his reaction to being bitten. Or the way his thumb moving in and out of my mouth is so erotic.

"I'll never hurt you," he murmurs, slipping his thumb from my mouth and swiping it across my lower lip. "I'll taste you. I'll make you mine in every way possible. I'll torment you until you're wet and begging for my cock. And I'll punish you if you're a bad girl, but I'll never hurt you."

I blink at his filthy words, my fingers curling around the necklace at my throat.

Dimitri smirks. "You're clutching your pearls. Did something I say shock you, *kisa*?"

When I don't respond, he leans in, his breath warm against my ear. "I bet if I slip my hand between your thighs right now, I'll find you wet for me, won't I? Is it my words that are turning you on, making you blush so prettily, or is it the taste of my blood in your sweet mouth?"

My pulse spikes and I'm at a loss for words. Never in my life has a man spoken to me like this before. It's utter filth. Scandalous. I clench my thighs together.

I probably shouldn't have lied about having past lovers. Now he's going to think I'm experienced in bed when I've never even been kissed. And the last thing I want to give to this terrible man is my virginity. That's mine to give, to someone worthy.

He's not worthy of a single kiss. My gaze drops to his lips. They're full and look soft, even with the healing split across them.

"Come." His voice is firm. "We're having dinner together at the dining table."

My brain finally restarts, and I remember where I am and what's going on. I certainly shouldn't be thinking about kissing or being in bed with this man. He's my stalker, my captor, he's pure wickedness.

But I've also never experienced attraction like this before. Even on my date with Connor Bane, who is beyond gorgeous, I found him nice to look at but there was no spark of lust. Honestly, I thought I was immune to such primal feelings as lust and desire. In this moment I realize how wrong that assumption was.

I swallow hard. This can't finally be happening now. Not with *this* man. It's all wrong. I refuse to give into my baser instincts.

Finally, I find my voice. "I'm not going anywhere with you. You don't deserve my company."

He stands up, gazing down at me from his imposing height. "Have you already forgotten my rules?"

"No. I'm simply choosing not to follow them." Gathering my fortitude, I fold my arms and sit up straighter in the bed. "There's nothing you can do to make me comply, so go away. Leave me alone."

He chuckles, the sound warm and vibrant. Quite opposite to the cold glare he has pinned on me.

Without another word, he lifts me up and hoists my body over his shoulder, then carries me from the room. Shock renders me compliant for all of two seconds, then I kick and scream at him, which he ignores. In the dining room, he drops me into a chair.

"Are you going to be a good girl and stay put?" He crouches down.

I shake my head, fuming. I'll never be a *good girl* for him. "Go to hell, *stronzo*."

"I didn't think so," he grumbles, reaching for me.

Cold steel encircles my wrist as he handcuffs me to the heavy metal table. I glare at him. He takes his seat and begins uncovering the dishes of tonight's dinner.

My stomach rumbles when the scents hit me. Cardamom, cumin, and garlic, then roast lamb and falafel. The spread contains all of my favorite Middle Eastern cuisine, including baklava for dessert. Next he pours us each a glass of Syrah from my favorite winery.

My chest flutters for a moment, until I remind myself that he's been stalking me for who knows how long, of course he knows what I like to eat. This has stalker vibes written all over it. There's absolutely *nothing* romantic about this dinner filled with all of my favorite things.

Absolutely nothing at all.

As much as I'd like to protest by not eating anything, I can't resist when he dishes up a plate and sets it in front of me. One bite and my gaze snaps up to meet his. "This is from Al-Amir isn't it?" I recognize their distinct spice mix.

Al-Amir is the best Lebanese restaurant in the city, but they're on the other side of town so I rarely eat there, unless it's a treat.

"It is." He looks proud of himself.

I ignore him in favor of the food. It's so good, I hardly care that I'm handcuffed to a table, forced to sit with this man who creepily knows my all-time favorite restaurant, and is surely manipulating me with this meal.

Moaning around my forkful of tender lamb, I close my eyes and savor the spices.

"Did Maks starve you today?"

I glance at him, his expression is serious, bordering on deadly. "No. This is so good, I could eat everything on this table even after having a full meal. But no, I had a salad for dinner earlier."

His green eyes warm, making the olive color rich and vibrant. The swelling of his one eye has eased, while the bruises have darkened. I'm tempted to ask him what happened, but he's not my host, he's my captor, and I have no interest in being polite to him. Heaven forbid he get the wrong idea and think I'm accepting this imprisonment.

He digs into the food on his own plate. I can't help but notice how his elbows rest on the table, and he wipes his mouth with the back of his hand instead of the provided napkin. What a brute.

I glance away, annoyed by his lack of manners. My parents put me through years of schooling in etiquette and social graces—only for me to end up here with this neanderthal. What a waste of effort. Which is exactly why I have to fight my way out of this situation. This is not where I belong.

I drink a sip of wine and clear my throat. "I need my phone back. I have work on Monday and I need to be online to do my job. I'll also need to be onsite at the venue some days, and there are vendors around the city I must visit."

My job is everything to me, an opportunity for freedom that I can't mess up. For the time being, I can work from this prison cell, but eventually I'll need to go to work in person.

"You don't need to work. You're my wife and I'll provide for you. Anything you want or need, all you have to do is ask." His heated gaze slides over my features.

He might as well pound his chest and say, 'I am man, I take care of woman'.

I narrow my eyes, tempted to find a way to stab him again, for all the good that would do. He hasn't even addressed the wound I gave him earlier, and I'm beginning to wonder if he's human at all. Surely it must hurt. Not to mention that the blood has ruined that shirt.

"You don't understand," I tell him, trying to explain this in simple enough terms for him to grasp. "I want to work. I need to have a job. If I sit around here all day, I'll go crazy."

The warmth fades from his eyes. "It's you who doesn't understand. You're mine. We will go out, together, when I say. Otherwise you'll stay here where you're safe."

"Where I'm safe?" I try to cross my arms, only remembering my wrist is restrained when I tug on it. "From where I'm sitting, you're the only person I need protection from."

CHAPTER 9

Dimitri

My wife is the most frustrating woman I've ever met. I gaze across the table at her pretty face, her disdain visible. Hell, it's nearly tangible how much she hates me. I thought offering her the world on a silver platter would make her happy. She doesn't have to work. I have enough money to give her anything she desires. But she doesn't want what I'm willing to give her for some reason.

Why does she want a job when she can have a life of leisure? Isn't that what most women want? To be doted on, cared for, the freedom to do whatever they want with their time? I don't understand why she's arguing with me about this.

Tonight I've presented her with her favorite food, the wine she loves, and the promise that she'll be taken care of, yet she glares at me. Sure, I wish she'd been good so I didn't have to handcuff her to the table. But what else was I supposed to do?

How do I make her cooperate? How do I make her see that I'll give her everything?

Maybe my expectations were too high going into this. Yes, I figured she'd be pissed off about how we married, but I hoped she'd get over it. I guess she just needs more time. It's only been twenty-four hours after all.

Impatience blazes through me. My entire body aches from fighting Boris last night, and now my side stings where she stabbed me with my own fucking kitchen knife—I'm going to have to talk to Maks about that.

I knew my *kotenok* had claws, but damn, everything I say and do with her seems to be the *wrong* thing. Even now, she watches me eat with disdain, like I'm not doing it right.

How can I catch a break?

I mull over my next words before speaking. "How about if you're good for the rest of this weekend, I'll give your phone back?"

"How about you give me my phone back and I won't suffocate you to death in your sleep?" she snaps.

I barely manage to suppress a grin. For months I've observed her out in the world. Her polite smiles, the way she keeps her back ramrod straight, and how capable she is at the events she organizes. I've known how driven she is to succeed, though I don't know what drives her to work when she doesn't have to, her family has plenty of money.

But experiencing Arianna up close and personal is more intriguing than I hoped. I'm learning that she has a temper, and she's not afraid to lash out. She seems unafraid, which is a first. Most people are terrified of me as soon as I walk into the room. My height intimidates them. The tattoos peeking out from my collar and my scarred knuckles tell the rest of my story.

But my *kisa*... she's not afraid, is she?

Shifting my expression, I scowl at her, showing my disapproval of her threat. "If you try to kill me again, I will have to punish you."

That statement gives her pause. Her gaze drops to her meal and she pushes the food around on her plate, sulking. She's stopped eating when moments ago she was devouring it.

My chest tightens with guilt. I want her happy, not looking like a whipped puppy.

"Please just let me go," she whispers. Some of the fight has gone out of her.

My gut twists this time, and my heart beats faster in panic. I can't let her go, I only just got her. After all this time... she's finally mine, and I'm keeping her forever. Not a soul can steal her away from me.

"I *can't*," my tone is tinged with regret. Because it's the truth, even if I wanted to let her go, to make her happy, I can't. Every fiber of my being recoils at the idea of being without her.

"Why?" Her searing hazel eyes are more blue than green right now. She's fucking gorgeous.

I should give her an explanation centered on my family's agreement with hers, which she already knows about. I should tell her all the business reasons why I have to keep her. How I need her to regain my standing in this city and show my enemies that I'm not weak.

But none of those reasons are the ones I want to give her. They feel shallow, lacking sincerity. On the other hand, I can't voice the truth either. She'll think I'm completely fucking insane—which I might be.

Instead I say, "You already know why. Now eat your food."

But she doesn't know why, not really. She has no idea how deep my obsession for her actually goes. I didn't know it for sure until I vowed to take her as my wife. Those two words—*I do*—set the beast inside of me free. The possessive creature that laid claim to this woman long before I wanted to admit it to myself.

I stalked her, forced this union between us, but ultimately she won. She owns me, through and through, and she doesn't even realize it.

When we go to bed that night, she silently agrees to sleep in my room. Not that I've given her any other choice. Dressed in a long satin nightgown, a robe wrapped around that and cinched at the waist, she lays stiffly beside me. She's gone from glaring daggers to an ice queen. I much prefer the passionate, spiteful side of her personality.

The strained silence hangs heavy between us until I finally drift to sleep.

"You should have wiped out the Pontrelli family for breaking their promise, not marry their daughter," Sasha complains, sitting on the opposite side of my office desk.

"That's none of your fucking business," I tell him.

He manages Riot, and his comments about my personal life and business decisions outside of this club are unwelcome.

He shakes his balding head, and mutters, "Vadim was weak for making that alliance in the first place. We don't need the fucking Italians."

"What the fuck did you just say?" I snap. My temper is getting the better of me today, but damn, sleeping beside my beautiful, sexy wife and not being able to touch her all night was absolute torment.

I'm not going to sit here and let my club manager talk shit about my deceased uncle—his former boss.

"Nothing, *Pakhan*, I'm sorry." He doesn't look fucking sorry, but he will be. Mentally, I add his name to my list of suspects who had a hand in Uncle Vadim's demise.

"Have you found out who helped Boris escape yesterday?" As if my life wasn't complicated enough. Boris not only survived our fight, but then escaped from storage. Which means someone let him out and helped him get away. Surprise, surprise that the security cameras for that time-frame weren't working.

This is why I don't fucking trust anyone these days.

"No, not yet. I'll have my guys keep looking." He sighs. "You should also know that there are some foreign Russians in town, not our guys. We don't know who they are or who they work for, but they busted up two of our guys pretty bad last night. Didn't even ask them any questions, just beat them and left them out back."

"Out back? Here at the club?"

He nods.

"Sounds like they know exactly who we are and where to find us," I muse.

"Yeah, that's what I got from their message too. *Pakhan*, we're losing face all over the city since those Italians fucked us over. First getting a shit ton of disrespect, then Vadim's death, and now unknown Russians moving onto our turf. You need to do something, *Pakhan*, before this city tears us apart."

"I am doing something. This all started with the Pontrellis going back on their word, so I've made that situation right."

He sighs and shakes his head. "They need to be punished."

Normally I'd agree with him. Except I still think this disturbance is coming from inside the Bratva, the Italians breaking their word was simply an excuse to set all this shit in motion and murder my uncle. We could have saved face by spreading the rumor that we were the ones who backed out of the Pontrelli deal, not the other way around.

In our world, deals are made, twisted, and broken all the time. What matters is who's left holding the bag. In this case, it was us, but it shouldn't have been. Most people didn't even know about our proposed alliance with the Italians, but somehow word of the deal got out and spread like wildfire.

It doesn't add up. In fact, the whole thing stinks.

I wish I could shake this feeling that my uncle was betrayed by his own men. Everything would be easier if I believed that it was the Italians who murdered him, but something about his death doesn't sit right with me when I try to blame it on the other families.

As for Boris, he challenged me to that fight with the intention to kill me. I wish I could believe that wasn't his goal. Call me paranoid, but everything about him doesn't sit right with me either. Boris has worked his way up through the ranks too quickly, first with my cousin's death, then my uncle's. Then he challenges me to a fight for leadership? He's guilty as fuck.

Now I just need to find him, confirm my suspicions, and put him down. He and whoever is helping him in his plot to overthrow me will die.

"I'll deal with the Italians," I tell Sasha. "You focus on finding Boris."

With one last nod, he gets up and leaves my office. Finally some fucking peace.

My mind immediately goes back to Arianna and how beautiful she looked when I left early this morning. I put fresh flowers by her side of the bed because I know she loves them. She's not a coffee drinker, so I left an insulated pot of English Breakfast on her nightstand along with an orange and almond biscotti.

I want to win her over, I'm just not sure how.

Maybe tattooing my name on her ring finger was too much? I don't know. She did seem especially upset about that.

I shake all thoughts of her from my head and refocus on my business. Picking up my cell, I dial Mr. Pontrelli.

"Kozlov," he greets, his tone mildly irritated.

"Pontrelli, I need your men on the lookout for my man Boris. He's a dead man walking. If you spot him, tell me and only me."

"Consider it done." He pauses. "How is my daughter?"

"Combative, stubborn, and pure hell."

He lets out a dark chuckle. "That's my girl. Remember if you hurt her, I will fucking skin you alive."

"She's safe with me," I tell him before ending the call.

Why does everyone have it in for me today? Fucking hell.

That evening after work, I head upstairs to my penthouse. It's Sunday night, but the club below is hopping. This city really never sleeps.

As soon as I step through the door, I hear raised voices coming from the kitchen.

"That was not a slappable pile!" Arianna shrieks.

"Yes it was," Maks says. "Look, there were two sevens."

"No there weren't, you put that second seven on top after you slapped it. You're a cheater!" She giggles.

"Prove it."

I enter the kitchen to find Maks with his hands full of playing cards held up over his head, and Arianna jumping up and trying to grab them. Maks laughs and taunts her.

Their easygoing banter and genuine mirth fills me with jealousy. My entire body stiffens.

"What the *fuck* is going on in here?" I glare at them both.

The smiles drop from their lips. Maks looks

panicked, he immediately sets the cards on the island and takes a step away from Arianna, who levels me with a cold glare. As if I'm nothing more than an annoyance, interrupting their time together.

She sits down and grabs Maks's cards. "I'm teaching my *cheating* bodyguard how to play Egyptian Rat Screw."

"*What?*" I blink. *Screw what?*

Maks holds up his hands in surrender. "It's not what it sounds like, *Pakhan*. It's innocent, I swear. Just a silly card game."

A silly card game. While I've been downstairs dealing with one headache after another, they've been up here playing card games and laughing? Sure she'll teach Maks something fun that she knows, but all she does is fight with me. I had to chain her to the fucking table just to have dinner with her last night.

What the actual fuck?

I know I'm overreacting, but I'm fucking jealous, envious, of their time together.

"Get dressed," I snap at Arianna. "We're going out."

"Why don't you try asking me nicely," she counters, shuffling the deck. "I'd rather stay here and play cards with Maks. He's much more fun than you are."

Fucking Maks. I shift my irritated gaze to him, and he looks guilty as fuck. Which he should.

If Arianna wants to play games, fine, we'll play games. I fish her phone out of my pocket and dangle it in front of her face, snatching it away when she reaches for it.

"If you're a good girl tonight, you can have this back. Tomorrow's Monday, you wouldn't want to miss work."

I see the defeat in her eyes before she caves, her shoulders slumping forward. "Fine."

"Good girl." I grin. "Now wear what I lay out on the bed for you."

As I leave the room, I hear her mutter, "Controlling *stronzo*," and Maks's answering guffaw. How the fuck did those two get so chummy in the span of one single day? If he weren't my childhood best friend, I'd fucking end him.

Just like that, I'm irritated and jealous all over again.

CHAPTER 10
Arianna

D imitri practically ignores me as he conducts business with various men throughout the night. I sit beside him in the booth, his arm draping over the smooth leather behind my back is the only indication of my existence. His colleagues ogle me from time to time and I feel like a trophy, a possession, nothing more than an ornament for their amusement.

If it weren't for the promise of having my phone returned to me, I'd tell Dimitri and his business associates to go fuck themselves. Instead, I keep my expression blank, my spine straight, and my chin lifted.

Every time I tug at this dress's short hem the deep neckline pulls down. It's a lose-lose situation. I feel like a cheap whore wearing this thing. And honestly, I'm surprised Dimitri would make me wear something like this, given his possessive nature. Maybe he wants to make some kind of statement, or perhaps he's simply doing this because he knows it makes me uncomfortable.

I don't really care for his reasons. He's a scoundrel.

He concludes his business with a pair of men in ill-fitting suits and they leave our table. One of them tosses me a lecherous glance and Dimitri's jaw muscles pop. Good, he's hating this as much as I am.

Dimitri removes his arm from behind me, and his massive palm landing on my bare thigh gives me a start. For the first time tonight, his gaze meets mine.

"You're being such a good girl, *kisa*. But I want you to smile, instead of looking like being at my side is torture."

I plaster a fake smile on my face, while shooting him a glare.

He chuckles, his fingers giving my thigh a soft squeeze. I absolutely *hate* how his touch makes my body warm. I do my best to ignore the unwelcome sensation. But he's a difficult man to ignore, especially when I'm sitting right next to his massive body, his spicy cologne invading my nose. Everything about him draws me in, makes me want things that I've never craved before, and I hate it.

While he's been chatting with his men, I've been daydreaming about ways to escape him. I don't normally consider myself a violent person, but every time I glance at the champagne bottle on the table, I imagine grabbing the neck, breaking the glass against the table's edge, and stabbing Dimitri in the throat. Then I'd gleefully watch as he choked on his own blood.

I wistfully sigh at my wishful thinking. If only I could turn my dreams into reality.

Dimitri eyes me. "That smile is much more genuine now, what's on your mind?"

"Murder."

"Of anyone I know?"

I nod and hum an affirmation.

He chuckles again, the sound deep and pleasant, and it goes straight through me. It's probably the only pleasant thing about him—not that I care. "Does my sweet wife really want to murder her husband?"

"Mariticide," I murmur, more to myself than to him. "I'm only your wife because of a forged document."

Irritatingly, he shrugs as if forcing me into this marriage is no big deal. "I had to do what needed to be done."

"Only because you know that I'd never willingly marry you." I give him my biggest fake smile. "You disgust me."

His green eyes flash with that hint of hurt that leaves me confounded. This man can't possibly be emotionally invested in this situation. In *me*. He doesn't know me well enough. Or maybe due to his months stalking me he thinks he knows me, even if he really doesn't. There's absolutely no history between us. I shouldn't be able to get under his skin, and yet...

"Mr. Kozlov, we have something to discuss," a man interrupts us. He and two others take the seats across the table without waiting for an invitation. As soon as they sit, the man openly leers at me.

My forced grin drops. I can't stand another second of sitting here like an idiot and taking their shit.

"Excuse me," I tell Dimitri.

His hand curls around my wrist. "Where are you going?"

I roll my eyes. "To the restroom. Relax."

He nods, as if I need his permission. Exasperation sweeps through me and I yank my wrist from his hold.

As soon as I exit the booth, the leering man smacks my ass. The sound cracks through the air. I gasp, taken completely by surprise, then round on him as fury sets in. I'm about to give him a piece of my mind when two muffled shots ring out.

His colleagues stand, drawing their guns and aiming them at... Dimitri. But then they hesitate.

I glance at Dimitri to find him holding a gun with a silencer attached to the barrel. Slowly, he shakes his head at the two men in warning. They decide to save themselves and drop their weapons as soon as the bouncers are on them. Then they're escorted out, leaving the dead man behind.

The man Dimitri shot and killed for... for smacking my ass.

I glance around at the club's VIP patrons, but hardly anyone pays much attention to us or the mess at our table. Those few who glance our way barely bat an eye at the blood. What *is* this place?

For a moment, I'm paralyzed, shocked by the casual violence. Dimitri takes my arm and steers us to a new table as a crew clears away the mess we left behind.

"Are you all right?" he murmurs against my ear. The sound is strangely comforting.

I gape up at Dimitri. "You killed him."

"I'm sure it won't be the last time I kill for you, *kisa*." He sets me on his lap and I go willingly, still stunned by his ruthlessness. Logically, I've known all along that he's a wicked man capable of terrible things. But it's different to experience that violence up front and personal.

A shiver runs up my spine and prickles over my

scalp. I should be much more afraid of this man than I have been.

Dimitri shrugs out of his leather jacket and places it across my shoulders. Warmth envelopes me, as does his spicy cologne. Briefly, I close my eyes, drinking in the newfound comfort.

Then I remember where I am and who I'm here with. *My enemy.* I try to wriggle off his lap, but his enormous hands hold me in place. I stop struggling when I feel him harden beneath my ass.

"You shouldn't solve conflict with violence," I chastise him, trying to distract us both from his erection.

"Is that so? Then how should I have handled that situation?" He sounds amused.

I turn my head so I can glare at him. "If you hadn't dressed me like a whore then maybe he wouldn't have thought it was okay to touch me."

"Oh, really?" He leans down and his breath teases my ear. "Don't you know that the way a woman dresses is never an invitation to be touched?"

I gawk at him. "What are you, a feminist now?"

"I just believe a woman should be able to wear whatever she wants without it being used as an excuse for another person to take advantage of her. Actually, I believe the same applies to men. I think everyone should take responsibility for their own actions."

"And does that belief apply to you?" I further turn in his lap to better face him and ease away from his rigid cock. "What about your actions? I don't see you taking responsibility."

"I take full responsibility. I know exactly what I've done to you and why I've done it." He threads his fingers through my hair, gripping it at the roots. "You're not just some pretty girl in a short dress to me, Arianna. You're so much more than that. I make no excuses for myself and I won't apologize either."

My breath hitches. He's looking at me like he wants to eat me alive, an expression that can only be described as hungry.

Ravenous.

I've never felt more like prey than I do right now.

But beneath his obvious hunger lurks something else, something almost desperate, or vulnerable. It's that look that frightens me the most.

"I know I'm just a pawn to you," I finally say. "I'm nothing more than the backup plan to join our two families."

"That's where you're wrong." He leans in, his lips brushing gently over mine. If I move at all, we'll kiss. I stay as still as possible, not wanting to encourage him. "You don't realize it yet, but you and I were inevitable. We're fate, *malyshka*."

"You're insane," I breathe the words.

"I know." That desperate vulnerability reappears in his gaze again. "And it's all because of you. You make me crazy."

I feel like I'm missing something monumental. Like, somehow, I should *know* him. But I don't. Maybe it's just the way he seems to be looking into my soul right now, and giving me a glimpse into his.

Or maybe he really is crazy.

He's my enemy, and I won't forget that. Ever. No matter how much he affects me physically. That's just biology, nothing more.

Abruptly, he stands with me in his arms. "It's time for bed."

Cold reality washes over me and dread settles deep in my stomach. Bed—with him.

Last night I barely slept at all for fear that I'd wake up to him assaulting me. He never touched me, and in the morning I woke to find him gone, but fresh flowers, tea, and my favorite biscotti were on the nightstand.

He's so confusing. So sweet, yet so infuriating.

I'm his prisoner, there's no denying that. Yet, up to this point at least, he's treated me like... I'm precious to him. It's unnerving. I don't know what to think.

Like right now, I'm wrapped in his jacket as he carries me through his club to the elevator. I loop my arms around his neck. His body feels strong, solid against mine. If the circumstances were different I'd consider this moment romantic.

But they aren't different. And this isn't romantic.

Even when we enter his penthouse, he refuses to let me down, instead carrying me into our shared bedroom where he sets me on the top of the comforter. He reaches for my cheek and I recoil from his touch.

His hand drops, and he sighs. "Let's get one thing straight, *kisa*, I'm not going to force myself on you. I like my women willing—more than that, I like them begging for my cock."

My cheeks flush at his vulgar language, even as heat pools between my legs. Why does he have this affect on me? I don't like foul-mouthed men.

"So until you're on your knees, begging for my cock inside your sweet pussy, that's not going to happen. Do I make myself clear?"

Hurriedly, I nod.

"Use your words, wife."

I lick my suddenly dry lips. "I understand."

"Good." He starts stripping right there in the middle of the room. First his shirt comes off, exposing his tattoos, then he kicks off his boots. His hands start in on his jeans and I know I should look away but I can't quite do it. He slides the zipper down and frees his erect cock.

My lips part with a mix of shock, horror, and awe. It's thick and veiny, bobbing as he slides his jeans off. Is he still hard because of me? Why?

His low chuckle sends a flush over my entire body, and finally I avert my gaze.

"I won't force you," he says, humor in his voice. "But I will tempt you every chance I get. I'll make you burn for me, *kisa*." He fists his dick, the motion drawing my attention. "Just think how good this is going to feel sliding inside your drenched little cunt. One day, I'm going to fuck you so good that you'll moan my name over and over. Then I'll give you the best orgasm of your life. You'll be so addicted to my cock that I'll ruin you for any other man."

Clenching my thighs, I clutch my pearl necklace, flustered by his filthy words.

"Arrogant much?" I snap at him, my gaze finally lifting to his eyes.

His smile is pure sin.

CHAPTER 11

Dimitri

T he blaring screech from my dream follows me into the waking world. I cough and roll over. Smoke. Fire alarms. My first instinct is to get to Arianna. I reach across the bed, but her spot is cold and empty.

"Shit." Pulling on a pair of sweatpants, I dart from the bedroom.

The smoke is thicker in the hallway. Frantically, I search for the source which seems to be coming from the kitchen. As soon as I set foot in there, I jerk to a stop.

Arianna is standing in front of the stove, burning newspapers. My living room drapes are on fire, the flame spreading rapidly, while Maks is doing his best to put it out.

"What the fuck are you doing?" I roar at my wife.

She's fully dressed, a small packed bag rests on the island like she's ready to go somewhere. The smoke is getting thicker by the second and I swear the temperature has risen since I stepped into this room.

Arianna glances at me and shrugs, then tosses a wad of flaming paper on the nearest area rug. The wool fibers smolder.

I stare at her, speechless. She's a fucking psycho!

Dark satisfaction unfurls in my chest. This woman, my fucking *wife*, just might be as crazy as I am. Crazier, judging from her calm demeanor as she literally sets fire to anything and everything around her. She's a goddess of Hell and I'd happily burn with her—just not today.

"Out. Now!" I bark at Maks. He nods and heads for the exit, opening the hidden staircase door in the entry closet.

Grabbing her bag with one hand, I firmly grip Arianna's arm and drag her away from the inferno. For her own sake, I'm glad she comes along without resistance. We need to evacuate and I don't really feel like hauling her out of here while she's kicking and screaming—though I would if she insists.

She coughs as we enter the stairwell that leads to the parking garage. I glance down at her, but she's plastered that aloof expression on her face that's unreadable. I'm looking forward to breaking through it to find out what the hell she's thinking.

Our rapid footsteps echo in the metal and concrete corridor. We meet Maks at the bottom of the stairs, where he's holding the door open.

"Fire department should be here any minute," he says, glancing up from his phone. "Where are we going?"

"Just take the bike and we'll meet you at The Manor."

Maks dips his head toward Arianna. "You really want to take her to that place?"

"Do you have a better idea?" I ask, shoving her through the door and walking toward my cherry red, Ferrari SF90 Stradale. "We'll be safer there than anywhere else until my penthouse is fixed up."

"All right." Maks hops onto my Harley and speeds out of the garage.

I buckle Arianna into the passenger seat, where she folds her arms and refuses to acknowledge me, staring straight ahead. I promised her punishment if she tried to kill me again, and I think attempting to burn me alive in my own apartment qualifies.

We'll be safe at The Manor in Manhattan, where violence is strictly off-limits and violators are dealt with swiftly. Of course the place is crawling with the worst of the worst, but since we're not allowed to murder each other beneath that roof, it's the safest place in the city.

I drop into the driver's seat and press my bare foot to the petal. Damn, I'm still only wearing a pair of sweatpants, but it's too late to go back for a change of clothes.

Sighing, I shift the Ferrari into gear and merge onto the quiet street. A quick glance at the dashboard shows that it's three in the morning. We'll still be able to get a few more hours of sleep after checking in at The Manor.

Unless I decide that her punishment can't wait until morning.

As I drive, my attention drifts to Arianna. She hasn't said a word. While I'm amused by her tenacity, I'm not fond of her murder-suicide attempt, or the destruction of my property. She could have burned down my entire fucking club. As it is, I'm sure the fire suppressant system activated and everything is going to be soaked.

"What the fuck were you—?" My question dies on

my lips when a spray of gunfire hits my bulletproof rear window. I grab the back of Arianna's neck and shove her head down. "What the actual fuck?"

Suspicion boils over in my mind and I glance at my new wife. Did she do this? Was her plan to flush us out of our safe haven just to send an assassin after me? I did give her phone back to her last night. Was that the first call she made, to have me killed?

That's harsh. Heartless—even for her. I really thought I felt *something* between us. A spark, mutual desire, passion. After all, the line between hate and love, loathing and lust, is a fine one.

How could I have been so wrong?

Another bullet hits my side mirror, shaking me from my thoughts. I auto dial Maks number from the dashboard and he picks up on the second ring.

"Yeah, *Pakhan*?"

"We have a very aggressive tail. Get rid of him. And change of plan, we're going to the estate. See you there."

Maks hangs up, and a few seconds later he's wedged the bike between us and the other car. He starts shooting at them to draw their attention. I speed up, trying to get more distance between us and our pursuers. Blowing through a red light, I change course away from The Manor and take the highway out of the city.

I dial my men that Maks recently, and thoroughly vetted, informing them that I want round the clock security at the estate. Then I call the caretaker to let him know we'll be there in an hour.

With all of that taken care of, I settle in for the drive and let my mind wander. Did Arianna do this, or does Boris have my place staked out, figuring he'd take me down before I managed to get to him? I don't have any answers yet, but I'm sure as shit going to get them out of my sweet wife once we're safe.

I glance at Arianna as we approach the massive iron gates, an ornate K between two eagle's heads sitting at its center. They swing open, and her lips part in awe. Despite her treachery, my chest warms. I have to admit, even in the pre-dawn light my ancestral home is a sight to behold. Its late eighteen hundreds Gothic revival style shows in its high, sharp peaked roofline. The house sits upon a hill, its sinister form giving the idea of an impenetrable fortress. Which is exactly what it is—massive, fortified, and surrounded by acres of woodland.

I'm satisfied to see a guard already stationed at the gate. He waves us through.

"What is this place?" She finally speaks.

"The Kozlov family estate, and my childhood home." I get out of the car and come around to her side to open the door. "Come. They're expecting us."

"They?" She grabs her bag from the floor.

"The caretaker and his wife, who is also the cook."

"Oh." She slides out of the car, her impenetrable mask firmly back in place.

I keep my own suspicions and anger at bay. This isn't the time or place for that conversation, but we *will* be having that discussion. Soon.

The rev of a motorcycle draws my attention as it comes up the driveway. Maks drives right up to us before killing the engine. His shaggy blond hair windblown.

"How'd it go?" I ask.

"As expected." Which means the guy was dealt with and won't be coming back. "Hey, do you recognize this guy? Nothing on him other than a Russian passport." Maks shows me the man's identification. I take a good, long look.

I make a mental note to look further into these mystery Russians. They could be responsible for Uncle Vadim's death. At this point, they seem to be trying to move in on my territory. First my men beaten and left at the club, now coming after me. I will get to the bottom of this.

"Never seen him before. He could be a hired assassin." I throw an accusatory glance at Arianna, who flips her hair over her shoulder, ignoring me again. My gaze narrows. I turn back to Maks. "Send his picture to all of our men, see if any of them recognize him."

"Consider it done, *Pakhan*."

I grab Arianna's upper arm and haul her toward the entrance, irritation crawling up my spine.

My wife thinks she wants me dead right now? Just wait until I bend her over my knee and punish her perfect ass, *then* she can fucking hate my guts.

CHAPTER 12

Arianna

Dimitri manhandles me up to the arched, double front doors. Even though he's been trying to hide it, I can tell he's livid. But I'm not sorry for what I did. His entire building burning to the ground would have served him right for ruining my life. Unfortunately, his place was much more difficult to set on fire than I expected. Mostly because it was so sterile. The damage will be minimal.

And at this point, I can't rely on my dark knight to save me from this wretched man. If he was going to appear, he'd have done so already.

I'm left on my own to deal with Dimitri Kozlov.

He just doesn't get it. I want him to let me go, to contact his lawyer and have them draw up divorce papers. I want as far away from this life as I can get, not to get sucked further into it.

If he's unwillingly to let me go, then I'll force him to do it. One day at a time, I'm going to make his life hell. Then, maybe, he'll wake up some day and realize that

I'm not worth the effort and the headache. He can find some other woman to be his trophy wife. Plenty of women would probably be glad to fulfill this role, just not me.

I want a man who will be a good husband, and eventually father. A civilized, sophisticated man. That is absolutely not Dimitri Kozlov.

The door swings open, and we're greeted by a couple in their mid-sixties. Dimitri introduces them as Kir and Nina, the estate's caretaker and cook. A thread of guilt tangles in my chest. It's because of my actions that they are up before dawn having to get ready for our arrival. If only I could spare everyone around us while taking out my wrath on Dimitri.

As soon as we're in the foyer, Dimitri, barefoot and shirtless, wanders off with them, discussing specifics about our stay, and I'm left to my own devices.

Spinning, I head toward the exit, where a guard blocks my path. He shakes his head, staring me down. Right. I'm still a prisoner.

Annoyed, I turn around and venture further into the mansion, taking in the green marble flooring, ornate trim, and high ceilings. Most of the furnishings are antiques by the look of them. I'd guess eighteen hundreds to early nineteen hundreds. Painted portraits hang on the wall in the foyer and the nearest sitting room, I also spot them decorating the stairway walls.

This... is not exactly where I imagined Dimitri growing up. There's so much lush culture in these two rooms alone. How did someone like *him* come from a place like this?

The mansion practically screams old money, sophistication, and nobility. All things that Dimitri Kozlov certainly is not.

Stepping into yet another room, I find a well-stocked and comfortable library, beyond that is a music room featuring a Steinway piano, then a lavish formal dining room done up in reds and golds. The place is massive, and pretty soon I'm all turned around as I try to find my way back to the entrance. Somehow I end up in the music room again instead of the foyer.

"Lost already?" Dimitri pushes off from the door-frame, and slowly stalks toward me. His clenched fists belie his casual tone.

Pointedly ignoring him, I pretend to be especially interested in the sheet music at the piano. I can practically feel the irritation radiating from him as he comes up behind me. Good. At least I know that I can get under his skin, even if I can't get through his thick skull.

"What the fuck were you thinking trying to get us all killed?" His tone is soft, lethal.

I pivot around to face him, crossing my arms. "You don't seem to understand that I am not your plaything. I've told you that I don't want to be married to you numerous times, but do you listen? No, you do not."

"So this is *my* fault?" His brows dip in either confusion or irritation, I can't tell.

"Exactly. You wouldn't listen to me so I have to act out instead. Do I have your attention now, Mr. Kozlov?"

His gaze darkens. "You've always had my attention, *kisa.*"

I ignore his pet name for me, and how it makes my stomach flutter, focusing on my demands instead. "Good. Now, you will have our marriage annulled as soon as possible. Then you will return me to my parents' house in the city. From then on, you will never contact me again. All of this you will agree to unless you want me to burn down this house to the ground." Though in all honesty, the very thought makes my stomach twist. I could never destroy a place this beautiful, even to spite this man.

But Dimitri doesn't know that. I hope at this point that he thinks I'm unhinged, completely psychotic, and true to my word.

He takes a step forward until I'm forced back. My backside bumps the piano, but he doesn't stop until he has me caged in, his palms resting on either side of my body, on top of the ornate grand piano. My breath hitches. He's so tall, he towers over me, displaying all of that tattoo-covered muscle.

"No, no, and *no*." His body heat seeps through my clothing, and I flush. "You're mine. You'll always be mine. The sooner you come to terms with that, the better. Besides, it's not safe for you out there. Or did you miss the part where the car was chasing us and the gunfire?"

I narrow my eyes at him. "They're after you, not me. Being with *you* puts me in danger."

Guilt and pain flash through his deep green eyes before both emotions are gone. He squints at me suspiciously. "How do I know you're not the one behind that attempt on my life? You probably weren't even supposed to be in the car with me, were you? Or was he your ride away from my penthouse?"

"You're kidding me, right?" I scoff when his expression remains hostile. "I should be flattered that you think

I'm such a devious mastermind. But no, my plan was to set your place on fire and walk out of there once the fire department arrived, then call my sisters to come pick me up. Unlike you, I don't have henchmen waiting in the shadows to do my bidding."

"So you're not trying to kill me," he muses, as his eyes search mine.

"Oh, I am trying to kill you, just not with hired assassins." God, he's so close, his proximity's messing with my head.

He pins me with a flat stare. "Stop trying to murder me."

"Then let me go," I plead.

He presses his body to mine. "Never."

I huff, frustrated, and trying to act like his nearness has no effect on me at all. When in reality, my heart's pounding so hard and fast I feel dizzy, and every molecule in my body is hyper aware of *him*. His scent invades my nose, his voice echoes in my ears, and my body sways toward his body heat.

"You're so beautiful when you're annoyed." His fingers trail across my cheek, his gentle touch startling me, leaving me more flustered than I was a moment ago. "You do remember my rules, don't you?"

Shakily, I nod. I'd been so sure that I was going to escape that I never stopped to consider what he'd do to me if I didn't manage to succeed.

"Then you know that I'm going to have to punish you for being a very naughty girl." He pushes his thumb past my parted lips, the same one I bit not so long ago. Although this time, I won't make the same mistake.

"Now turn around and bend over the piano bench. You deserve a spanking."

I shake my head and his thumb slips from my mouth. "No. I'm not a child and I'm not going to let you spank me like one." My pulse thunders in my ears.

"You can either take your punishment willingly, or I will bend you over my knee and we can do this the hard way. The choice is yours." His voice is so soft, the tone in contrast with his statement.

That's not much of a choice at all. I have no doubt he'll follow through on his threat, so reluctantly I nod and move toward the piano bench. Facing it, I lower my hands to the seat and bend over, presenting him with my backside.

This is the most humiliating position I've ever been in. I hate him for demanding that we do this at all. It's juvenile.

My cheeks flush when he lifts my skirt up, exposing my satin panties. I grit my teeth, wishing he'd get on with it so this would be over already. I can feel the heat of his gaze across my skin, and when his palm smoothes over my ass, I swallow hard.

Smack! The force of his hand coming down on my butt cheek has me gasping and rock slightly forward. My face flames with both embarrassment and anger.

He smacks my ass again and a third time, then massages my heated skin with his massive palm, rubbing away the sting. I press my lips together, refusing to utter a sound as he punishes me. I won't give him that satisfaction.

"You're taking your punishment so well, *kisa*. Such a good girl," he croons. "Such a *good girl*."

His tone and praise sends a delicious shiver along my spine and my skin tingles. I despise how he has such an unwanted effect on my body, how his deep voice resonates beneath my flesh, and how his pet name for me releases butterflies in my stomach.

It's all so wrong. Without thinking, I rub my thighs together.

He spanks me again, lower this time, his palm coming in contact with my pussy. It should hurt, and I'm completely unprepared for the wave of pleasure that spikes through me. To my absolute horror, a low, breathy moan escapes my throat.

Before I can further react, Dimitri smacks my pussy and I nearly come. My nipples strain against my shirt. A tremble shakes my body. He slides his fingers up and down my soaked satin panties and hums with approval.

"You're so wet, *kisa*. Fuck *malyshka*, this is supposed to be a punishment. Not..." He trails off.

A punishment, *right*. All I can feel is his fingers teasing my clit through the fabric and how painfully sensitive my nipples have become. To my shame, I rock back against his hand, my body demanding more. No one has ever touched me like this before and it's so... *good*.

CHAPTER 13
Dimitri

My wife's breathing in rapid, shallow pants as I toy with her clit through the saturated fabric of her panties. She looks so beautiful bent over for me, her ass pink from my spankings, and those throaty little moans she can't suppress. My cock strains against my sweatpants. If she glanced behind her, she'd see how hard I am.

She whimpers, slowly riding my hand, and all the remaining anger drains out of me. All I want to do is sink my fingers into my wife's hot pussy and worship every inch of her body.

But I don't, and won't. If I take her right now, she'll hate me for it in the morning. So I pull my hand away from her heated skin. She groans in protest.

Leaning over her, I ask, "What do you want, *malyshka?*"

Nothing between us is going to happen without her enthusiastic participation. I want her to want me and everything I can give her.

"You have to use your words. Tell me what you want and I'll give it to you."

She remains silent, refusing to tell me what she desires.

With a sigh, I straighten, pulling her up with me. "Let's go to bed. We can still get a couple hours of sleep tonight."

She nods. When she faces me, my heart stops for a split second. Her cheeks are rosy, her blue-green hazel eyes glassy and shining. Her chest heavily rises and falls. She's a sight to behold.

My gaze dips to her pretty, parted lips, the temptation to kiss her threatens to overwhelm me. So much so, that I ball my fists to keep from giving in, and turn on my heel. I'm sure she's exhausted, it's been a long night. Her tiredness is probably why her shields against me are thinner than usual.

She doesn't want me, not really, she's just too tired to resist. I don't want to take her like this. It's all or nothing. Which means tonight, both of us go unsatisfied.

"This way," I mutter.

Arianna follows me through the house to the second floor where our bedroom's located. We walk in silence. She pointedly avoids looking at me, and I know she's continuing to fight our physical attraction to each other. If only she could understand that, for me, this is about so much more than sex. I'm not sure how to make the clear without coming off as insane.

My obsession with her engulfs all of who she is, including her body, her mind, and her very soul. I want her hopes and dreams, her fears, and her secrets. Most of all I want to be the man she turns to for anything and everything.

In light of all that, maybe punishing her wasn't the right course of action, but she needs to know I'm serious. She can't act out without consequences. Even if those consequences morph into something neither one of us expected in the moment.

Her soft moans replay in my memory. My cock grows harder—like that's even possible. Fuck, this woman is going to be the death of me.

We enter our bedroom and she makes a beeline for her side of the king bed. Not bothering to undress, she curls up on top of the comforter, and her eyelids fall closed. She's out in a matter of seconds.

Carefully, I remove her shoes. Then grab a throw blanket and cover her sleeping form. She doesn't stir, even when I brush a strand of dark brunette hair away from her angelic face. When she's asleep she looks so peaceful, that scowl she wears for me fades away. I wish she always looked this content.

With a sigh of longing, I place a soft kiss on her temple.

I'm in the middle of going over the damage report to Riot and my penthouse when my phone rings—again. I know that number, and I don't feel like conversing with him right now. Of course his call was inevitable. In fact, I'm surprised he waited until after the weekend. It's been three full days since I took Arianna.

I press the button to send the call to voicemail. Moments later, my phone pings with incoming text messages. I can't get a fucking break.

ROMAN DE LUCA

I know you're ignoring me.

ROMAN DE LUCA

Pick up my fucking call, Kozlov.

ROMAN DE LUCA

We both know you're in deep shit.

Then my phone starts ringing again. *Fuck.*

I answer the call and bark, "What?"

"Don't *what* me, you son of a bitch, you know full well that the Pontrelli women are under my protection. What the fuck were you thinking?" De Luca's tone has me gritting my teeth. Fucking no one speaks to me like this and lives.

"Watch it, De Luca, I'm the head of the entire Kozlov Bratva now. Show some fucking respect."

"I'm ready to go to war for my wife's sister. Ask yourself, do you really want to go up against me and Blake Baron? They don't call him the *Black Baron* for no reason. He eats *pakhans* like you for lunch. And I can close down any import/export business you have with a snap of my fingers. So don't fucking threaten me, Kozlov, I'm not in the mood."

Shit. Frustrated, I run a hand through my hair. With all the other troubles I have going on, I don't need to add

De Luca and Baron to the mix. Everyone in the city knows not to cross them.

Which is exactly why I have a get out of jail free card with them both. It's time to cash it in.

"You owe me, remember?" I ask, leaning my elbows on the smooth desk in what used to be my uncle's home office. "I told you where to find my cousin when he took your wife captive. In exchange, you promised me a favor from both you and Baron. I'm cashing it in. Don't get between me and Arianna. She's *my wife*, De Luca. My *wife*."

A strained silence comes through the phone. He's probably trying to find a way out of this, but there isn't one, not without destroying his word of honor. Which is his main currency.

"Fine," he says. "I'll inform Baron about our arrangement."

"Good," I grunt.

"You may or may not know this already, but the Pontrelli women are tough. Arianna's going to make a meal out of you if you're not careful. And if you hurt her in any way, I'll gut you myself."

"You can keep your threats to yourself, De Luca, I have no intention of harming her. She's my wife and I take that as seriously as you do."

"Did she agree to the marriage?"

I hesitate. "Not exactly, but she'll warm up to the idea eventually."

"I doubt it. You can't force a Pontrelli to do anything she doesn't want to do."

"You'd know all about that, wouldn't you? After all, you did kidnap Sophia, before she became your wife, from her own damn engagement party to my cousin. You shouldn't throw stones."

"I don't know what you're talking about," he drawls. "That was the best decision I ever made."

I snort. What an arrogant bastard. He stole his woman away from her fiancé, but when I snatch Arianna from a date, *I'm* the bad guy? She was out on a date with Connor *fucking* Bane of all people. He's the biggest playboy in New York City. If anything, I saved her from getting wrapped up in his bullshit. She should be thanking me.

Instead she avoids me. All day she's been sitting at the breakfast nook table buried in work. Whether it's answering emails, making phone calls, or jotting down notes, she acts like I don't fucking exist. It hurts.

"How, uh," I clear my throat. "How did you win over Sophia?"

His chuckle's full of dark humor, as if he knows exactly what I'm going through with Arianna. Is it really that obvious?

"It wasn't easy, but we negotiated an arrangement that worked for both of us. A marriage of convenience. But then she tore down all my barriers, exposed my deepest, darkest secrets, and I had to confront all of my fears to win her back." He pauses. "Are you sure you're ready for that, Kozlov? Wouldn't it be easier to just let her go free?"

"I don't have anything to lose by keeping her, and everything to gain." As I say those words, unease settles in my gut.

"Sure you do. You know what, granting you the favor you're owed is hardly necessary. Baron and I will stay out of your way, you have my word. We're going to sit back and watch while Arianna chews you up and spits you out. Do you really think you're the one in control?" He laughs. "Good luck, Kozlov. Oh, and welcome to the family."

The call ends, and I stare at my phone, annoyed. What the fuck is he even talking about? I *am* the one in control. I've orchestrated this entire situation from its inception.

Crazy motherfucker.

CHAPTER 14
Arianna

For the first few days, I worked in the breakfast nook, until I discovered that the library's not only quieter, but more comfortable. Tarina has done her best to ease me into my workload, which gets heavier every single day, but I don't mind. Losing myself in work means I'm not thinking about Dimitri.

It means I can avoid thinking about how his hands felt on my skin, how his accented voice makes my body come alive, and how I acted like a wanton woman the other night. I blame it on the adrenaline from the fire and car chase, my general state of stress, and the lack of sleep that entire weekend. That's all it was. So I have no idea why I keep replaying the roughness of his hands on me that night.

I don't want him. Really, I don't. He's the last man on earth that I'd ever be happy with.

For now, we seem to have come to a kind of truce. He's as busy with his work as I am with mine, and the only time we see each other is at dinner. Lately, he hasn't even come to bed until I'm asleep, and he hasn't touched me since that time in the piano room. Which I should be grateful for instead of antsy about.

I haven't tried to escape again. Where would I go, if I did? More than likely, Dimitri would catch me and take away my phone, which I simply can't risk. My job is too important to lose.

I'll suffer through dinners with him, and whatever else, as long as it doesn't rock the boat too much. He seems truthful about not forcing himself on me, and since I'll never get down on my knees and beg for him, then sex is not something I have to worry about.

At some point he'll grow bored of me, then hopefully let me go. Or we can just keep to the status quo. I really don't care as long as he doesn't interfere with my life any more than he already has.

"Miss?"

My head jerks toward the library door. "Hi, Maks."

He shoots me a brief smile. "I brought the rest of your clothes over from the penthouse. I thought you should know."

"Thanks, I really appreciate it."

Now Maks? He's a sweetheart. Dimitri could learn a thing or two from his best friend. Never mind that. If Dimitri was anything like Maks then I'd *like* him, and I don't want that.

Maks grins. "I'll let you get back to work." He starts to close the door.

"Hey, Maks," I call after him. "Did the club reopen this week?"

A pang of guilt hits me in the chest. My intention had been to escape Dimitri, not put a bunch of people out of work while the fire was investigated and the club was shut down. I was so narrowly focused on punishing Dimitri that I didn't think about the other people my actions would hurt.

"Yeah, it opened last night. Repairs to the penthouse will take a while longer."

I give him a smile as he leaves the room. The damage to Dimitri's apartment I'm not so ashamed about inflicting. He deserves every bit of that inconvenience.

My phone vibrates and I check it.

SOPHIA

Just checking in on you again. How are things?

Ever since I managed to catch up on all of my sisters' missed calls and panicked texts, we've been checking in with each other at least twice a day. They are another reason I need to keep my phone.

Annoyance runs through me. I hate the kind of control Dimitri has over my actions, and I wish I could find something to help balance the scales. So far, he doesn't seem to have any weaknesses, but there must be something. No one is completely invulnerable.

I reply to Sophia's text.

ARIANNA

I'm doing okay, just focusing on work, so that I don't have to think about him. How did you survive the first few weeks with Roman?

SOPHIA

> Good question. It wasn't easy. But once we came to a kind of truce, he started to open up and I realized that I'd misjudged him.

Fat chance I've misjudged Dimitri. Though we do have our own truce.

ARIANNA

> Yeah but he rescued you a few times, so you already knew there were some good parts to him. Dimitri has no such qualities. I can't stay here with him forever. I can't.

SOPHIA

> I know. We're working on it. Dimitri has Papa doing something for him, maybe after that's done he'll be able to negotiate with Dimitri. If not, Roman will have to step in.

As soon as she sends that text, the three dots appear, showing she's typing some more. I wait.

SOPHIA

> I'm not going to leave you to the same fate as Ilaria.

Ilaria. I stare at the name. It's been ages since I thought about her.

ARIANNA

> I know.

Ilaria grew up with us, her family was close to ours. She was an only child and the three of us were like sisters to her. In our minds we *were* family.

Then she turned sixteen, the same year I did, and everything changed. Her father literally sold her at auction. No matter how hard we tried, we never figured out who bought her or what happened to her after that day. She simply vanished from our lives.

But her impact remains. For years after that, I thought that being good and making my father proud would guarantee that I wasn't sold off to a strange man. Once, I even told Sophia that it was our duty to fulfill our father's wishes and marry whoever he chose for us. I thought Sophia's arranged marriage into the Kozlov Bratva would pave the way for good matches for myself and Gin.

How wrong I was then.

After seeing everything Sophia went through with Roman—before she fell in love with him—I knew that I had to get out of this life. Even though father changed his mind and told us we could marry for love, I knew this world wouldn't let us go so easily.

Here I am, caught in its clutches, paying for my father's debt to the Kozlovs. It will never end. Not until I'm a thousand miles away, starting over with a new identity.

Sophia has sealed her fate with Roman, but at least they love each other, they're happy together. Ginevra still has a chance to escape this life too, and I hope she'll seize the opportunity once it presents itself. Before it's too late.

SOPHIA

I'm sorry to bring up Ilaria, you were so close growing up. I know it's been a long time.

It's fine. I need to get back to work.
Chat later.

Sophia sends a hug emoji.

I swipe over to my to-do list and try to focus on the next task, but my mind keeps drifting to Ilaria. What has her life been like for the past five and a half years? Is she still alive? How much has she suffered?

The library door swings inward, and Dimitri's broad form fills the opening. Abruptly, I stand up, immediately regretting the move when he stalks toward me, his eyes taking in my silk blouse and trousers. His gaze leaves a heated trail down my body.

I worry my bottom lip. I hate how one look from his intense, mossy green eyes gets me all flustered.

"How can I help you?" I curtly ask, crossing my arms, not at all noticing how his dark T-shirt stretches across his muscular chest and around his arms. Obviously, he should wear a larger size.

He stops in front of me, his body much too close to mine, forcing my head back in order to meet his gaze. Why does he have to be so damn tall? And smell so good?

I try to step back, but the desk I've been working at is right behind me. I'm essentially trapped between Dimitri and a hard surface—again. Irritation mingles with the nervous butterflies in my stomach.

"We're going out on Friday night." He studies my face as he speaks. "There's a big fight at The Pit that we need to attend."

The Pit. *Charming.* That definitely inspires my enthusiasm.

"Oh, so you're going to show me off to all your friends again?"

He scowls at my sarcastic tone. "I don't have any friends. It's the biggest fight of the year, everyone who's important will be there. I need to make sure you're going to behave yourself."

"I make no guarantees." Haughtily, I flip my hair over my shoulder and glance away. Pretending that he doesn't exist has been my go-to coping mechanism.

He places a finger under my chin, forcing my gaze back to his. "You will behave yourself, *kisa.*"

"What are you going to bribe me with this time? Or will it be a threat instead?" I stare into his eyes, noticing the tiny flecks of light and dark green and his thick black lashes. *Pretty.*

Mentally, I shake away that intrusive thought. What is *wrong* with me?

"Arianna," he says in a warning tone, then sighs. "What do you want? I'll give you anything—except a divorce."

I mull that over. What do I want from this difficult, brutish man?

"The freedom to come and go as I please," I reply. "I need to go into the city for work on a regular basis. I want to see my sisters and cousins, too."

"Done. Maks will drive you."

"Done?" I frown up at him, there has to be a catch. Dimitri is never this agreeable.

"Yes, done." He trails his fingertips along my jawline, the gesture both intimate and reverent. "I know you don't believe me yet, but I want you to be happy. You're *my wife*. I'll move heaven and earth for you, *kisa*."

My eyes widen at the sincerity in his voice. They're surely empty promises—*lies*—but that doesn't stop my stomach from swooping. My brain and body are not on the same page when it comes to Dimitri Kozlov. He leaves me confused, and agitated, and... warm and tingly whenever I'm around him. It's disconcerting.

Desperate to change the subject, I glance past him at a gold-framed painting above the fireplace. "This place is for royalty. How did your family end up here? Are you secretly a prince or did you steal all this stuff from one?"

I've spent days poking around this mansion, growing more and more confused by its contents. The place looks like a museum rather than a family home. A memorial of another era.

"Well, *kisa*." Abruptly, he picks me up and sets me on top of the desk, then steps between my legs, drawing our bodies even closer than before. My breath hitches when he plants his palms on my thighs. "You should know where your husband came from." His eyes search mine, but I'm not sure what he's looking for. Reading my reaction to his touch, maybe?

"I was born in Russia. My mother was a prostitute, who died when I was two years old. And my father gambled away what little money we had. When I was seven he sold me to pay off his debts, then he also died not long after. A couple years later, my uncle found me and brought me to America and raised me as his own. My cousin and I were like brothers."

My lips part in shock. *Sold?* Young girls like Ilaria are

sold, not men like *him*. I'm unable to imagine this huge, powerful man ever being so small and helpless.

I certainly didn't expect him to be so forthcoming about his upbringing.

For a moment my chest clenches to think of him so young and all alone. Abandoned by his own father, then orphaned. No child deserves that.

Without thinking, I reach for him, placing my hand on his T-shirt clad chest. His heart pounds, strong and rapid. I didn't mean to touch him, I just...

"I'm sorry," I tell him, retracting my hand, but he places his palm over mine, holding me in place. "Your uncle sounds like a good man."

"He was." Pain mixed with grief and loss lingers in his eyes.

If he were anyone else, I'd pull him in for a hug. But Dimitri Kozlov is not the huggable type. He's too large, too intimidating, too... much.

Instead, I settle for a proper response. "I'm sorry for your loss."

Somewhat to my surprise, I am sorry. Truly. I'm sorry for the loss of his uncle, but also for losing his childhood. Losing everyone and everything at seven years old had to have been hard, not to mention the trauma of his own father selling him. I can only imagine what that's like. What kind of man grows out of such a terrible childhood?

I'm looking at him, but I don't think I've really *seen* him until this moment. He's a person like the rest of us, with a whole lot of baggage.

His brow pinches, and his fingers dig into my thighs. Not in a way that hurts, more like I'm an anchor and he's trying to hold on, to ground himself in something solid. He nods, accepting my condolence.

When he hangs his head, my hands automatically slide up and around his neck. He leans forward, resting his forehead on my shoulder, and sighs like he carries the weight of the world on his back.

Uncertainty rattles me. This position is too intimate for us. Yet I don't push him away. In this moment, he's not a ruthless, manipulative asshole. He's a grieving man, who had a terrible childhood, who just wants solace. And for whatever reason, he's finding momentary peace in my arms.

I'm not sure why I don't hate it, but I don't.

I stiffen when his arms wrap around my waist and he hugs me close. When he doesn't try anything inappropriate, my body relaxes against him.

His soft sigh speaks volumes. Did this man ever get any physical affection as a child? He did grow up without a mother, as far as I know his uncle was a widower. Besides, how affectionate could a Russian mafia leader really be to his nephew?

CHAPTER 15
Dimitri

Every time we have dinner together, Arianna pretends that I don't exist. However, she can't hide the way she blushes when our fingers brush as we reach for the same dish, or her sweet little moans as she eats her favorite dishes. Nina is an extraordinary cook and she's taken up the challenge of recreating the Middle Eastern, Thai, and Italian foods that Arianna loves.

She contentedly groans around a forkful of pasta. "This is so good, I can't believe my mama didn't make it." She grows still, as if she didn't mean to speak out loud, and her gaze lands on me.

"Nina is up for any challenge. If there's anything you want, just ask her to make it for you."

She nods and goes back to staring at her plate. I watch her as I shove the delicious food into my mouth and chew. Honestly, the main reason I put the having dinner together every night rule into place is because I love watching this woman eat. She's so expressive.

I love it when she moans, when her eyelids flutter closed and she tilts her head back. I imagine that's how she looks during sex. My cock grows harder as we continue to eat, and my mind wanders to other things I'm desperate to taste. What would she do if I crawled under the table and ate her pussy for dessert?

Would she moan louder? Would that color on her cheeks deepen? I bet I could make her breathless in seconds. Someday I'm going to find out.

She drains her wine glass, and I stand up, approaching her to refill it. I don't bother trying to hide the bulge in my jeans. Sure enough, as I fill her glass, her gaze drops to my erection and she blushes again.

I lean over to murmur in her ear, "This is what you do to me, *kisa*. Tell me you want it and I'll give you the best orgasm of your life."

She meets my gaze as I pull away. "You don't know anything about women, do you?"

I lift a brow in question.

"You strutting around shoving your dick in my face doesn't make me want you." She sniffs, glancing away. "I'm attracted to a man's mind, his thoughts and feelings, and how well he can keep my interest in conversation."

I scoff. She must be lying. Women have the same urges as men. "I know you want to ride my cock as badly as I want to fuck your pussy. You just won't admit it."

"Think again." She swallows a bite of pasta. "I get more pleasure from eating this delicious meal than you could ever give me in your bed."

"Do you want to bet?" I sit down, my gaze never leaving her gorgeous face.

She lifts one shoulder in a shrug. "If only I was interested in finding out, too bad I'm not."

I scowl at my plate. Does she really want thoughts and feelings, and conversation? Or is she just fucking with me? I already told her about my childhood. What more does she want?

We make our way down the stairs at The Pit to find our reserved front row seats. Arianna, wearing a long blue silk dress that hugs her curves, looks like every man's wet dream on my arm. I want nothing more than to tear that dress from her body and fully make her mine. A lesser man would have taken her by now, but I'm not that weak. My patience is endless. I *will* have her on her knees, begging. It's only a matter of time.

I've seen how she reacts to me every time we're near each other. There's chemistry, attraction, whatever you want to call it. Try as she might, she can't hide her flushed cheeks, the way her pupils dilate at my touch, or how flustered she becomes when we're close to each other. She wants me. She's just too stubborn to admit it.

If I didn't have to show her off publicly, to let them all see that I take what's mine, settle a debt owed, I'd hide her away from all of their leers. I hated the way people looked at her that night when I took her down to Riot. Tonight's no different. My lip curls as men, and women, explore my wife's body with their heated gazes.

I wish I could pluck their fucking eyeballs out.

At least I don't have to worry about her acting out tonight. She's been nothing but perfect since we arrived, all smiles and polite charm for everyone—everyone except for me. I try not to show my annoyance.

We take our seats, then order drinks. A vodka for me and Syrah for her.

As the crowd around us grows and becomes louder, I watch my wife. She sits with her back straight, head held high, sparing a polite smile for everyone who stops to say hello. She even sips her wine like a goddamn queen.

For the first time, I fully realize who she is in our world. She's smart, strong-willed, and not afraid to speak her mind. She's mafia royalty, the daughter of a don, a powerful woman in her own right.

And I stole her under the guise of upholding an agreement that we both know was broken and buried. But that hasn't changed her. Even with a suit-wearing thug for a father, she radiates pure class. She's become more refined since spending time with Roman's mother, Isabella De Luca, the matriarch of Manhattan high society.

In contrast, I'm the son of a gambler and a whore. I was born into this world destined to be a nobody. No wonder she looks at me like I'm trash.

My fingers ball into fists and I glance away from her, only for my eyes to be drawn right back to her profile. She's impossible to look away from for any length of time.

The crowd around us goes wild as the fighters enter the ring. They're announced, and then the fight begins. Normally, my full attention would be on the combatants, looking for their tells, sizing them up, but not tonight.

Tonight a lead weight has settled in my gut and suddenly I'm conflicted. The differences between Arianna and me seem more vast than before. I've never been comfortable in a suit, or among sophisticated people. Hell, I should be in that ring right now, covered in sweat and blood, not here in the front row, and certainly not the owner of this venue.

Deep down, I'm just a fighter. Always have been, always will be. I let my knuckles do the talking.

This goddess beside me deserves more than that. She should be with a man who's her equal in every way, and for the first time, I'm beginning to doubt that man is me.

Having her for myself is probably a temporary reality, one that's not going to last. She already knows she's too good for me. Instinctively, I know that too, but I refuse to admit it to myself. So why is this coming up now?

Then it hits me. It's because she doesn't fit in here with this blood-thirsty audience. Her beauty clashes with this crass, brutal environment. I never should have brought her here. She already thinks I'm a brute, this further supports her bad opinion of me. Damn it.

It's not like I can change who I am.

But you also don't have to force her into your ruthless world. I sigh, hating that nagging voice in the back of my mind.

I glance back at the ring just as one fighter slams the other against the cage's wall. Arianna gasps and clutches my arm. The fact that her immediate response is to hold onto me for safety sends a thrill up my spine.

Of course the moment is ruined when she releases her grip, like touching me burns her skin.

But... her reaction, to turn to me in the first place, gives me hope.

Dangerous fucking hope.

I can't help but smile.

R ound after round, Arianna kept her eyes glued to the cage as if she couldn't look away for even a moment. I can't tell if she was horrified or enthralled. Maybe a bit of both.

Silence weighs heavily between us in the back of the car on our way home to the estate. I brush a stand of hair from her shoulder and she shivers.

"You were a good girl tonight," I praise her. "Maks will drive you to work on Monday, as I promised."

Her gaze finally finds mine. "Thank you."

She's so distant and polite, it grates on my nerves. I prefer her fire, the way her eyes flare when she argues with me, over this superficial façade she puts on. But we also can't be arguing all the time. It's counterproductive.

"I have another reward for you, too." My chest tightens, hoping she'll like the gift I bought for her.

She lifts a perfect eyebrow, and her cheeks grow pink. "Oh?"

Her reaction makes me suspect that she's thinking dirty thoughts. I search her gaze, trying to read her mind and how she feels, but I come up empty. She leaves me off balance all too often. I can't tell if I'm making progress with her or if she hates me more with each passing day—she's just getting better at hiding it.

I clear my throat. "It's at the house, in my office."

"What is it?" Her tone's wary.

"You'll see." I rest my hand on her thigh and she tenses before angling away to gaze out the window. The small rejection tears at me, just like every other time she's acted like I don't fucking exist when I'm sitting right here.

Will she ever see me as anything other than her abductor?

We pull into the garage and I help her out of the car. She only hesitates a moment before placing her hand in mine, but I can't tell if she wants my help or if she's just being polite. God this woman drives me crazy.

Getting a better grip on her, I entwine our fingers and lead her into the house. She doesn't resist as I tow her along to my office. And her passive acceptance makes me fucking giddy. What's wrong with me? I'm acting like I've never held hands with a girl before. Which come to think of it, I haven't.

Inside, I lead her to the package sitting on my desk, reluctantly releasing her hand. "Open it."

She gives me a suspicious look, but does as I ask. Opening the package, she finds my gift to her, and I swear my heart stops as I wait for her reaction.

Opening his gift, I discover it's a laptop. Confusion creases my brow and I glance up at him. "Thank you. This is... unexpected."

He rubs the back of his neck, as if he's uncertain or embarrassed. "I've seen you working all week on your phone, checking emails, and trying to keep all of your work information organized, and I just thought it would be easier on a laptop."

Shock momentarily renders me speechless. He bought me a gift to make my work easier?

"This is very thoughtful of you." I smooth my fingers over the slick metal. "But, I thought you hated the fact that I work."

"No, *kisa*, I don't understand why you insist on working, but I don't hate it. If anything, I admire your drive, and your independence. If you want a career, then I want to see you dominate it."

Once again, I'm not sure what to say. Who is this man? Where did he stuff that overbearing jerk for the night? More importantly, what do I do with this very kind and thoughtful version of Dimitri that has seemingly appeared out of nowhere?

I settle on honesty. "I do plan to have a career, and I will dominate it. My plans are already set in motion. Thank you for the laptop, this is a game-changer for my workflow."

He smiles, genuinely for the first time. The expression lights up his striking features, even softening that faint scar across his eyebrow, and he looks terribly handsome.

If we'd met under more agreeable circumstances, how differently would we regard each other?

I mentally shake that thought away. He's not my type and he never will be. The situation between us can morph and change, but that doesn't matter. He kidnapped me, forced us into marriage, and tattooed his name on my ring finger. The past can't be altered and I'll never forgive him.

Not that he wants my forgiveness, all he desires is my acceptance of this situation.

"Good night," I say, hugging my new laptop to my chest, and brushing past him. He murmurs the statement in return, letting me go.

On the best of days this man leaves me teetering off balance, then he goes and does something like this and I... I don't know what to think or how to feel. Between him telling me about his childhood, the fact that he chose this elegant and appropriate dress for tonight instead of something revealing, and now this thoughtful gift, my defenses are starting to weaken.

I can feel my walls cracking and I don't like it one bit.

I have to hate him. Because if I begin to not hate him, then I'm lost.

I meet my sisters, Sophia and Ginevra, and our cousin Ravenna, at my favorite bakery in Manhattan. It feels so much longer than a week and half since I last saw them. I've missed them terribly.

As expected, they launch right into grilling me about Dimitri. It's quite reminiscent of how we all did this to Sophia less than a year ago. I let them swamp me with questions, while they debate points with each other, too anxious to let me answer.

Finally, I silence them with a raised hand. "Honestly, just let me explain."

They nod in unison.

"I'm fine. He's treating me well enough, better than expected honestly. Even so, I hate him and hope that this ridiculous marriage will come to an end sooner rather than later." Which leads me to what I really want to know about. "Sophia, you said Papa is doing some work for Dimitri. Do you know what it involves?"

"As far as I can tell, it's a man hunt."

"Do you know who they're after?"

Sophia shakes her head. "I don't. And so far, Roman's not involved. Papa hasn't told me any details about it."

I sag. This is a dead end. "I'm just trying to figure out his motive for taking me, you know? Like for Roman he kidnapped you as revenge against your fiancé at the time. And Ravenna, Cian married you to stop a war. Can it really be as simple as Dimitri needing to uphold our family's agreement? That seems petty."

Sophia and Ravenna both send me sympathetic glances. Maybe Dimitri really is that petty.

Ginevra wistfully sighs. "I can't wait to get kidnapped and fall in love."

"I'm not falling in love," I snap. "Be careful what you wish for, Gin, it just might come true."

My youngest sister rolls her eyes at me. "Well, as romantic as it would be, I don't think it's going to happen. I met someone. His name's Oliver. He's a real sweetheart. I might fall for him."

Putting my own drama on the back burner for a while, I catch up on my sisters and cousin's lives. Gin seems serious about this man she's seeing and I hope she doesn't get herself into trouble. She views the world in such a positive light that I'm afraid one day it's going to tear her apart—and she won't see it coming.

I share a weighted glance with Sophia and she dips her chin, acknowledging my silent plea to have Roman look into this Oliver guy. I need to know that my sister's safe.

"You can come back for me at five o'clock, there's no need for you to hang around here all that time, Maks."

He shuts off the engine and shifts in his seat. "I'm not just your driver, I'm also your bodyguard, so wherever you go, I go too."

I sigh, tired of arguing with him about this. "Fine. Let's go in before I'm late for work."

"Yes, ma'am." He gives a curt nod and a smile. I swear he's as stubborn as his boss.

We exit the car, and Maks hands the keys to the valet, while I jog up the marble steps, then make my way to Tarina's office. She's waiting there for me along with two other women and a man. The rest of the event planning team, who I've only interacted with via email.

"Good, we're all here." Tarina claps her hands together and stands. "Today we're finalizing the layout, catering needs, and decor for every single room as well as the grounds. Let's get to it."

Maks shadows me as I walk around Leonidas with the rest of my team members, Ben, Charlotte, and Shantel. I had no idea this venue had this many rooms, it's massive.

After the first twenty minutes or so, I lose myself in the planning process. While we each have different responsibilities, it's good to see the big picture and how it'll come together for New Year's Eve.

Tarina has tasked me with the ice sculptures, of which there will be several, and the plethora of floral arrangements. Leonidas is certainly going to live up to its reputation of hosting elaborate, over the top celebrations. And I'll be one of the people to make it happen.

By the time we break for lunch, I'm giddy. This is exactly what a dream job should feel like—inspiring, challenging, and oh so rewarding.

I glance around the private room where we're having a catered lunch. Ben and Charlotte sit close, heads bowed in conversation. Shantel eats quietly by herself, scrolling through her phone. I notice that Maks is missing. Did he finally get bored and go back to the car? If he did, I can only assume that he realizes how safe I am at this private club where access is extremely limited.

"Are you overwhelmed yet?" Tarina asks, sitting beside me.

"Not at all."

She smiles. "Then perhaps I did underestimate you in the beginning. You've certainly been on top of everything I've sent you so far."

"That's my job." My chest fills with satisfaction. Impressing Tarina could lead to a full-time position at Leonidas, which I desperately want.

We spend the rest of the afternoon in the brisk autumn outdoors, going over the plans for the terraced garden, fireworks display, and basically the total transformation of the grounds.

Once we're back inside, Tarina dismisses us. "You all have your tasks, let's see some real progress this week. We will meet here every Monday going forward to review and make sure we're on schedule. Have a good evening."

Armed with vendor contact information and specifications, I'm looking forward to a week of appointments and purchase orders. With luck and diligence, I'll have minimal tasks left on my list by next Monday.

I enter the foyer, heading for the door, when my gaze clashes with bright blue eyes. My heart lodges in my throat, and I come to a stop.

"Arianna?"

"Connor." I'd ask what he's doing here, but he already said he's a member of this club.

He rushes toward me, closing the distance between us, and sweeps me away to a small alcove. "Are you okay? You never returned any of my texts. I've been worried."

Guilt twists in my stomach. I didn't want Dimitri to have any further reason to hurt Connor, so I blocked his number. Stupid, and rude, I know. It was only a matter of time before our paths crossed and I'd have to explain myself.

"I'm sorry. It's complicated, but I'm fine."

"Are you sure?" His penetrating gaze studies me, then he grabs my left hand. "What happened?"

He's referring to the Band-Aid that I wrapped around my ring finger this morning to hide Dimitri's tattoo. Horror and embarrassment grip me tight.

"Nothing." I pull my hand out of his. "I should go."

He snatches it back and tears the bandage away, revealing the tattoo. As he reads the words his features darkens with fury. "You are *not* the property of Dimitri Kozlov."

My mouth opens and closes, but no sound emerges. How do I explain this to him? Why does he even care?

"I had no choice. He forced me to marry him, even forged my signature on the marriage license," I blurt out. "It's fine, I'll get a divorce. Eventually. But you have to leave me alone."

Connor's gaze is pleading. "That is *not* fine. Arianna, let me help–"

"What's going on here?" Maks steps into our alcove, his deadly blue gaze locked onto Connor Bane. "It seems we should have done more than left you unconscious on the side of the road."

Connor squeezes my hand before he drops it and steps toward Maks. "Go fuck yourself." He glances back at me, his expression unreadable. Then he's gone.

"Come on, let's get you home." Maks ushers me toward the door.

"Where have you been? You weren't there for lunch."

Maks looks down, but not before I catch the glint of guilt in his eyes. "Nowhere important."

The valet pulls the car around and we climb inside. As we drive away, I notice Maks glancing into the rearview mirror and follow his gaze to Leonidas. There, in an upper window, is a man staring at us. I can't make out his identity, but he watches the car until we exit the gates.

Who is that man?

CHAPTER 17

Arianna

"*N et, Papa, net. Pochemu ty brosayesh' menya?*" Dimitri groans in his sleep, waking me, and I turn toward him. "*Ne. Pozhaluysta, Papa. Ya budu khoroshym, ya obeshchayu.*" He's muttering in Russian, I can't understand anything other than *papa*. Is he dreaming about his father?

"Dimitri?" I reach for his bare shoulder, he's warm to the touch yet he's shivering. "Wake up."

"*Net.*"

I shake him a little harder. "Wake up, Dimitri."

"*Net!*" He grabs me and rolls us until he's on top, pinning me to the mattress. I can barely breathe beneath his weight. "*YA nenavizhu tebya, sukin ty syn! Kak ty mog postupit' tak so mnoy, c nami?! YA, blyat', ub'yu tebya!*"

He's screaming in Russian, and I tremble beneath him. Even though I'm pretty sure his anger isn't actually directed at me, I'm terrified, having never seen him this upset before. Tears trail down his flushed face, his eyes closed.

"Dimitri, please wake up." I gasp for breath, my lungs seizing, unable to draw in air.

"You fucking bastard!" His eyes snap open. The moment he realizes where he is, and who I am, his gaze clears. Abruptly, he slides from the bed and stands, raking his fingers through his hair. "I'm so sorry, *kisa.*"

I suck in a much needed lungful of air. Sitting up, I pant, trying to fully catch my breath as the fear leaves my body. Adrenaline makes me tremble, and Dimitri notices.

"*Fuck!* I'm so sorry." For a second, it seems like he's going to sit down and come in close. He takes a step toward the bed, his arm extended. Then he drops his hand and rushes backwards. Turning, he bolts out the door, leaving me all alone in the pre-dawn gloom.

I shake off the remnants of terror, briefly hesitating before I pull on a robe and go after Dimitri. I'm not sure why I'm driven to do such a thing. It must boil down to this overwhelming need to make sure he's okay. It's human instinct. I know I won't sleep a wink if I keep wondering about him.

It takes a while to find him in this massive house, with its winding corridors and endless rooms. What finally tips me off is the noise. I follow the sound of grunts into a part of the house I swear I've never seen before, and find Dimitri, opposite a tired looking Maks, as they spar with each other. The room appears to be a gym, with a boxing ring in the middle.

I hesitate in the doorway. He's obviously fine, and now I feel like I'm intruding.

Maks murmurs something to Dimitri, who glances

over his shoulder at me. His gaze is tinged with guilt and embarrassment. He quickly looks away, and I know I've been dismissed.

Backing into the hall, my chest tightens and twists. Why on earth did I follow him? He doesn't need me. He's a grown man who can take care of himself.

My logic tries, and fails, to overrule the unwanted feeling of hurt. His obvious rejection stings. It shouldn't, because I don't care about him at all, but it does. Straightening my spine, I remind myself of everything horrible he's done to me and that helps to ease the discomfort. By the time I'm back in the bedroom, my heart has completely shut out Dimitri Kozlov.

That entire week Dimitri avoids me. He rises early, and doesn't return home until after I've fallen asleep. I should be the happiest captive alive to no longer have to endure dinner with him, or the tension of preparing for bed together. But I'm not.

I'm pissed off. How dare he?

How dare he treat me like one moment he desires me, and the next he can't stand to be in the same room. It's rude.

Ugh, what is wrong with me? I should take this opportunity to ask for that divorce I desperately crave. Instead, I've been taking the wonderful dinners that Nina makes me to the cozy home theater every night.

Tonight I'm watching *Pride and Prejudice* for the millionth time.

Maks sits in the recliner next to mine, eating popcorn, and complaining about my movie choice, like he does every night. "How can you watch this boring shit?"

I'm curled up around my bowl of Pad Thai, the best of comfort foods. "It's not boring. Jane Austen knew exactly what women want. Mr. Darcy is perfection."

"Mr. Darcy is an asshole."

I glare at him. "Obviously you have no idea what kind of man women want."

"You've got that straight." He snorts. "Here we go again with the melodrama."

"Says the man who cried at the end of *Anna Karenina*."

He tosses popcorn at me, and I use my fuzzy blanket as a shield. "I did *not* cry! Even if I did shed a single tear, it's a tragedy, people are supposed to feel sad. The fact that you showed no emotion at all is kinda concerning."

I scoff in mock outrage. "I showed emotion, just not outwardly. Inside I was all teary."

"Bullshit." He focuses on the movie. "Turn it up, will you? I can't hear their terrible lines."

I hide my smile as I increase the volume. "Are you sure? What about your rule of always watching TV on mute so you can hear if we're being attacked or whatever?"

"That was at the penthouse. There's so much noise in the city. Out here we're surrounded by nothing but a top-notch security system that pings anything suspicious right to my phone. I know about every wild animal that crosses through the garden out back."

"I'm glad you can finally enjoy some quality entertainment to its fullest extent." I chuckle at his teasing glare.

He gazes at the screen, tossing popcorn at it a minute later. "Look at that asshole just ignoring her every chance he gets."

Reminded of Dimitri, I glance away from the television. "Dimitri had a nightmare the other night," I blurt out, before thinking it through.

Maks's brows rise. "Really? It's been a while, I thought the nightmares were gone."

"You know about them?" That catches my full attention. "Do you know what they're about? He was speaking Russian, I couldn't understand much at all. Other than the word *papa*."

His usually open expression shutters closed. I pushed too far, didn't I?

While Maks has been fun to hang out with when he's around, and when he drives me in town, he's never been forthcoming about information regarding his boss. His loyalty speaks volumes.

"Never mind, I—" I start.

"We met when he was seven years old and I was nine on the streets of Moscow. I saved him from getting caught by these two bullies who had it in for him. Since that day, we've been inseparable. I told him about all the best places to beg and taught him how to pickpocket." He gazes down at his hands, frowning. "Those were rough times. I think that's where most of the nightmares stem from."

Pickpocket? Begging? "But I thought... I thought his father sold him to someone."

Maks clears his throat. "He did. The man who bought him only needed him once a week, so the rest of the time we lived on the streets." He glances over at me. "Don't tell him I told you any of this. It's not really my story to tell. So don't ask for more."

I nod, understanding.

Why is it every time I think I've figured out who Dimitri Kozlov is, another layer comes to light? How can a man who seems so simple be so complex?

CHAPTER 18
Dimitri

Tonight's the first time we've had dinner together in a while, and I've avoided it for this very reason. Arianna looks at me differently, like she knows all my secrets and can see into my soul. I hate it. I don't want her pity. Hell, I don't want that look of compassionate understanding either.

After all these years, I thought the nightmares had run their course. I was wrong. Was it because of opening up to her about my childhood that has those memories resurfacing? Or is it because of my uncle's sudden death?

I don't know, and I don't care. All I'm concerned about is looking weak in front of my wife. I'd rather she see me as the monster she thinks I am than a sad, little boy, crying because his daddy abandoned him.

Fuck. The only way I can think of to deal with this situation is to ignore it ever happened.

I awkwardly clear my throat, avoiding her gaze. Now that she's finally giving me her attention, I don't fucking want it. "We're going to a charity dinner and auction next Saturday. You know how it works, be good and—"

"I'll behave, Dimitri. You have my word." Her tone is gentle and soft—pitying. I fucking hate it.

"Good. See you then." I stand up, quickly glancing at her stunned face as I leave the dining room in the middle of our meal. I won't sit there for another moment while she pities me. She doesn't know a fucking thing about my life. Unless...

I pull my phone from my pocket and text Maks asking him where he is.

MAKS

I'm in the gym. What's up?

Instead of replying, I head for the gym.

Inside, Maks is punching a heavy bag, and continues even when I march up to him and demand, "What the fuck did you tell my wife?"

"What makes you think I told her anything?" He grunts, his gloved fists jabbing at the bag in quick succession.

"Don't fucking lie to me."

He shrugs. "She mentioned you had a nightmare and wanted to know why, so I gave her the highlights of our growing up."

Fuck, fuck, *fuck*. "Why the hell would you tell her about that?"

He catches the bag to stop it from swaying, then faces me. "I think the real question should be why the fuck haven't *you* told her about that? She's your wife and she barely knows anything about you. Do you think keeping parts of who you are a secret is going to make her like you? It won't. Part of the reason she hates you so much is because she only sees your worst side. Give her some perspective, for fuck's sake."

I scowl at him, annoyed and confused. "Why would I tell her about my weaknesses?"

"Because it shows her your vulnerability." He sighs, clearly exasperated. "Vulnerability builds trust and open communication. I've seen you obsessing over her for what seems like forever, and now that you have her, you're pushing her away. I know you want her. And honestly, I think she could be good for you if you'd just let her in."

"What, are you a fucking relationship counselor now?" I snarl, irritated by his perceptiveness, and glance away.

"I just want to see you happy, Dima. Is that such a bad thing?"

Something like hope blooms in my chest. "And you think I could be happy with her?"

"I don't see why not. She's the only woman I've ever seen you this... focused on. Stop holding yourself back."

Slowly, I nod, taking in his words. "Just because I want her doesn't mean she wants me in return."

"Then why don't you give her a reason to like you?"

"Like what?" I glance at him.

"I don't know." He shrugs, then turns back to his heavy bag. "I'm sure you'll think of something."

L ying awake in bed, I think over what Maks said earlier this evening. Do I have any redeeming qualities? What does Arianna want in a man? I've never given either of those questions much thought. I just... I don't know, figured that I'd take her for myself and somehow she'd be as obsessed with me as I am with her, because our connection has to be fate, right?

I'm starting to think I was wrong. She doesn't return my feelings for her—she hates me, and now she pities me, too. If anything, this situation has gone from bad to worse.

Sometimes I wish I didn't want her so much. That this craving for her could be cured, and I didn't ache for a mere glimpse of her. But I do, she's an addiction, one I couldn't go for more than a few days without giving in to. Now that she's under my roof, in my bed—so close, yet still so far away—my obsession with her has only grown.

Turning my head, I gaze over at her slumbering form. I still love watching her sleep, and now I can do it without breaking into her parents house.

Tonight, her back's turned toward me and she's curled into a loose ball under the blankets. I wish the bed was smaller so she couldn't leave so much space between us. Resisting the urge to reach for her, my fingers curl into a loose fist.

She's made it very clear that she doesn't want my touch, or at least she refuses to admit to her desires. I can tell how much our physical contact affects her—it does the same to me, that warmth, the shock of electricity that surprises me every single time, and the way my heart pounds faster. I know she feels it too.

Arianna whimpers, and my attention snaps to her. Through the faint light, I see her shoulders moving with quick, shallow breaths. Is she awake? Her next pained moan has me sliding across the bed, eating up the distance between us.

I gently place my hand on her delicate shoulder. "*Kisa*, are you all right?"

She nods.

I'm about to back away when she whimpers again. "What is it?" I ask, my tone laced with sincere concern. "Are you in pain?"

"It's nothing. Go away." She gasps, her breathing rapid as she groans.

I peek at her pinched expression, it's all the answer I need. But why is she hurting? What happened?

Fully alert, my gaze roams over her body, seeking clues. What's hurt and who's responsible? I'll make them pay whoever they are. That's when I notice how she's holding her lower abdomen. That must be the source of her discomfort.

"Is it cramps?" I ask, my voice low and soothing.

She nods, squeezing her eyes shut.

"Okay, *malyshka*, I've got you." Getting out of bed, I grab a couple of pain pills from the bathroom, along with a glass of water and the heating pad I sometimes use after a fight.

Returning to her side, I hand her the pills which she shallows down, then I plug in the heating pad and place it across her stomach. She murmurs something that sounds like *thanks*, before settling down.

I round the bed and climb into my side. For all of two seconds, I hesitate before scooting close enough to her that my body heat warms her back. She might not want my touch, but right now she needs it.

As soon as I reach her, she freezes. Ignoring her reaction, I start massaging her lower back, using my thumbs to loosen the knots. A soft moan escapes her lips and she relaxes.

Another wave of cramps assault her and she cries out. Shifting closer, I massage her lower stomach beneath the heating pad. At first, she whimpers in distress.

"Shh, *kisa*, I've got you. Just relax."

Her pained sounds soon turn to blissful sighs of relief, then contented moans. It's fucking music to my ears.

I continue massaging her until her breathing slows and she falls to sleep. Being able to sooth her like this warms me with pride. Did I finally do something right? Taking care of her, touching her like this, like no other man ever will again, sends a coil of possessiveness straight through me.

I could use this and other tactics to manipulate her into trusting me, into liking me. But I find that's not my intention at all. I *want* to take away her pain. This is something I'm proud to do as her husband.

I'm having tea and working on my laptop at the breakfast nook table when Dimitri comes into the kitchen. He grabs some cereal and pours it into a bowl, then opens the refrigerator.

This morning, I woke up to his arm draped over my waist, his soft breath in my ear. It took me a few minutes to convince myself that everything that happened last night was real, and not a dream. Now, I find my emotions surrounding Dimitri in a state of flux.

How can I reconcile the arrogant brute that I know, with that understanding man in bed with me last night? It's almost like that abandoned child living on the streets split into two completely different adult men—one I loathe, and the other... I don't know what to make of the glimpses he shows me of his softer side.

The fact remains, he took care of me when he didn't have to.

"How are you feeling?" he asks, drawing me out of my thoughts. He clears his throat, his gaze not quite meeting mine. "I mean, how are you feeling after last night?"

"Much better, thank you." It's the truth. About twice a year, I have a really rough start to my period, like last night. But after that part's done, I always feel better.

"Maybe you should take the day off." His green eyes finally lock onto mine. "Soak in the hot tub or something for a while. There's, uh, chocolate in the pantry, but if you want something else I can go get it for you."

My stomach flip-flops and I smile at him. This version of Dimitri pulls at my heartstrings, and I have no clue what to do with him.

"I'm better now, I promise."

He steps closer, his awkwardness suddenly gone. When he's towering over me, he finally pauses, his fingertips sweeping my hair out of my face. It's a gesture he does frequently. One I usually recoil from. But not today.

He drops into the chair next to mine, then wraps his arm around my waist, transferring me to his lap. I gasp at how easily he can pick me up, like I'm a doll, practically weightless.

"I can make you feel even better than I did last night, if you'll let me." He brushes my hair behind my ear. "Come on my fingers, *kisa. Please.*" His other hand dips between my thighs, brushing against my clit.

My cheeks flame. I grip his wrist, intending to shove his hand away, but I simply hold onto him while he rubs me through the fabric of my leggings. Is it him saying *please* that makes me hesitate, or the fact that this feels so good?

He applies more pressure, and I sharply inhale, his

spicy cologne invading my senses. I don't know how, but I'm so close already.

When I squirm in his lap, he works my clit faster, his movements deliberate, rapidly sending me closer to an orgasm. Holy, God, how can this be so wrong when it feels so right? I try not to give that much thought, instead losing myself in the moment.

My head falls back against Dimitri's shoulder and my back arches. An orgasm sweeps through me with so much intensity that my whole body shakes.

"Oh, *God!*" I moan, quaking in Dimitri's arms as he continues to stroke me. Once the tremors stop, and I fully realize what just happened, my entire face grows hot. "I—"

Dimitri places a finger across my lips. "Shh, *kisa*. Just relax. I won't demand anything more from you right now. I just wanted to make you feel good."

My gaze clashes with his, and I can only describe what I see in his eyes as hunger. He's holding himself back and we both know it.

I shift in his lap, and he hisses. That's when I notice his hard length pressed against my back. He rolls his hips, the movement small. My eyes grow wide. He feels... huge, long and thick. I didn't think my face could feel any warmer, but it does. I'm burning up.

Without a word, Dimitri lifts me up and sets me back in my own chair. He studies me for a moment. I'm not sure what he's looking for. I've barely reacted to what transpired between us. I think I'm still in shock.

His gaze does one final sweep over my features, then he takes his bowl and retreats from the kitchen, leaving me to stare after him.

FORCED UNION · 149

What just happened? Did I really come for my captor, on his lap, in the middle of the wide open kitchen? Oh my god, what's wrong with me? I should have stopped him, I could have at any point, but I didn't.

I expect shame to consume me, like it did after he spanked me on piano bench, but this time it's absent. All I feel is... good. *Great.* My muscles are like jelly, my skin buzzing with post-orgasmic bliss.

I'm even finding it difficult to figure out what's so wrong with feeling this good. Of course I've touched myself before, but it's never felt the same as what he just did.

Would it really be so bad to experience more of this kind of pleasure? Willingly?

God, I can only imagine what he'd do to my body if I let him. More heat floods my cheeks as I think about that. How his rough, strong hands would roam over every inch of my body. How it might feel to be naked in his arms, skin to skin. Would he make me come over and over again until I'm satiated?

I shake my head at myself. Am I really toying with the idea of giving into him?

That's a *terrible* idea.

Shakily, I drain the rest of my tea, ready to head into the library to work—and hopefully clear my head of Dimitri Kozlov—when Nina appears with an armful of blue hydrangeas and sets them in the sink. Thankfully she didn't show up any earlier or she would have gotten a shock.

Reckless, that's what that was.

"Good morning, Mrs. Kozlov."

I grimace slightly at that name, certainly not feeling

like I'm married, especially to him. "Good morning, Nina. What pretty flowers."

She swipes the vase of wilted forget-me-nots from the table, and mumbles, "I'm sorry these weren't replaced sooner, ma'am."

"It's fine, Nina. Really." I recall how the many vases around the mansion are always filled with fresh-cut flowers. "Dimitri really has a thing for blue flowers, doesn't he?"

Nina cuts the hydrangea stems, shooting me a glance. "He said the flowers are for you, ma'am."

For me? I vaguely remember him telling me that when I hurled the vase of delphiniums at him my first morning at his penthouse. At the time, I thought he was just trying to make me feel guilty, or distract me from my rage.

"Nina." My tone is hesitant. "Has Dimitri always had fresh flowers around this place? Or maybe his uncle did?"

She glances at me like I must be joking. "No offense, but neither of them are the flower type. No, it's only since he came home with you that he's insisted on the floral arrangements, saying that you like them, and to change them out regularly."

It's true, I do like them. At my parents house I always had a vase of flowers in my room, refreshed each week. But they weren't always blue, I love all colors, so that part is particular to Dimitri.

I wonder what it means.

More importantly, was Dimitri looking in my bedroom window? I wouldn't put it past him.

CHAPTER 20

Arianna

Groggy from sleep, I stumble to the bathroom and relieve the pressure in my bladder. My half-awake mind immediately drifts to work as I sit on the toilet. This past week has shown me exactly what Tarina meant when she said two of my co-workers combined were barely doing the work of one person.

Shantel is great to work with, but Ben and Charlotte seem to always mess up their tasks. Tarina has to come in and fix it. Honestly, I'm not sure why she doesn't fire those two.

I step out of the toilet room, and instantly freeze. The shower is running. On the other side of the steamy glass, Dimitri fists his erection and groans, his head tilting back. The sight is so unexpected, and erotic, that I can't tear my eyes away as he strokes his cock, slowly at first, the building up speed.

"Arianna," he groans my name. I startle, thinking he's spotted me, but then he moans. "*Fuck.*"

Oh my god, he doesn't realize I'm here, watching him. I'm intruding on a very private moment. But my feet may as well be glued to the floor, they refuse to move.

He moans my name again, and a wave of satisfaction rushes through me, knowing that I'm the reason he's masturbating, that I'm the woman he's thinking of right now.

That satisfaction is quickly replaced with horror. I most certainly don't want—

Dimitri's free palm lands against the glass, smearing a section clean, and I can more clearly see his face. Eyes closed, brows furrowed, and lips parted. He looks sexy as hell. He groans, and heat shoots straight between my thighs. I swear I might come just from watching him.

With a curse, his body jerks, and his eyes snap open. He's staring straight at me. My knees are weak, like they might give out any moment. Then he smirks. That slow, sensuous smile curls his lips, and I immediately know he knew I've been here the whole time.

He's teasing me. Tempting me.

"Like what you see, *kisa?*" His voice is still thick with sleep. "Do you want to join me here?"

Finally, I snap out of my daze and glare at him. But words fail me.

Unable to think of anything better to do, I bolt from the bathroom.

Annoyingly, Dimitri seems unaffected by our encounter in the bathroom, while I spend the next few days unable to stop remembering every detail of the incident. Each time I do, I have the shameful urge to touch myself. God, what is this man doing to me? It's completely unfair.

It's like his touch has awakened a need in my body that I never knew was there before. When I'm not feeling ashamed about it, I'm frustrated and needy. Several nights now, I've been tempted to roll over and do what he wants—beg him to touch me.

Thankfully, my pride won't let me.

Giving in is not an option. I'm still waiting for the opportunity to escape, and it better come soon because I don't know how much longer I can hold out. Not when he's playing this dirty.

This afternoon I'm returning from an errand Tarina sent me on, when I run into Dimitri in the library. *Speak of the Devil...*

He's wearing a black T-shirt and dark wash jeans with boots. His unruly hair is a little messier than usual, giving him an extremely sexy vibe. It's completely unfair. Why couldn't he be ugly, or smelly, or completely vile? Why does he have to be... well, himself? The man who's driving me absolutely out of my mind.

The slow grin on his lips says it all. He knows exactly how he affects me.

"I have something for you," he says, prowling closer.

"Oh?" I linger by the doorway. He's obviously been waiting in here for my return, so this run-in isn't spontaneous.

"Next Saturday we have that charity event, and since we'll be around polite society," he grimaces, "I figured you might want this."

My breath still in my lungs when he reveals a black velvet ring box and pops the hinged lid open. Inside is a wide gold wedding band, studded with tiny diamonds. It's actually quite stunning.

"This should cover your tattoo." He plucks the ring from where it's nestled and reaches for my left hand. I stare, wide-eyed, as he slips the ring on my finger, the fit perfect.

He leans in. "No more wearing Band-Aids to cover this up."

He knew? How long has he known I've been doing that to cover his mark on me?

Sharply, I glance up at him. "Does this mean you're sorry for branding me?"

"Not in the slightest." He lifts a brow at my outrage. "I did what had to be done and I won't apologize for any of it, *ever*."

"Did what needed to be done." I echo his phrase, yanking my hand out of his. "I don't see why you had to do this at all. If you really wanted my family to join with yours, there are other ways it could have happened. You could have talked to my father and come up with a solution. Unless this is all some kind of power trip for you."

His features darken, and his lips press into a thin line. "By breaking our agreement, your father disrespected us. When my uncle refused to make an example of Mr. Pontrelli, insisting on forging a new agreement between our families that didn't involve marriage, everyone saw us as weak."

Dimitri grabs my jaw, lowering his face to mine. "It's because of your father that my uncle was murdered. I knew I had to see the original agreement through in order to save face and regain whatever respect I could, but it's too late. The man who murdered my uncle escaped and I can't find him." He releases me, stepping back.

Papa going back on his word for his daughters sakes is the reason Dimitri lost his uncle? I had no idea. When Father said we were free to choose our own husbands, that he'd never force us into an arranged marriage, I thought this was all over. I had no idea of the lingering consequences.

Another thought occurs to me. "That's who you have Papa looking for, isn't it, this man who killed your uncle?" I ask. He nods, but that leads me to another question. "Why aren't your own men after him? Don't they want vengeance?"

He sighs. Dragging his hand through his hair, he glances at me. "The man I'm having hunted down used to be my second in command. He's one of my own men. Which means I can't trust any of them. Worse, someone helped him escape and I haven't figured out who yet." He sounds defeated, tired.

Those lower in rank murdering their superiors to take control is not uncommon. From what Dimitri's telling me, it sounds like he's surrounded by men he can't trust, but he's also outnumbered. How long until that man comes for Dimitri, the last obstacle standing in the way to the top?

"What about the guards outside?" I ask. "Do you trust them?"

He shakes his head, and my heart races. "Not one hundred percent, but I do trust Maks. He's vetted them, and keeping an eye on them."

"Except when he's driving me around," I point out. "He's either here watching them, or he's with me in the city. He can't be in two places at once. What if something happened while we were away?"

"That's a risk I have to take. These guards I do trust more than others, just not one hundred percent." He gently rubs my arm. "As long as Maks and I are alive, you're safe, *kisa*. Soon I'll have Boris, he can't hide forever, and then he's going to tell me who sided with him and betrayed my uncle. I'll purge the Kozlov Bratva and we'll be strong again."

"Will you let me go after that?"

He frowns, his gaze dropping to the floor. "I don't think I *can*. Not now, not then, not ever."

So the only way to escape him is if he dies—or someone murders him.

I've never seen a man look so uncomfortable in a tuxedo until tonight. The fit is perfectly tailored, but that doesn't stop Dimitri from pulling at his cuffs and collar. He's going to tear off a sleeve if he keeps that up.

Tonight's charity dinner is in a luxurious Manhattan hotel ballroom, followed by a silent auction in another part of the venue. We arrived in the middle of cocktail hour and have been slowly working our way around the reception area.

The first person I spot is Connor Bane, surrounded by his brothers, all lurking in a corner. His bright blue gaze traps mine for several intense moments.

A rumble emits from Dimitri's chest, and I turn to find him glaring at Connor. I place my hand on his arm. "Not here."

He grunts, and we both walk away from the Bane brothers.

"Arianna, my darling." Mrs. De Luca floats up to us, kissing me on both cheeks. "How wonderful to see you. Congratulations on your position at Leonidas, I knew they'd love you."

"Thank you for being my reference, Mrs. De Luca." I motion toward Dimitri. "Let me introduce you to Dimitri Kozlov, my... husband." My cheeks warm. I've never referred to him as either mine or my husband. But how else would I introduce him? I am wearing a wedding band, after all.

Mrs. De Luca pins her hawk-like gaze on him, extending her hand. "Pleasure to meet you, Mr. Kozlov. I've heard all about you." She assesses him. "You'd better be treating Arianna well, or I'll make sure that you—"

"*Mother*," Roman De Luca approaches our rapidly growing circle. "Are you threatening other guests already? The night is young."

Mrs. De Luca beams up at her son. "Oh good, you're here. I only make the threats, darling, I expect you to fulfill them."

Dimitri seems completely caught off guard by the De Lucas and I can't blame him. Sometimes it's impossible to tell if they're being serious or not. Then there's the plain aggression they hide behind their social graces. Like how Roman is shaking Dimitri's hand, trying to crush it by the look of that grip.

Inwardly, I roll my eyes.

"Arianna!" Sophia appears from behind her husband and we embrace. She holds my shoulders, leaning back to get a better look at my dress. "Are you seriously wearing a Skye Adair gown tonight? I'm so envious!"

I glance down at my ivory dress and blush. To say I was shocked when I saw the Skye Adair label inside the garment earlier tonight would be an understatement. My mind still hasn't stopped reeling with questions. One, how does Dimitri even know about Skye's designer line? Two, how on earth did he manage to get his hands on this dress since her inventory sells out within minutes? And the price tag... her designs are anything but inexpensive. I'm astonished at how much money he spent on me for this one evening. Especially when you add in the Skye Adair shoes and clutch.

"No you're not," I tell my sister. "You're wearing one too." Sophia's obsessed with Skye Adair and has been following her career since the beginning when she started as a fashion forward social media influencer.

Sophia releases me and smiles. "This old thing? You're right it is, but your dress is from her newest collection. How did you score it?"

My gaze wanders to Dimitri, who's getting an earful about my accomplishments from Mrs. De Luca, a quiet smile on his lips. The pride shining in his eyes when he looks at me makes my stomach flutter with a million butterflies.

"Oh. I see." Sophia latches onto Roman's arm. "We'll see you after dinner." She studies me for a few seconds longer, her gaze silently asking if I'm okay. I give a subtle nod, then Roman pulls her away. Mrs. De Luca follows after them.

"Hello, handsome." A woman's sultry voice purrs, her gaze locked on Dimitri.

My jaw drops when he acknowledges her, a genuine smile lighting his features as they hug.

A sensation I haven't experienced before swims through me. It's burning, yet icy cold, and suddenly I'm irrationally angry. Who does this woman think she is? More importantly, who is she to him?

I want to drag her impossibly tall, blond, skinny ass away from him this instant.

Dimitri gestures to me. "This is Arianna Kozlov, my wife."

I arch a haughty brow at her, but all she does is grin, which further infuriates me. She extends her hand. "It's nice to finally meet you. I'm Skye Adair."

For a second, I simply blink at her offered palm. Skye Adair? As in *the Skye Adair*?

Snapping out of it, my cheeks hot, I shake her hand. "Nice to meet you," I say, but my words are rushed.

"That dress is perfect on you. When Dimitri came by my studio and told me your tastes, and which event you two were attending, I knew this outfit was the right choice." She appreciatively gazes down at me.

"Thank you," I murmur, my manners on autopilot.

He went to her studio? Were they alone together?

"How, um, how do you two know each other?" I ask,

my gaze flitting from her stunning, pale green eyes, to his darker ones.

"You didn't tell her?" Skye giggles, the sound light and airy. "We went to high school together. Which seems like ages ago now. We had our ten year reunion last summer."

A gong sounds, instructing us all to find our designated dinner seats. Skye waves goodbye to us as she goes in search of her own date.

I'm left speechless. I should have recognized her immediately, I've seen her social media profiles, but all I saw was a beautiful woman draping herself on Dimitri. And that smile he gave her was far more intimate and relaxed than I've ever seen from him.

Dimitri steers us into the ballroom to locate our seats. He leans down and whispers in my ear, "Jealousy looks good on you, wife."

A fierce blush creeps up my neck. "I'm not *jealous*."

As soon as I utter the word, I finally identify how I've been feeling. He's right. I'm *jealous*. For the first time in my life, I'm actually jealous because I thought a woman was throwing herself at a man I claim to have no feelings for, least of all ones powerful enough to inspire jealousy.

This is a disaster. I'm a hot mess.

I glance up at Dimitri and my mood further sours. He can wipe that smug grin right off his face.

We're seated in the traditional pattern of alternating women and men around the twelve top tables. The man beside me is an older gentleman with a pretty young date next to him, wearing a massive diamond necklace. The woman seated to Dimitri's left is a stern looking grandmother, who barely spares him any notice

Without the distraction of friends and family, Dimitri tugs uncomfortably on his tuxedo jacket, earning a distressed glance from the woman beside him.

"What's wrong?" I lean toward him to ask.

"Nothing."

Fine, if he doesn't want to tell I won't push. I place the cloth napkin in my lap, noting that Dimitri does the same. It's the first time I've seen him use one.

Servers surround the tables, handing out small plates of sweet potato chips topped with goat cheese and caviar. I nibble on mine. Dimitri picks his up and pops it in his mouth. He grimaces as he chews. I pretend to ignore him.

Next is the soup course. The sweet, earthy aroma of pumpkin and spices makes my mouth water.

Once we're served, I steal glances at Dimitri. He's frowning at the nine pieces of silverware on his place setting. Only two of them are spoons, a much easier decision to make than when it comes to the forks. He looks half tempted to pick up the bowl and bring it to his mouth.

Once again, I lower my voice for his ears only and ask, "What's wrong?"

He tugs at his collar, his brow dipping lower. "How do you know which one's right?"

"The spoon and fork at the top are for dessert." I pick up my soup spoon. "Start from the outside and work your way in with each course."

He dips his chin in acknowledgement. Carefully, he takes his spoon in hand, then watches me eat the tangy pumpkin soup before diving into his own. He mimics my mannerisms, his back straight and shoulders square, one forearm resting on the table, and every so often he dabs his mouth with the napkin.

We make it through the soup course, the appetizer, salad, fish, and first main course without incident. The palate cleanser is a citrusy Prosecco, which Dimitri scowls at before downing his glass in one go.

The conversations around us ebb and flow between the most common topics—politics, gossip, and the stock market. But we rarely join in.

By the time we get to the end of the twelve-course meal, Dimitri's shoulders have relaxed some. The servers clear away our dessert dish, and replace it with a bite-sized macaroon.

"What's this?" he asks. "Didn't we just eat dessert?"

I hide a smile behind my napkin. "It's called *mignardise*. It's kind of like a second dessert. A finishing touch to the meal."

Dimitri shakes his head, muttering, "Crazy fucking rich people." Which earns him a startled glare from the woman beside him, as he pops the macaroon into his mouth.

CHAPTER 21

Dimitri

After that torture, which these people call dinner, we're finally free to explore the items up for auction. Arianna wraps her small hand around my arm, her body swaying against mine, like she actually wants to be here with me. That's a first. I can't deny the satisfaction that unfurls in my chest. I must have done something right for a change.

We mingle in and around the others, going from one display to the next of items up for auction. The room is moodily lit, with spotlights shining down on the individual, glass-encased objects.

When we stop in front of a five strand pearl necklace, Arianna draws in a quick breath. Together, we circle it, taking in the whole thing, and I notice the single string of pearls that trails down the back, ending in a teardrop shaped diamond. Arianna would look stunning in this piece—especially if she was naked, wearing only this...

I open the app for the silent auction and start bidding as we move on. Apparently the necklace is originally from Russia, possibly part of the Romanov treasures that were taken out of the country during the Russian revolution a hundred years ago.

I can't imagine a more perfect piece of jewelry for my queen.

Smirking down at her, I press the button to bid again. It seems that some asshole also has his sights set on this necklace, because each time I bid, the same anonymous user does too. But it will be mine, to give to my wife, no matter the cost.

We circle back around to the beginning, and I lean down to murmur in her ear. "Did you see anything you liked?"

Her lips part, but then she shakes her head. "Nothing I can't live without."

I know she's lying. Well, maybe she can technically live without it, but even now her gaze is locked on that pearl necklace across the room. The way her eyes light up tells me everything I need to know.

She lifts her face toward mine. "But it's a charity auction so we should bid on something."

"I already have. Just a bit on some random pieces." I'm sure my grin takes on a wolfish quality. "Like you said, *we* should bid on something."

Pink blooms on her cheeks "I-I obviously meant you. You should bid, for the sake of the charity part."

"Uh-huh." My smirk widens and her flush deepens.

A throat clearing nearby draws our attention. Connor fucking Bane swaggers up to us and I'm tempted to punch his pretty boy face just for kicks. Unfortunately, three of his brothers appear behind him as backup. Another one circles around to the side.

How many fucking brothers does this guy have?

I can tell they're Banes because they all have that irritating aristocratic look about them—like they think they're better than us common folk. Fuck them. Let my brass knuckles at their faces and they won't be so high and mighty anymore. These fuckers could use a few scars.

Arianna squeezes my arm in warning, as if she can read my thoughts. "Hello, Connor," she says, her tone polite.

"Arianna." He bows his head, then his gaze snaps to mine. "You're going to regret ever laying a hand on me, Kozlov. We'll make sure of that."

I jerk toward him, just to see what he'll do, and he fucking blinks. What a pussy.

"Any time, Bane. You just come on down to Riot and get inside that cage, and I'll knock your ass out—again." Honestly, I should have finished him off the night he tried to steal Arianna away from me, then I wouldn't have to deal with his shit. I knew he wasn't about to let it go. Though even if I had killed him, then his brothers would be on my ass. The situation is fucked.

"Listen here, you Russian piece of—"

"Is there a problem, gentleman," Roman drawls as he approaches.

Blake Baron comes up beside him. Lifting his head, he sniffs. "I smell something nasty. Do you smell that? I can't quite place it, but I think it starts with a B..." He snaps his fingers. "Bane. That's it. That's the stench. Multiple Banes, no wonder it smells so awful in here." Blake sneers.

All four Bane brothers glare at him in unison. It's fucking comical.

Connor points to me, backing away. "I'm coming for you. Watch your back, Kozlov."

I shrug, which further pisses him off.

Arianna angles toward me. "Thank you for not starting a fight in here. I appreciate it."

"I guess that would be inappropriate, huh, *kisa*?" I gaze down at her, amused by how uncivilized she thinks I am. Though she's mostly right. But I don't want to ruin our nice evening out by spraying Connor fucking Bane's blood all over the place.

"*Kisa*?" Blake Baron raises a blond brow. He glances at me and chuckles. "I figured you had to be pussy-whipped when you called in your favor." Snorting, he saunters off with Roman at his side. Arrogant prick.

"What favor?" Arianna asks, looking up at me.

I hold back a groan. "Blake Baron and Roman De Luca both owed me a favor for something I helped them with once. I called it in when Roman threatened me for... taking you. He and Baron were going to intervene, but my favor was for them to stand back and do nothing. They had no choice but to either agree or break their word."

"Ah. So that's why they haven't murdered you and rescued me. Totally makes sense now."

I chuckle. "Doesn't it though?"

Taking a chance, I loop my arm around her waist and

pull her closer. She briefly stiffens before melting against my side. I've never cared for public displays of affection, but with Arianna, I want everyone to know she's mine.

I pull out my phone and check the bidding app again. The necklace is at six million dollars, and I add another five-hundred thousand to that number.

As I'm about to pocket my phone again, it vibrates with an incoming call from Maks. I swipe to answer.

"Maks, what's—"

"It's not looking good out here, *Pakhan*. Two vans just pulled around back and they look shady as fuck. Get the hell out of there. I'm picking you up at the side entrance ASAP."

Ending the call, I grab Arianna's arm, and start walking toward the exit. "We're leaving. Right now."

"What's going on?" She jogs to keep up with my long strides.

I scan the area for immediate threats. "Don't know yet."

The doors up ahead silently swing closed, and I look for another exit sign. Except those other routes are blocked by men in dark suits, and I doubt they're hotel security. A glint of metal in the low light confirms my suspicions.

Two men step further into the room and shoot multiple rounds into the ceiling. People shriek at the loud noise.

I pull Arianna down, covering her body with my own. Going for my gun, I remember that I don't have it because the venue made everyone walk through metal detectors.

Screams echo through the space as everyone else ducks for cover too, and at first I think this is a robbery. There are plenty of high value items on display tonight. It's the perfect kind of loot.

But then four more gunmen join the first two and start sweeping the room. They aren't smashing cases or taking the valuables. They're looking for someone. I have a bad feeling that it might be me they want.

When one man glances our way, I read the satisfaction in his eyes. He's found me.

I don't recognize him. Boris must be working with men from another part of the city, or even out of state.

The guy turns his head to speak to one of his comrades in Russian, and I strike.

Bouncing to my feet, I punch him and he drops like a ton of bricks. He's out cold. His gun leaves his grip, skidding across the floor.

People all around shriek, and I catch quick movement out of the corner of my eye. Roman and Blake are wrestling one gunman to the ground. Across the room, the fucking Bane brothers are taking down three more. I guess they are somewhat useful.

The last shooter standing is making a beeline for me.

I reach for Arianna, my grasp coming away empty. I glance down. She's gone.

Where the fuck did she go?

An audible click sounds from behind me. I spin around, coming face to face with the barrel of the handgun she's holding. Pointed at my chest.

Malice flickers through her beautiful hazel eyes. I swallow hard. This is the moment she's been waiting for, biding her time until she can off me and escape. This is her chance at freedom.

And from the look in her eyes, she's going to take it.

Fuck.

I didn't see this coming. I should have. All the signs were there, but deep down I didn't think she'd actually do it.

Her finger presses on the trigger. Our gazes lock, my jaw sets, and I silently dare her to do it. See this through to the end.

Fucking shoot me already.

Releasing my breath through my nose, I give in to my fate. Murdered by my own wife, by the woman who I've been obsessed with for longer than she'll ever know. I had one taste of her and it wasn't enough. Not by far.

Her gaze flits over my shoulder. She takes aim and shoots.

A heavy thud sounds from behind me, and I look down to see the sixth gunman's skull blown to pieces. His blood seeps toward my shoes.

"We should go." Arianna's calm voice captures my attention.

Our gazes clash. I'm sure she sees the surprise in mine.

I'm alive. I can't fucking believe it.

She hands the gun to me, and I sweep her up in my embrace, hustling us toward the exit. Roman, Blake, and Sophia appear at our side, and together we leave the scene.

Blake, a gun in his hands, walks ahead of us, making sure our way is clear to the hotel's side door off the ballroom hallway. We push open the doors, exiting to a brisk autumn evening, sirens wailing in the distance.

Maks is there for us. Arianna and I pile into the limo, just as Blake ushers Roman and Sophia into a waiting SUV.

CHAPTER 22

Arianna

My heart's pounding, adrenaline shaking my entire body. I held Dimitri's fate in my hands, and instead of shooting him, I saved his life. That man wasn't paying attention to me, his focus was on Dimitri. Since none of the shooters had put a bullet in him, I can only assume they wanted him alive.

That was my one chance to end this between us and get away.

But I didn't pull the trigger.

Now I know that I never will.

Silence stretches between me and Dimitri. We sit opposite each other in the limo, the air between us thick with tension and unspoken thoughts. When his gaze locks with mine, my heart skips a beat.

We look into each other's eyes, mesmerized and vulnerable, for what feels like an eternity. His gaze shines with wonder bordering on disbelief, then uncertainty, until finally transforming to smoldering heat.

The tension between us ratchets high. I can feel its pressure against my skin, like a living, breathing entity.

My chest rapidly rises and falls. I grip the seat to hold myself in place, the need to touch the man in front of me suddenly becomes overwhelming, nearly impossible to resist.

He moves first, and the atmosphere bursts. I'm reaching for him. Our lips crash together. He thrusts his tongue into my mouth and I suck on it. My fingers thread through his hair that's just long enough to grip and pull. One of his hands roams my hips and waist, while the other cradles my head, keeping me pressed flush against him.

We're on our knees on the limo's floor, tangled up in each other, our bodies telling truths that our tongues won't dare speak.

I want you.

I need you.

I hate you.

I'm obsessed with you.

Dimitri peppers kisses along my jaw, licks my neck like it's his favorite flavor of ice cream, then goes lower, nipping my flesh along the way. He lifts me back onto the seat and clasps the seat belt around my waist.

I frown at him. That's it? Are we done?

His answering smirk tells me otherwise. Slowly, he lifts my skirt, his fingers gliding up my bare thighs, and I sharply inhale. He pulls my hips forward, positioning me at the edge of the seat, then ducks down, disappearing beneath the fabric of my dress.

My lips part, shocked when he tears off my panties. His hot breath heats my pussy. Then he tastes me.

Tentative at first, as though he's sampling a new flavor. He murmurs something in Russian against my flesh. His tongue delves deeper, licking, lapping at my molten core.

With a moan, my head falls back against the seat.

He drapes my legs over his broad shoulders, then grabs my hips. The new angle gives him better access and I gasp. His tongue circles my clit. The sensation is unlike anything I've ever felt before. So good.

My fingers dig into his shoulders as he increases the pressure and pacing. *Oh my god.* A loud moan escapes my throat.

When he pushes one finger into my soaked pussy, I come apart. The best orgasm of my life overtakes my body. My mind blanks. All I know is pleasure, wave after wave of pure, all-consuming bliss.

Dimitri eventually rocks back on his heels, his heated gaze settling on mine. "You're delicious, *kisa.*" He pops his finger into his mouth, sucking it clean. "Has any man ever made you come on his tongue before?"

I shake my head. I have no energy for anything other than telling the truth.

"Good. Because you taste better than I imagined. Your sweet pussy is all mine, it belongs to me. Actually, I haven't had enough of your sweet, hungry cunt yet."

He parts my legs and buries his face between them again. I squeak in part surprise, part protest. He can't possibly...

But he does. This time he works me up so slowly it's the best kind of torture. Two of his fingers slip into my pussy, stretching me, and he grunts at my low whimper.

All the sensation is too much, yet not enough at the

same time. Soon he has me panting, begging for more. Pleading in a way I never thought I would.

"Dimitri, *please*."

His low rumble vibrates against my sensitive flesh. I try to roll my hips, needing more, but the seat belt keeps me trapped in place.

"Please, Dima." I use his nickname. I'm not sure why it slips out.

"Fuck," he mutters, curling his fingers and finally giving me what I want. He sucks on my clit and I come. This orgasm is stronger than the last. I'm afraid I might actually pass out as pleasure jolts through me.

I shove at Dimitri's shoulders but he doesn't stop. "Please, it's too much."

"I know you can take it. Come for me again."

"I can't—" Another orgasm courses through me and I cry out. *Holy fuck!*

"Such a good girl." Dimitri blows air across my hot pussy, and I whimper. "I'm nowhere near done with your delicious cunt, *kisa*. You fucking belong to me. Do you understand?" He leans back, gazing at me. "You're *mine*."

Panting, I glare at him. "I hate you."

"I know." He smirks. "Show me how much you hate me, *malyshka*."

His mouth captures mine, forceful, demanding. I taste my own tanginess on him. He runs his tongue across my lips, demanding entry. Instead of allowing him in, I suck his lower lip between my teeth and bite down. A coppery taste teases my tongue. He groans with pleasure.

The car stops, and I'm surprised to find we've arrived back at the Kozlov mansion.

Dimitri unbuckles my seat belt and pulls me from the limo. With a muttered Russian command spoken to Maks, Dimitri lifts my body over his shoulder and carries me into the house, up the stairs, and straight to our bedroom.

"Hey!" I protest at his manhandling.

He swats my ass. "You want to draw blood, *kisa?* I'm all yours. Show me how much you hate me."

As soon as he sets me on my feet, I attack him. My arms loop around his neck as my legs wrap around his hips. I smash my lips to his.

He walks forward until my back's pressed to the wall. This time, I give his tongue entry, our breaths mingling, our touch conveying our desperation. I shove off his tux jacket, then tear at his shirt. One solid tug sends his buttons scattering across the floor. My fingers trail over his tattooed chest.

He pulls back. "You want me." He says those words like they're a revelation.

"I'll never want you." I grind my pussy against his steely erection, contradicting my lie.

"You need me," he murmurs against my lips.

"I'll never need anything you're willing to give me." My voice is throaty, husky with desire.

His breath tickles my ear. "I'm going to fuck you until you admit out loud that you want me, need me, and that you can't live without me."

I scoff. "Don't press your luck. I'll never admit any of that."

"Oh, you will." He rocks his hips into me. "But first, I believe I promised to make you beg for my cock. If you want this, you need to get on your knees and beg, *wife*." He rolls his hips and I moan. Why does he have to feel this good?

I might be inexperienced in the bedroom, but there's no way in hell I'm going to let him call the shots.

By the time I'm done with him, *he'll* be the one begging.

CHAPTER 23

Dimitri

My eyes widen slightly in disbelief when Arianna releases me and sinks to the floor, to her knees. I didn't think she'd do this so willingly. But fuck does she look like my very own heaven-sent slut, kneeling, ready to beg for her husband's cock.

I grow painfully hard just from looking at her. Fucking perfection.

She surprises me all over again when she reaches for my belt. My head tilts back on a moan as her delicate hands work to free my dick.

In the limo, when I fingered her tight cunt, there was a moment when I thought she might be a virgin. She's so damn tight I couldn't fit more than two fingers in her pussy without the experience becoming uncomfortable.

But now, with her eagerness to get at my cock, I know she's no shy virgin. She's hungry for me.

A wave of possessiveness rushes through me. My

dick might not be her first cock, but it will be her last. I'll make sure of it. And she can tell me all the lies in the world about how she hates me, how she doesn't want me, when her need is written clearly on her beautiful, flushed face.

Right now, she'll do anything I tell her to do. I guarantee it. First, I'm going to watch her beg.

Sliding my slacks down, she wraps both hands around my cock and I groan. It's much larger than my two fingers, but I know my good girl can take it.

"You want that?" I ask her, my voice gravelly with desire. I slowly fuck her palms. "Beg for it."

A flicker of hesitation crosses her features. In a flash it's gone, replaced by pure defiance in her gorgeous eyes. She leans forward, flicking her tongue across the head of my dick, tasting, like I did to her pretty cunt earlier.

Fuck, that feels so damn good. Too good. Like heaven.

My deep moan seems to encourage her, and she parts her lips, taking my aching cock into her hot, wet mouth.

My hips jerk. *Fuck.* I'm going to come too soon if she keeps this up. I haven't been with a woman in... far too long. Almost two years. All because of *her.* She steals away my every sexual thought, it's her face I see when I get myself off, and the only woman I want to sink into is her—she's my obsession.

Now she's on her knees, swallowing around my cock, sucking on it like she can't get enough. She's fucking perfect.

"Fuck, *kisa*, you're going to make me come. Stop. That's enough. I want my cum in your pussy not down your throat."

At my command to stop, she takes me further down her throat. *Holy fucking shit.* Pleasure races up my spine. My balls draw up, tightening. I narrow my eyes at her. She's playing dirty.

My cock leaves her mouth with an audible pop. She gazes up at me through thick lashes. "You'll be the one begging, Dima." Then she sucks on my dick.

Dima. I don't know where she learned that nickname for Dimitri, but I love the sound of it on her lips. Okay, not as much as I love the feel of her lips around my cock. *Christ.* My fingers thread through her silky hair.

"You dirty, dirty girl. Do you really think you're going to win this game?" My voice is a strained, guttural growl.

She nods, a smirk shining in her eyes.

Fisting her hair, I shove her mouth further onto my cock, making her take more of it down her throat. Her eyes grow wide and tear up. Which makes me think I'm the largest man she's ever had. Good. At least I'm her first in that way.

And the first to eat her pussy, I remind myself. Satisfaction coils in my gut.

However, the memory of her orgasming on my tongue brings me that much closer to coming down her throat.

"Fucking hell, what do you want?" I ask her.

She lifts a haughty brow. We both know exactly what she wants.

I shake my head. "You can't win this, *malyshka.* Just give in. I bet if I slip my fingers into your pretty little cunt I'll find you dripping for me, won't I?"

She visibly shudders, her skin flushing pink and I

know she's as turned on as I am right now. But as she'll soon learn, I'll outlast her. My self-control is formidable. There's nothing she can do to—

Arianna slides her hands around my hips, then presses forward until my entire cock disappears down her throat. Holy shit that feels like heaven. She must be holding her breath because there's no way she can breathe around that.

When she looks up at me, tears leaking from her eyes, I fucking break.

This woman. Fuck.

She swallows and my balls tighten.

"*Please*," I groan. "Please let me fuck your perfect cunt."

Her eyes dance with triumph. She may as well enjoy the moment, because I'm going to make her pay for this dirty trick.

Grabbing her under the arms, I lift her off my dick, and set her on her feet. With one brutal tug, I tear off her dress. The fabric pools on the floor. Underneath, she's completely naked.

My hungry gaze eats her up. She's absolute perfection.

Blushing beneath my scrutiny, she goes to cover herself.

"No." My command rings out. "Now is not the time to get shy with me, *kisa*."

She swallows hard, her gaze darting around the room. What's wrong with her? A moment ago she was teasing the shit out of me, taking charge, being so fucking confident. Now she seems uneasy, and I don't know why.

Slowly, I lean in and kiss her. She steps forward, melting against me as I reignite the smoldering passion between us. My fingers dip to her pussy, and she's soaked. She's more than ready for me.

I push her onto the bed. Her back hits the mattress, and I flip her over, dragging her to her hands and knees at the edge of the bed. I circle her clit, working her up again, and this time she moans my name.

She'll be screaming it soon enough.

I tease her until she comes, then I line myself up, and thrust balls deep into her wet heat. I hiss at the tight fit. Her body tenses, her pussy squeezing me harder than I've ever experienced before.

I grit my teeth, not wanting to come just yet. I promised to fuck her, not go off like an adolescent boy.

Pulling almost all the way out, I glance at my dick and my blood runs cold. The pink tinge coating my cock tells me everything I need to know. She's a virgin.

Somehow, she's a fucking virgin, and she hid the truth from me.

Slipping from her pussy, I make her roll over, then climb onto the bed, covering her body with mine. I gaze into her eyes. Like this, she can't fucking hide from me.

"I'm your first," I say. "Why didn't you tell me?"

She huffs. "Like I would ever admit to being a virgin to the man who kidnapped me and forced me to marry him. I didn't want you to think that you could have my virginity too. I didn't want to be a prize."

"What? But here we are..."

"I know. I never expected to give myself to you." She glances away.

I smooth her hair back. "You should have told me, I could have hurt you worse than I already have."

The possessiveness I've felt toward her since saying my vows grows stronger. I'm her first. I feel both honored and unworthy. That seed of doubt is shut out when my inner caveman growls. This woman is mine. *Mine.*

"I'm going to do this right," I tell her, sliding my fingers between us. I line my cock up with her entrance and slide just the tip in. Teasing her clit, I rock my hips, easing in little by little. "That's right, just relax, *malyshka.* You're doing so good."

Her eyelids flutter, lips part.

"Eyes on me, *kisa.* Keep your eyes on me."

Her gaze snaps to mine.

Gently, I rock into her, kiss her lips, and look into her beautiful eyes. It feels a whole lot less like fucking and more like making love. My heart twists. Could she ever love me?

Before long, she's rolling her hips, meeting me thrust for thrust. A soft moan leaves her throat. "More," she begs. "Please, Dima, give me more. I can take it."

I give her what she wants. Driving into her harder and faster, she comes apart so prettily on my cock, and I follow her right over the edge.

Then I take her in my arms and hold her as she dozes. I've never wanted to cuddle after sex before, but everything is different with Arianna. She makes me want things I've never dared dreamed about before. I crave... *her.* Only her.

No amount of time with this woman will ever be enough. I could fuck her a billion times, and I'd still want her again and again.

The power she has over me scares me, because even though I can force her to stay with me forever, I want her to choose me for herself. Could a woman like her ever choose a man like me?

CHAPTER 24
Arianna

Dimitri is out trying to get IDs on the men who attacked the hotel charity event last night. Apparently he has men he relies on for information who work for the police department. He seems to have contacts all over the city, not just in the area run by his bratva. I'm sure my father is helping with some of that too, allowing Dimitri to use his own network, now that our families are joined.

I don't know how, but Dimitri managed to keep me away from the police. According to the official report, I wasn't involved at all.

I shift uneasily in the bathtub. Last night...

Well, last night was quite the turn of events, and I'm not sure how I feel about it. The adrenaline from everything at the hotel certainly pushed me over the edge, but I can't blame all that happened between us on brain chemistry, that would be unfair.

Dimitri has unexpectedly grown on me. That's the truth.

I might even like parts of him. Dare I admit that I also might want to explore whatever this is between us a little longer? He's not the man I'll settle down with, and one day he'll have to let me go, but until then I want more. More of him.

This morning my body aches, but it's a delicious kind of ache. My cheeks heat from the memories of last night. I can't believe I did all those things. I made him beg.

Then my stomach twists. The way he took me slowly, our eyes on each others, that look of pure reverence in his gaze... It was enough to undo me, to make me question everything I know about him and myself.

That scares me to death. I feel out of control.

Waking up with his arm draped across my waist, his body flush against mine, didn't help either. I never would have pegged Dimitri as a snuggler. But he is. He wraps his body around mine like he's never going to let me go again. We've never touched like that before, and now that the physical barrier between us has come crashing down, I'm feeling so much more vulnerable.

More than I've ever felt before. But that's the thing with Dimitri—he makes me experience all kinds of emotions I haven't before.

My phone chimes. My sister is finally texting me back.

> **SOPHIA**
>
> Last night was crazy. How are you doing? You shot a man. Are you feeling okay about that?

Right. I did shoot and kill a man in front of a whole bunch of witnesses. I should be freaking out, but I'm not.

In fact, that man's death seems so trivial to me that I'm actually a little worried about myself.

Though I've always known that, if given the right reasons and circumstances, I could kill a man.

Papa trained us all how to use a gun, but I was his star pupil. Partly, I think, because we both knew that I took the training very seriously, always expecting that someday I would shoot someone because that's simply the world we live in.

I just never expected to do it to save my captor's life. I groan.

What is seared into my memory is the look in Dimitri's eyes when I had the gun trained on him. The anguish, the gradual acceptance, and then the defiance, like he was daring me to pull the trigger. That gave me pause.

He's the type of man who would kill for me, but I had no idea until that moment that he'd also die for me.

A chill runs across my skin and I shiver despite the warm bath.

ARIANNA

I'm fine. You know the world we live in, so is it really that surprising what happened?

SOPHIA

No. But everyone handles it differently. I can come by if you need someone to talk to.

ARIANNA

Really, I'm fine. Just don't tell Gin what happened because she'll ask me a billion questions that I don't want to answer. Okay?

SOPHIA

My lips are sealed.

ARIANNA

Thank you.

I relax back against the soaking tub and sigh. I love my little sister. It's just sometimes she's a bit dramatic.

My phone pings again, but this time it's Tarina asking me to call her. I immediately dial her number.

"Arianna, I'm sorry to bother you on a Sunday, but Mr. Hyde has changed the design of two whole rooms, and I'm scrambling to get us back on the timeline with these changes. Can you come to the club today so we can walk through this?" She heaves a sigh. "He's such a pain in my ass."

I smile at her exasperated tone. This isn't the first time Mr. Hyde has swept in and shifted the function of a room once the layout and design was all set. I'm starting to suspect he enjoys flustering Tarina.

"Yes, I can come in. See you in an hour."

"You're a Godsend, Arianna." She hangs up.

I text Maks to tell him we're going out. Then I ease out of the tub. It's time to get back to work.

"Just so you know," Maks says. "Leonidas is the only place you're allowed to go outside of the estate. Dimitri's orders. He wants you straight back home after work."

"I'm well aware." I wave him off as we enter the building. Leonidas Gentleman's Club probably has one of the best security systems on the planet. They have to, given who their members are, and the type of security they need, without each person who enters here having to bring their own bodyguard.

Maks settles into a chair in the foyer. He likes to people watch.

I head up to Tarina's office, finding her and Ben working together. She shakes her head at him. "I want elegant and lavish, Ben, not tacky."

He frowns at his laptop screen. "Fine. I'll find something else."

"What can I help with?" I ask, setting down my purse.

Ben glances up, shooting me an annoyed look, like he blames me for his poor design choices. Honestly, I don't know why Tarina keeps him around.

"Let's walk," Tarina says to me, and I follow her through the hall. "This room was going to be the gambling den, but Mr. Hyde wants to make it a speakeasy instead. Which means the gambling has to move to the East wing. So..." She fills me in on all the change orders and how to work with it all given our current timeline.

I need to order some additional supplies to pull off

the speakeasy vibe, and the room layout will alter slightly.

As we head to the East wing to take a look at the new space we'll be working with, I spot Maks disappearing up a staircase. Isn't he supposed to be waiting for me in the foyer? What is he doing this far into the club? He's not a member. How did he get access?

I slow down and pat my trouser pockets. "You know what, I left something in your office. You go ahead, I'll catch up with you."

Tarina glances back at me, giving a curt nod. "Be quick about it. I'll start sketching out the layout for that room."

"I will."

She turns a corner, and I dart for the staircase that Maks ascended. At the top is a long hallway with doors along both sides. I believe these are private rooms. Frustratingly, I have no idea which one Maks entered.

Then I hear it, his distinct low rumble with that Russian accent. I step closer to the sound and press my ear to the door. There's two men on the other side having a conversation, but I can't make out their words.

Who could Maks possibly know at Leonidas?

The club is secure, discreet, the perfect place to meet with someone. But who, and why? It's really none of my business, I realize that, but Maks acts so strangely every time we're here. Like he's hiding something.

Heavy footfalls approach the door. I jerk back, frantically looking for a place to hide.

The handle turns.

I sprint up the stairs to the third floor, just as the door

opens and Maks steps out. Crouched against the banister, I peek down. Maks shoves a thick envelope into his breast pocket, glancing up and down the hall. Then he descends the stairs to the main level.

Was that a payoff? That sure looked like an envelope stuffed with cash he just pocketed. Is he acting on Dimitri's orders or someone else's? There's only one way to find out.

Leaving my hiding place, I step downstairs. Maks is strolling through the hallway, and I pretend to have just spotted him.

"Maks, what are you doing in this part of the club?" I casually approach him with a friendly smile.

He stiffens, then slowly spins around. His Adam's apple bobs as he swallows. "Nothing. Just needed to stretch my legs."

"Oh. So you weren't looking for me?"

"Nah. If I was looking for you, I'd send a text." His posture is relaxed, but it looks forced because his gaze keeps darting to the side. I'm surprised that he's such a terrible liar. In his line of work that could get him killed.

I don't want to push him too hard so I table the rest of my questions. "Okay then. I'll be about an hour, I think. I'll text you if work keeps me longer."

He nods, relief radiating off of him in waves. Turning away, I walk toward the East wing, my mind reeling.

If Maks was on an errand for Dimitri, he'd say so. We've stopped at places in the past around the city when Dimitri needs something done that isn't too dangerous. So that leaves me with one conclusion: Maks is going behind Dimitri's back.

Is he working with Boris, the guy Dimitri's trying to find? Or is he an informant of some kind, maybe with the FBI? The possibilities are endless. And not a single one of them looks good for Maks.

CHAPTER 25
Dimitri

"Listen, Pontrelli, I get it that Boris has left the country, but that doesn't mean your work on this is done. I need to know who helped him escape. You have my suspect list, any leads?" I lean forward, elbows on my desk, phone to my ear.

Pontrelli snaps, "No. No leads. Those other Russians have disappeared too. I'm finished with being your hound dog. Use your own resources if you want to follow around your men. Mine are busy with more important tasks."

"This isn't over until I say it's over. Remember, your daughter's life is on the line." I threaten, my tone menacing, even though my words are empty. I'd never harm his daughter, but he doesn't know that.

"Don't," he says. "Just don't. I'll put my men on it."

"Good." I press the button to end the call.

Boris has left, right after those fuckers tried to grab me from the charity event. The one dead man on the scene had no ID on him. So far, nothing has come back from running his prints either.

My guess is that Boris is regrouping. He's pig-headed, there's no way he's giving up. He'll either lead this Bratva or he'll die trying to step into my position.

The one thing that confuses me is why he wants me alive. Why didn't they shoot me at the hotel? They had plenty of opportunity. I don't get it.

A knock comes at my door.

"Come in," I bark.

I do a double-take when Arianna enters my office. Standing up, I motion to a chair in front of my desk, which she hesitantly approaches. Our gazes meet, but she quickly glances away, a faint pink staining her cheeks. It's obvious she's thinking about last night. Does she regret it? Worse, did I hurt her?

She sits and folds her hands in her lap. All prim and proper. Her shields are up, and I'd honestly do anything to get beneath them.

I clear my throat. "What's on your mind, *kisa?*"

After a strained moment, her eyes finally lock onto mine. Her pretty blush returns full force. Christ, I love that look on her.

"Do you trust Maks?" Her question takes me by surprise.

"Why? Did he touch you?" My fingers ball into fists on my desk. I don't care who it is, if anyone touches her they die.

Arianna's jaw drops. "No! Nothing like that... It's just that he met with someone at Leonidas and it struck me as suspicious. Was he running an errand for you?"

My fingers relax. "No. But believe it or not, Maks has his own life too. Not everything he does is for me."

"Oh. Okay." Her gaze lowers.

Could Maks betray me? The simple answer is *yes*. Do I think he'd ever turn against me? No. We have too much history together. He's been my one and only constant, reliable confidant. My friend.

At least I hope all of that is true.

Though Maks isn't the one intriguing me right now. *She* is.

I study my wife where she sits in front of me. She seems far more nervous than I've ever seen her before. Yet she's the one who came into my office, she sought me out, not the other way around.

"So," I lean forward on my elbows. "One night of my cock is all it took for you to go from wanting to kill me to warning me against potential threats? If I didn't know better, I'd think you're starting to like me, *kisa*."

Her face flames, her luscious lips parting as she clasps her pearl necklace, giving me all kinds of naughty ideas. Abruptly, she stands, narrowing her eyes. "You know what? I should have put that bullet in you last night."

I sit back and run my palm over my unshaven face. "Fuck, do you have any idea how gorgeous you are when you're feisty?"

My comment seems to throw her off. She stands there, staring at me like I've lost my fucking mind. Which is probably true. Especially where she's concerned.

Slowly, I stand up and move around the desk toward

her. Our gazes collide. I'm sure she can see the hunger in mine, because I'm nowhere near done with her. When I reach her, I slip my fingers around her throat and pull her close. She glances at my lips, then licks her own.

My mouth captures hers in a demanding kiss. She moans, her body melting against mine. All the awkward tension between us drains away as she lets me plunder her mouth with my tongue.

She tastes so fucking good. I'll never get enough of her.

Pulling slightly back, I murmur in Russian, *"Ty tak chertovski sovershenna, ya khochu tebe poklonyat'sya."*

You're so fucking perfect, I want to worship you.

Her pupils blow wide and she trembles. It's not the first time I've noticed that my native tongue affects her. She likes my filthy words too.

Lifting her up, I spin us around and place her ass on my desk. The little gasp she lets out has my cock growing harder. The need to feel her overtakes me, and I strip off her pants.

"Arms up," I demand, pulling her blouse over her head. All of her clothes hit my office floor, until she's sitting naked on my desk. Her breasts heave with each breath she takes. Such a perfect sight.

I step between her legs, still fully dressed, and take her nipples between my fingers, rolling them. She gasps, her back arching. She may say she wants to murder me, but I know what she really wants, and I'm more than willing to deliver.

Once her nipples are hard, I skim my fingers down her stomach, then dip my hand between her thighs. She's fucking soaked. She rolls her hips, demanding more. I love how responsive her body is to me.

"Do you want to come for me, *kisa?*" I whisper against her ear. "Do you want to come on your husband's fingers?"

She closes her eyes and nods.

"Eyes on me, *malyshka.*" I stop teasing her clit until her eyes snap open, finding mine. "That's right. Now ride your husband's hand like a good girl." I glide two fingers into her needy pussy. She obeys, rolling her hips, sliding up and down on my hand. As a reward, I circle her clit with my thumb. My free hand tangles in her silky hair and I lean down, taking one nipple into my mouth, and suck on it—hard.

"Dima!" she gasps my name as her cunt contracts around my fingers. Fuck she feels amazing.

Withdrawing, I go for my belt, but she beats me to it. Fumbling—so fucking adorable in her desperation to get to my cock—she undoes my belt, then the zipper on my jeans.

I snatch her hands away before she can further take charge, pinning her wrists behind her back. I line myself up and thrust into her pussy. Her breath hitches from the impact, but she doesn't give any sign of pain. If anything, she's in seventh heaven.

Letting her wrists go, I shove her back flush against the cold glass surface, then position her hands above her head. "Stay like that. Don't move."

She nods, her gaze trained on me as I fuck her into the desk. I lose myself in the feel of her, the intense pleasure on her face, and that look of wonder in her striking blue-green hazel eyes. There's no going back from this. I've had a taste, and I want more. So much more.

Gliding my hand between our bodies, I pinch her clit, and she comes on my dick. Satisfaction settles in my gut.

Two more thrusts and I'm about to follow her over the edge. I pull out, stroking my cock to completion. I give her a pearl necklace of my own. Ropes of my milky white cum cover her neck and tits. Such a beautiful sight.

With my free hand, I grab my phone and snap a picture of her. Fucking gorgeous.

"Dimitri!" She's obviously shocked.

Good. I like seeing her wide eyes and parted lips.

"What? You're a masterpiece, *kisa*. Here, look." I position the screen for her to see. She glances at the photo, her already flushed cheeks color crimson, but she doesn't argue.

"Stay right there." I tuck my dick away and pocket my phone. Then dart across the hallway to the bathroom, returning with a warm washcloth in hand.

I'm delighted to see that Arianna obeyed. She's laying back on my desk, completely naked and covered in my cum. She's such a good girl for me.

With the washcloth, I caress her smooth skin, cleaning her up. She watches my every move, seeming mesmerized. I take my time, loving touching her in any way I can.

"You're not the man I thought you were," she says in a quiet voice.

I quirk a brow. "Oh yeah?"

"Yeah. You're... complicated, unexpected? I'm not sure how to describe you."

A smirk touches my lips. She has no idea. Our time together hasn't given her much chance to really get to know me. Not the real me. That's about to change.

I want to show her all of myself. Even the parts that I keep hidden from the rest of the world. Even my secrets.

CHAPTER 26

Arianna

Today Dimitri's driving us in one of his sports cars further into the country. We're headed toward a small town in the mountains. The crisp, autumn air is sharper up here, but the scenery is beautiful. Even so, my gaze keeps sliding back to Dimitri's handsome face, and dropping to his hand resting on my knee.

He absentmindedly rubs my skin with his thumb, and my stomach flutters. His touch drives me crazy, whether it's sexual or a simple, small contact like this. I'm still not entirely certain how to think or feel about him.

However, I am willing to admit that Dimitri is alluring in ways I never expected. I could easily become addicted to him, even if just for a little while. Why not play along with this fantasy for however long it lasts? I'm not risking my heart, and the things he does to my body... Those things I crave.

The reality is he'll grow tired of me at some point. After all, I'm nothing more than a possession to him, a power move, and once he gets everything he wants, he'll pursue the next woman. I may as well enjoy him while I can.

My stomach twists. The thought of him with another woman doesn't settle well with me. That same jealousy I experienced at the charity event rises up, making me frown.

"We're here." Dimitri's voice jolts me from my thoughts. He pulls through tall iron gates and parks in front of a stately mansion with a sprawling lawn. The sign above the door reads: *Rurik Orphanage.* I frown at it in confusion.

"You brought me to an orphanage?" I face Dimitri, who nods and gets out of the car, coming around to my side to open the door. "Why?" I ask as he helps me out.

He pins me with his intense deep green eyes. "Because of what you said in my office about me not being the man you thought I was. And, well, I wanted to show you more of who I am." He rubs the back of his neck, looking doubtful. "I'm not all fights, and clubs, and guns, you know."

Without further explanation, he takes my hand and we enter the building. As soon as we step inside, a horde of children come running down the stairs, their expressions bright with excitement.

"Uncle Dima! Uncle Dima!" They scream as they surround him. He drops my hand so he can pick up the little girl that can't be any more than five years old. She hugs his neck, looking smug at being in his arms.

Dimitri claps several older boys on their backs and pats the heads of the other children. All while I stare in shock and wonder. This is like entering an alternate universe.

What are we doing here, and who is this smiling man in front of me surrounded by happy children?

A matronly woman sweeps into the room, grinning up at Dimitri. "As usual, you're right on time. The children have been looking forward to your visit all month. If you can untangle yourself from them, we can speak in my office." She gives me a polite smile, before shooing the kids away. "Go play outside, all of you."

The five year old tightens her hold on Dimitri. Pouting, she shakes her head. "No."

"Katerina," Dimitri croons. "Don't you want to go play with the other children?"

"No," she says, her stance firm.

Dimitri's smiles indulgently. "In that case, I want you to meet someone." He turns her toward me. "This is Arianna."

Katerina blinks, taking me in while keeping her arms wrapped around Dimitri's neck.

"Hello." I wave at her, and she ducks, suddenly shy, hiding her face in his shoulder. The sight is so cute, and unexpected, that my heart squeezes. I smile at the both of them.

Dimitri whispers something to Katerina. She glances up at him, then nods. He sets her on her feet. She waves at us as she runs out the door to play with the rest of the children. The look on Dimitri's face is that of a doting father.

Is he her father? After that interaction I witnessed between them, I can't see Dimitri leaving his child in an orphanage. Not for any reason. Even so...

"Is she yours?" I ask, hesitant.

His gaze snaps to mine. "No. Of course not. She was abandoned on our doorstep when she was three days old."

"Oh." I release the breath I didn't realize I'd been holding and step forward. "What did you say to her?"

"I promised her a piggyback ride later if she'd run off and play with the others for now." He shoots me a dazzling smile, like he's looking forward to it as much as she is. Then he gives his attention to the woman who runs this place, I'm assuming, and his demeanor shifts to all business.

"Mila, this is Arianna, my wife. Give me this month's update."

We shake hands, before she escorts us into her office, where we all take our seats. She gets straight to the point. Obviously familiar with Dimitri enough to not keep him waiting long.

"We've placed the twins in a good home—together. The couple adopted both of them just as we hoped," she says. "The babies are always easier to find homes for though. To think that at least three of our eldest will be turning eighteen in the next few months. I haven't told them yet, but I have their life start packages all ready for them."

"That's good." Dimitri bobs his head in approval.

"What is that?" I ask him. "A life start package?"

He glances at me, then clears his throat in that way that indicates he's nervous. "Money mostly. At least for those who don't have a college scholarship, or some other opportunity to help them start their adult lives."

"Oh." I take a second to digest that information.

He goes back to discussing details with Mila, while I try, and fail, not to stare at his profile. This ruthless mafia man has a hand in running an orphanage and gives his money to children in need? I'm quite confused right now. No one can be this full of surprises, can they?

"You should know that we have an inquiry," Mila says hesitantly. "It's for Katerina."

Dimitri's brow furrows. He's not happy with that news, but he's trying to hide his emotions. "That's good. Do me a favor and vet them thoroughly. Twice. Make that three times."

"I understand, sir." Mila sighs. "Well, that's all the news I have for you this month. We are at your disposal today for anything else you need."

"I'm going to give my wife the tour. Then we'll spend some time with the children."

Mila softly smiles. "Thank you, sir."

As soon as we exit her office, I pull Dimitri to a stop. "What is going on here? You're obviously an investor or something. Why?"

He takes my hand in his and we start walking. "I bought this place ten years ago, knowing I wanted to open an orphanage—a good one, a safe and comfortable place for children to grow up—since I came to America to live with my uncle. Having experienced how rough the streets are, and the type of hands the young and innocent can fall into, I wanted to spare others from the same fate. No orphan should grow up like I did before my uncle saved me."

"So you opened an orphanage," I muse, squeezing his hand to show my approval. "You're a sweet man."

He shoots me a dubious glance. Maybe *sweet* is the wrong word to describe him.

We round a corner, ending up in a quiet, empty hallway. Dimitri pulls me into him, then steps forward until my back hits the wall.

"I am not *sweet, kisa.* Don't be delusional." His body presses flush against mine and my nipples pebble. "My need for this place was brought about by trauma and pain. I'm no saint. I'm not doing this out of the goodness of my heart. This place gives me a sense of control in an otherwise chaotic world. Don't you ever paint me as the good guy. That way of thinking will only lead to disappointment."

I cup his face, my thumb brushes over his bottom lip. What he won't say out loud is that this place helps heal his broken soul. That it's his way of giving back for the life his uncle gave him. But I don't need him to tell me that to understand.

"I'll never expect you to be anything other than what you are, Dimitri." Every day I'm still finding out who that person is, and the glimpse I've gotten today is one I like very much.

Dimitri ducks his head, capturing my lips in a toe-curling kiss. By the time he pulls away, I'm breathless.

"Come. I want to show you around." He takes my hand again. "And, *kisa,* don't tell a soul about this place. Not even Maks."

Quickly, I nod.

So this is his secret? One he hasn't told Maks about, his best friend, but he's willing to share with me?

Butterflies erupt in my stomach. He's letting me in, allowing me to see beneath his bad boy exterior to the heart of gold underneath. In this man is the last place I ever expected to find such a heart.

This light and airy feeling stays with me all day as I tour the orphanage, learn about everyone there, and watch Dimitri interact with the kids. He keeps his word and gives Katerina a piggyback ride. She shrieks and giggles, and the grin on his face couldn't get any bigger. The sight further warms my heart.

So much so that on the drive home I'm quiet. I suddenly have this dreadful feeling that my heart may be more at risk than I initially thought possible.

I've always imagined myself with a highly educated, sophisticated man. Nothing like Dimitri Kozlov who is pure heart and raw passion. His energy is all-consuming, addicting. But there's nothing safe or stable about him.

More and more I have to remind myself that I don't want to be with him. He's my captor. My stalker. He forced his agenda on me and I have no choice. I want to escape him—yet I let that opportunity come and go.

Lately I feel my convictions are not as strong as they used to be. I'm struggling to keep our relationship in perspective. Even though one thing is certain—I cannot fall for Dimitri Kozlov.

I'd be betraying the very essence of who I am.

Worst of all, that way lies heartbreak.

CHAPTER 27

Arianna

"Where are we going?" I shiver on the tarmac in my wool coat. Crisp autumn has given way to winter as we approach Thanksgiving. It's the Tuesday prior to the holiday, and we're hustling toward a private jet instead of cooking a feast at home.

Dimitri wraps his arm around me and I lean into his warmth. Then pull back, narrowing my eyes at him. "Are you trying to get out of having Thanksgiving with my family?" When he gives me that innocent look, I chastise him. "*Dimitri.*"

"I'm not *trying* to get out of spending the holiday with your parents." He lifts me in his arms, and I release a startled cry as he starts climbing the jet's stairs. His grin transforms into a dashing smirk. "I'm *successfully* doing just that."

I slap his chest. "Put me down. We're going back home. I can't believe you'd try something like this." Though actually, I can. The very notion of sitting around a table, surrounded by the Pontrelli family, must terrify him. After all, he's not exactly in their good graces.

"Not trying, *kisa*, doing. Remember?" He sets me in a seat and immediately fastens my seat belt. "You can call them once we're in the air and tell them we're not coming on Thursday."

"We're not coming? I think you mean to say that you're *kidnapping* me—again." I cross my arms and huff in mock annoyance.

His smile widens. "Kidnapping you might be my favorite pastime. No, actually, my favorite is—"

"Fine." I cut him off before he can get too descriptive, because I know exactly where his head is at. "We can get out of going to my parents place for Thanksgiving, but we absolutely have to be there for Christmas."

"Deal," he says like he just won the better end of this bargain.

The jet begins to roll, and in minutes we're ascending into the air.

I shift toward him. "You still haven't answered my question. Where are we going? I'm literally your captive audience, will you tell me now?"

"It's a surprise." His mouth twitches with amusement.

I groan.

"You're going to love it." He clasps my hands in his. "If you don't, then we'll turn right around and come home. But you're going to love it."

"Okay, fine. I'll let you know my decision after we arrive at this mystery destination."

His smug expression gives me pause. Where could

we be going that he's this excited about? And secretive about.

Shaking my head in exasperation, I take in my surroundings. The jet is comfortable, with cream leather seats and an airy interior. Dimitri's bad boy appearance is at odds with this posh environment. He looks like walking sin in his jeans, dark T-shirt, and leather jacket.

"Wherever we're going, we could have traveled a lot less expensively than this, Dimitri. First class would have been a luxury. You don't have to try so hard to impress me, you know."

It's no secret that my family has money, but I don't want him to think I expect to always live that wealthy lifestyle. One day, when I'm on my own, earning my own money, I'll have to embrace a simpler existence to make ends meet. Which I'm perfectly fine with doing.

I'm startled when he laughs outright, the sound rumbling through his chest. It shoots pleasure straight between my thighs.

"What's so funny?" I ask, trying not to squirm.

"Why do you keep treating me like I'm an impoverished club owner? Hmm?"

I arch a brow. "Because I'm fairly certain you spend all your money on sports cars and orphans. My father's a don, I know how men in our world spend pretty much everything they make to sustain their outrageous, enviable lifestyles, but the truth is they're practically broke. It's not like you're a Colombian cartel boss making bank on importing drugs." I shift in my seat. "All the flowers, the new laptop, the Skye Adair ball gown, now this private jet. It's too much. You've spent a fortune in less than two months. It makes me...uncomfortable."

He leans back and scrutinizes me. I'm completely serious.

Papa always treated us well growing up, made sure we had a proper education and designer clothing. After all, he wanted us to attract the wealthier dons and their sons. But he's always been strategic with how he spends his resources. Relatively speaking, he's frugal.

Of course now that Sophia is married to a billionaire, she can have whatever she wants. I, on the other hand, aim to work for my money. I can make a good life for myself in the event planning industry. Honestly, I prefer a more cautious and realistic approach to wealth management. I can't stand the idea of bouncing around between plentiful and poor. Stability is what I crave.

When he doesn't say anything, I sigh. "Just stop spending so much money on me. Give it to the orphanage instead. Add it to their life start funds."

"Wouldn't want to spoil them that much, *kisa*. They already get a hundred grand when they turn eighteen." He rests his elbows on his knees. "Don't worry, it's in a trust until they're twenty-two so they can't spend it all in one place, or before they've learned some responsibility."

I stare at him, slack-jawed. "You're... You're actually serious. You give them a hundred thousand dollars when they age out of the system?" I've never heard of such a thing.

"One hundred percent serious. Do you really think I'd give those children a place to live then toss them out without any means of survival, or opportunity, when they turn eighteen?" He scoffs. "Don't be ridiculous, only the government does that to this nation's orphans. And as far as spending my money on you goes, I'll do as I damn well please. I'm going to spoil you every which way I can, and you're going to take it like a good girl." He grins wolfishly.

I blush and look out the jet window. Obviously there's no sense in arguing with him.

My family's more than a little disappointed that I'm not spending the holiday with them, but all thoughts of that vanish from my mind when Dimitri welcomes me to his island.

"What do you mean *your* island?" The jet dropped us off at a private airfield. From there Dimitri drove us to a sprawling ocean-side villa. The blue waters glitter with the early evening sunlight and a slight breeze kicks up, taking the edge off the heat. I ditched my wool coat as soon as we landed.

"I mean *my* island as in, I own it." He deposits our suitcases in a bedroom that overlooks an outdoor pool, the view drawing the eye to the beach and ocean beyond. "I bought it a couple of years ago, as an escape from the city. Then I decided I needed a jet because that's the fastest way to get here."

Wait. He owns the jet and a private island in the Caribbean?

I gape at him. "Who *are* you?"

"More than I appear," he says, his breath tickling my ear. He walks past me, into the main living space and opens a bottle of wine. "Come. Sit with me."

In a state of disbelief, I do as I'm told. Taking the wine glass he offers, I sit on the sofa and admire the view. I've only been on this island for about an hour, yet I already feel my muscles relaxing. There's something about this environment that makes my mind automatically unwind. It reminds me of vacationing in Italy. The warmth, the sparkling water, the easier pace of life. I love it.

Dimitri sits beside me, his body angled toward mine. "From what my uncle's told me over the years, our family fled Russia in the early nineteen hundreds during the Russian Revolution. We came here, bringing all of our wealth with us. Or at least as much as we could. My father is the only one who ever returned to our Motherland and that's how I was born there, but that's a story for another time."

He swallows a mouthful of wine. "Anyway, prohibition started soon after and my ancestors saw their way into positions of power and profit in the United States. They opened speakeasies in New York City, which today are the clubs we run, that still offer illegal substances, gambling, fights, and anything else we want. But my family also invests heavily and our net worth is pretty much up there with all the other greedy mother-fuckers in this country. Basically, I'm rich, *malyshka*. Filthy rich."

Not just rich, but old money wealth. The Kozlov Estate's mansion now makes more sense. The art, the culture, the lavishness is all because of his family's history.

I cock my head to one side, teasing. "Are you sure that story's true? Maybe your ancestors just stole it all."

He chuckles. "Maybe they did. Or maybe I'm a Russian prince in disguise."

We both laugh. Though now that he mentions it... Honestly, I could see that. Dimitri is a never-ending source of surprises.

"Are you hungry, *kisa?*"

I enthusiastically nod. "Are there any restaurants on this island?"

"Not a single one. It's just us and a couple of caretaker cottages on the other side of the island. We have a cook and a housekeeper. I had the place fully stocked before we got here. Come." He holds out his hand and I take it, his palm warm and dry in mine.

He leads us to the beach. I don't see anyone else around, but someone set up flickering torches and a candlelit dining table at the water's edge. Native flowers decorate the tabletop between the covered dishes. The scene's absolutely stunning.

I glance up at Dimitri, who's watching me closely for a reaction. I smile, completely blown away.

He pulls out my chair and I take a seat. He sits opposite of me.

"It's not twelve courses, but I think you'll like it." He uncovers a large platter, revealing the best smelling Bistecca alla Fiorentina. The steak looks done to perfection. My mouth waters as the rich aromas reach my nose. Dimitri uncovers the rest of the traditional Italian dishes and serves us.

"This is amazing." I moan around a mouthful of the tender steak. "Compliments to the chef."

"I'll be sure to tell him."

As we eat, I glance up to find him studying me like

there's something on his mind. After the fifth or sixth time, curiosity gets the better of me.

"What?" I ask. "Why do you keep looking at me like that?"

"Like what?"

I finish my glass of Syrah. "I don't know. Like *that*."

He leans forward. "What's your favorite color?"

"You don't already know?" I lift a brow, challenging him. He did stalk me for quite a while. How does he know my favorite foods but not my favorite color?

"Surprisingly, I don't. Enlighten me."

I ponder my answer while he refills my wine glass. It's a simple question, but I actually don't have a simple answer. "I guess I don't have a favorite. My favorites are blue, green, and purple. But I can't choose between them."

He hums. "So that's why I could never figure it out."

"I guess." I motion toward him. "Yours must be blue given all the blue flowers around the house."

He chews on a bite and shakes his head. "It's green." His gaze grows hesitant. "I like the blue flowers because they remind me of what you were wearing when I saw you for the first time."

"Oh." Slowly, I nod. I've worn blue countless times, and I have no way of knowing which of those times he first started stalking me. I shift uncomfortably in my seat. How can I reconcile my terrifying stalker with this fascinating man seated in front of me?

Lowering my voice, I ask, "Why did you terrorize me? Why the stalking? Did you think breaking me would work in your favor? That I'd give in to you sooner, easier, if I was terrified when you forced me to be your wife?"

"No." His jaw clenches. "I was punishing you for your father's mistake. For our broken alliance that led to my uncle's death. I wanted someone to pay, anyone, since I couldn't find my uncle's killer. So I took it out on you."

"I see." My tone is brittle. It's times like these that I'm reminded of how I'm nothing but a pawn in his revenge game. An object to take out his frustrations on, to marry and seal a broken alliance, and to use in order to have power over my father.

I stab my risotto with more force than necessary.

"I won't apologize because I'm not that kind of man. But sometimes I wonder how things would be different between us if we met under other circumstances. If I had asked you on a date rather than sent you threatening text messages."

"Honestly, it wouldn't have mattered." I haughtily look him up and down. "I never would have given you a chance." I don't mean to say that to hurt him, it's simply the truth. Okay, maybe it's also an attempt to shield my heart. "You're not the type of man I envision myself with and you never will be."

His brow creases. "What kind of man do you want, *kisa?* What future do you envision for yourself?"

Is he serious right now? Why does he care?

Done with dinner, I set down my fork. "I want an educated man. One who is suave and charming. But he also has to be loyal, honest, and supportive. I want a man who will be a good father to our children." I lick my lips. "I didn't know that I wanted this before, but now I'm sure I want a man who's head over heels in love with me." *And in lust with me.* Though I won't say that part aloud.

Eyeing me, he gulps down the rest of his wine, then refills his glass. "You're right, I'm not the man you want."

I stare at him for a beat. I didn't expect him to so easily admit that. At least we're on the same page.

He leans his elbows on the table. "On the other hand, you're exactly the woman I want. One who's honest, independent, and stubborn. Fiercely loyal to her convictions and to those she loves. A woman who will make an excellent mother some day."

My cheeks warm. Is that really how he sees me? It's in a much more positive light than I would have guessed.

"I want children," he continues. "I want a home full of love and warmth, the kind of family I never had."

Family seems to be a value we both share. While I grew up in a strict yet nurturing environment, Dimitri was abandoned, orphaned, and endured so many hardships.

My heart breaks for him a little more.

Suddenly, seeing how he interacted with the kids at the orphanage casts him in a whole new light. He feels a sense of family and connection there that he didn't have growing up. Maybe he even feels like he can experience a different type of childhood by being around those children. In a sense, they are his family.

"You deserve the kind of family you want," I tell him. "Plenty of women would love to create that life with you."

"Just not you?" His expression shutters, impossible to read.

"Just not me." For some reason this statement doesn't land quite right. It burns like a lie on my tongue.

"Maybe I can change your mind." He stands,

prowling closer to me. His impassive features give way to lust.

"You can't," I say, but my heart races. "Above all else, I want out of this life. As far away from the mafia world as possible."

Dimitri drops to his knees in the sand. He lifts and repositions my chair so I'm facing him, his fingers curl around the sides. "Why? Why do you want out so badly?"

A rianna's brows draw together, her expression tormented. My heart twists, pulse accelerating with the need to protect her from any and all potential danger. Except I can't, because whatever's hurting her comes from within. I don't want to interrogate her, but I need to know the truth.

I dip my head, capturing her tortured gaze. "Tell me, *kisa*. Let me understand you."

"I-Ilaria." Her voice breaks. "We grew up together. We were so young when we met that I don't even remember it, she was just always there, like a third sister." She closes her eyes and releases a shaky breath. "Until one day she wasn't. Her father sold her when she was sixteen. We never even had a chance to say goodbye."

A lead weight drops in my gut. A father sold his own daughter? I can relate to that all too well.

"That was the first time I realized how messed up

this world is," she continues. "When parents sell their own children, who they're supposed to love and protect, there's no safe place for anyone here. I became terrified that my father would do the same to my sisters and me. In a way, I was right to be afraid."

She lifts her sorrowful gaze to mine. "Arranged marriages are much the same thing, under a different name. After everything that happened with my older sister Sophia's engagement, I knew I had to leave. This cycle will never end—not really. If I have children with a man like you they'll never be safe."

For a second, I'm speechless. Is that what she thinks of me? That I'd sell off my own children? *Really?* White hot fury burns in my chest.

"I was fucking *sold* by own father. I know exactly what that feels like and I'd never do that to another person, least of all my own child," I say vehemently. She needs to understand my sincerity.

"But you already have," she whispers. "You bought me. Not with currency, but with threats. Which means you forced my father to sell me. To you. How do you not understand that?"

"I—" My brows crash down.

She's right.

I thought I could claim her as my own, and by pure force of will she'd eventually want to be mine. How could I have been so wrong? I've been fucking blind to the suffering I've put her through. I need to wake the fuck up.

I've already tied her to me in every way possible—except her heart isn't mine. She can wear my ring, be my wedded wife, and share my bed, but if I don't have her heart then what's the point? If I can't win her over... then I have to let her go, don't I? As much as I can't stand that idea.

How is it that she's taken over my heart in such a short amount of time? To the point that I actually would let her go because I... *I love her.*

There. I admit it. But when did she become so much more than an obsession? Can obsession turn into genuine love?

Stalking her meant I only saw the shell of who she is inside. Bringing her into my life was my undoing. She stole my heart away with her pearl-clutching innocence, the defiance she showed when trying to burn down my penthouse, and when she helped me through that agonizing charity dinner. She could have turned her back on me that night and made me look foolish, but she didn't.

The final moment, the one in which I think I completely fell for her, is when she pulled that trigger. She should have killed me, we both know it, but she saved my life instead.

She chose me and now my heart belongs to her. Too bad she doesn't feel the same way, at all. To her I'll forever be her stalker, her captor, the man she loves to hate.

"You're right," I finally say. "I did buy you. I treated you like a commodity." *I'm sorry.* The words linger on the tip of my tongue, but refuse to be spoken. My throat closes around them, keeping them trapped inside.

My fingers itch to touch her, even though I know I'm

not worthy. I've treated her terribly, like a prisoner, an object, bringing her worst fears to life. As much as I wish I could put an end to this here and now, I can't. I'm not that good of a man—which makes me even more unworthy of her love.

She'll never love me the way I want, but I can't give up just yet. If all I have with her is this slice of time between now and when I find Boris, then I'll take it. I'll drink up every moment with her until I can't make her stay any longer.

Do I hope to win her heart? Yes. Do I think it's going to happen? No. Not in this lifetime.

"Thank you for admitting to it." Her hands land on my chest. Fuck, the way she touches me, even this innocently, sets me on fire. I set out determined to make her burn for me, but I'm the one engulfed in flame.

I cover her hands with my own. "I haven't been completely honest with you. The truth is, I don't care about the broken agreement between our families. I could hunt down my uncle's killer without your father's help, without having forced you to marry me." My grip tightens. "I've been obsessed with you since the first moment I saw you. All I want is a chance. This was the only way I figured I'd get that chance with you."

Her eyes widen, the whites sparkling in the firelight.

Before I lose my nerve, I plow ahead. "I knew a woman like you—no, that's not right," I mumble and start again. "I knew *you* wouldn't look twice at me. You admitted that I don't stand a chance and never have. So I forced you into this, and I'm not sorry. Because this is the only way I could get your attention."

"That's really messed up, Dimitri." She frowns,

concerned. "Maybe it was too harsh of me to say I'd *never* give you a chance."

"No. You were honest. But, *kisa*, I'm on my knees right now begging you to just look at me. To just see *me*. Not the dangerous world we're part of, or all the preconceived ideas we both have." I heave a frustrated sigh. I don't have the words to tell her what I want or make a good enough argument for her to understand my desperation.

She leans in. "I do see you, Dima. And honestly, what I see terrifies me."

I cringe. I'm an idiot. Of course trying to lay my soul bare to her she'd find disgusting. There's nothing pretty underneath my exterior.

"You've been more honest with me in the last ten minutes than you have in weeks." She cups my cheek, and my gaze darts to hers. "When I see you like this it scares me because you break through my defenses. I don't know what to do with this version of you."

"What do you want to do with it?" I ask, swallowing hard.

"This." Arianna brushes her lips against mine, once, twice. "But I know I shouldn't want you."

She wants me? She *wants me*.

I claim her mouth in a kiss full of longing. Our tongues tangle, licking and tasting, needing more. I pull her toward me and her legs part, instinctively wrapping around my hips. If only our minds could be as in tune with each other as our bodies are.

Pushing her thighs down and pinning her in the chair, I ease back. "Stay with me this weekend."

Slowly, I lift her skirt, bunching it around her waist,

then slide her underwear down her shapely legs. She obediently steps out of them.

"Please," I beg. I don't think I've craved anything more in my entire life. Not even food when I was starving on the brutal winter streets of Moscow. No, this is the moment when I will shamelessly beg.

She nods. "I'll stay."

The tightness in my chest eases. "Good girl." I lower my face to her pussy. "Now it's time for my favorite dessert."

My brass knuckles smash into the Russian's face, his teeth fly across the room in a spray of blood, but my mind is a million miles away reliving the days Arianna and I spent together on my island.

Something changed between us after that first night. The crystal clear waters, passionate nights, and isolation seemed to strip away every wrong that was between us. Until there was nothing left but our carefree souls, our true selves, gazing back at each other. We spent the days snorkeling, lazing on the beach, and making love in the tranquil water.

We hiked to my favorite waterfall—where I learned that Arianna's not a hiker, she's a city girl through and through. She developed blisters and I fucking grinned like a love-sick fool as I carried her all the way back to the villa.

For those few days I wasn't a Bratva boss, or a club

owner, or a man grieving the loss of his uncle. I felt light and free. Like a man who'd found the love of his life.

And Arianna allowed me to indulge in that fantasy.

Since we've been back, some of that easy energy between us has remained. I'll catch her secretly smiling at me when she thinks I'm not looking. She comes willingly when I reach for her, and I can't seem to stop touching her, whether it's having her hand in mine or my cock buried deep inside her hot cunt.

She's pure heaven. A fucking angel who lights up my dark existence.

"Who do you work for?" Maks's voice pulls me out of my thoughts and back to the present. My men caught this Russian foreigner poking around one of my clubs. We thought they'd all left the city, but we were misinformed.

So far he's been a tough son of a bitch and is refusing to speak a word. But he isn't from around here, and he's certainly not one of mine, so my best guess is he's working for Boris.

Boris fled the country and I don't need a professional tracker to tell me where he went. Russia. That's where he is, in the Motherland. Well they can fucking have him. If he steps one foot back in this country he's dead. Just like this associate of his will be dead soon.

I'll make sure of it.

One last blow to the side of his face and he's out cold. I straighten up, annoyed at the amount of blood splattered on my T-shirt. This fucker sure is a bleeder.

"We're not going to get any answers out of him like that," Maks notes.

I shrug. "He wasn't going to talk anyway. When he

wakes up, get Anton in here and tell him he can do whatever he wants. If it leads to answers, great. If not, oh well."

"Will do, *Pakhan*."

I clean up in the wall-mounted steel sink, scrubbing this fucker's blood from my hands. I wash the brass knuckles clean and pocket them.

Glancing down at my shirt, I sigh. Maybe I have a spare in my office.

I don't usually do the dirty work myself—that's Maks's job. But today I felt like getting hands-on with this guy while Maks asked the questions. This is what I get for it, a filthy shirt and no damn answers.

Maks calls Anton, our best torturer, and follows me to my office where I rummage around for a clean shirt and come up empty handed. My leather jacket will cover it up enough. That's the best I can do. When I get home I'll shower and change.

"Anton will be here soon." Maks puts his phone away.

Just as I sit down behind my desk, the office door bangs open. Maks draws his gun, narrowing his gaze on my red-faced club manager. When he realizes there's no immediate danger, he holsters it and leans casually against the door frame.

"Those fucking Italians were sniffing around here again," Sasha practically snarls.

"I told you, let them. They are working with us." Impatiently, I wave him off. I have more important business to attend to than arguing with Sasha about the Italians—*again*.

He braces his hands flat down on my desk and leans

in. "You don't know what they've been up to because you were away all weekend with that Italian whore. I told you we should have taken them out, not married into that family. That Pontrelli *slut* is—"

The silenced shot rings out in my office. Sasha's brains explode across the opposite wall and his body drops to the floor. I glance down at the gun in my hand, unable to recall exactly when I grabbed it. Somewhere between *whore* and *slut*.

Only *I* get to call my wife those words. And only when she's being a good girl.

Maks sighs. "Wasn't that a bit of an overreaction?"

"Nope." I drop the gun back into my desk drawer. "No one talks about my wife that way and lives. Be sure to tell the others just in case anyone is unaware of my expectations."

"Okay. I'll get this mess cleaned up and interview for a new club manager." Maks sighs like I'm a pain in his ass.

I stand up, any other business on my agenda today can wait. "Good. I'm going home."

"Okay, *Pakhan*, do you—" He interrupts himself and reaches for his phone, glancing down at a text. "I—I have an errand to run, but I'll make sure to get this all done."

"An errand?" I fold my arms, noting the way Maks won't meet my eyes. Arianna suspects him of betraying me, could she be right? I hope not. Maks is family to me and that level of backstabbing would fucking gut me. But everyone seems to have a price they can be bought for these days.

"Yeah. I'll see you later." Maks tosses on his coat and fishes out his keys.

"I guess we're both heading out." Grabbing my leather jacket, I walk with him to the parking garage under Riot. While I go for my bike, he heads for an SUV. I wait for him to pull out first, then start up my Harley and follow him.

CHAPTER 29
Dimitri

Maks parks in front of a seedy motel outside of town. We're outside of Bratva territory, in an unmemorable location that blends in with its surroundings. If Maks is going to betray me, this is the place to meet someone to do it. No man's land.

Fuck. I really don't want to have to kill my best friend.

Maks knocks, and enters room number two fourteen on the second floor. I drive around the block and find parking a little ways away, then hoof it back to the motel. I'm getting some fucking answers. Right now.

I jog up the stairs and approach the room. On the other side of the thin door, rumble two deep voices, one is Maks. The other sounds distressed. A third baritone roars in surprised fury, and two shots ring out.

That's it, I'm going in. One shove of my shoulder into the flimsy motel door and the frame cracks. The door slams into the wall with an audible *whack*.

I raise my gun. Then stop dead in my tracks.

What the fuck?

Maks is standing over a man's dead body. The stranger's blood seeping into the dirty shag carpet. The guy's hair is wet, with a towel wrapped around his waist as if he just got out of the shower.

A younger man sits on the bed, shaking, his feet drawn up to avoid the bloodshed. His lip is split, and the fresh bruises on his face are already starting to darken from red to purple. For some reason he looks familiar, though I swear I've never seen him before.

"What the fuck is going on?" I holster my gun, because this is definitely not a traitor's planning meeting, or anything else I expected to find.

Maks glances at me, resignation in his expression. "Dimitri, meet Liam Baron. Liam... this is my boss."

"Liam Baron? As in Blake Baron's younger brother?" No wonder he looks familiar. He has the same blond hair and aristocratic features as his brother.

Liam rises from the bed, harshly swiping away his tears. "Nice to meet you, Mr. Kozlov. I've heard a lot about you."

He's heard a lot about me? From who?

Maks shoots him a warning glare and shakes his head. Liam's lips press together. He hangs his head, looking like a sad, abused puppy.

The fuck is going on?

Sirens wail in the distance, spurring us into action. "Let's get the fuck out of here. We can talk on the way."

After Maks and I do our best to wipe the place clean, the three of us pile into the SUV out front. I send a text to one of my guys to have my bike picked up from here and brought back to Riot, grateful that I had the foresight to park a couple blocks away from this shitshow.

I drive, with Maks in the passenger seat and Liam Baron in the back. Glancing at them both, I try and fail to piece together how the fuck they know each other, and why Maks would be killing for Blake Baron's baby brother at a seedy motel.

The silence stretches on, until I break it. "Explain yourself."

"It's complicated." Maks glances at Liam.

"Then start talking," I command, impatience roiling through me. I want some goddamn answers.

"I will, once Liam's injuries have been looked at."

I tighten my grip on the steering wheel. Maks rarely disobeys me, and he's the only one I let get away with it. I'm tempted to pressure him right now, but there's something in the way he's looking at Liam that makes me hold my tongue.

Plus, I trust him enough to respect his decision. If he doesn't want to talk now then so be it. I'm sure he has a good reason.

I'll get answers out of them both soon enough.

One thing I'm pretty sure about is that Maks isn't working with Boris. The sense I got from that scene in the motel room is, whatever this is, it's personal, not business. Though fuck if I know how Maks and Liam Baron are connected.

I glance at Liam in the rearview mirror. He's in pretty rough shape. The last thing I need is Blake Baron coming after us because he thinks we fucked up his little brother. My gaze slides to Maks's knuckles. They're undamaged, so I doubt he beat Liam, unless he used something other than his fists.

Forty minutes later, this quiet, strained car ride comes to an end. We're at the estate. I park in the garage and usher them into the gilded sitting room. Maks goes straight for the medical supplies to deal with the worst of Liam's injuries.

I pour three vodkas and pass them around. "Start talking. Now."

Maks tends to Liam's cuts and the kid flinches, but doesn't complain. Looking at him a little closer, I'm guessing he's around twenty years old. Ten years younger than Maks.

"Liam?" Arianna steps into the room. "Oh my god, what happened?"

I frown at her. "You know him?"

"Of course. He's Blake Baron's brother. We've been at a number of the same events over the years." She pins him with a worried expression. "What happened?"

"That's what I'd like to know," I mumble.

Silence weighs heavily in the room. The tension's palpable.

Liam breaks first. He downs the glass of vodka in one swallow and sputters a cough, clearly not use to straight liquor. "I'm so sorry, Maks, I shouldn't have gone there with that man. When you told me you didn't love me, I... I did something stupid. I'm sorry."

What did he just say? When Maks told him—

I freeze, my muscles rigid. I feel like I'm intruding on a very private conversation. Awkwardly, I clear my throat and refill Liam's glass. The kid looks like he could use it.

With a nod of gratitude, he downs that glass too and I fill it for a third time.

"We'll talk about this later," Maks says to him. Turning, he gazes at me. "We've been seeing each other for the last few months."

"At Leonidas?" Arianna asks, and Maks nods.

Well, that explains that. I guess.

Maks sighs, burying his head in his hands. "I thought we were being discreet. I'm a fucking Bratva enforcer, and being with a man like me could put a huge target on Liam's back. He's a fucking billionaire heir, and I'm... from the wrong side of the tracks. It's a mess. There's no way it can work."

Liam flinches. His expression wounded.

My gaze flits to Arianna. She's technically a mafia princess, but sometimes I feel like we're from two completely different worlds.

"So," I say, glancing at the two men. "I'm guessing you came to Liam's rescue, and that you're not the one who did that to his face."

Arianna gasps like I'm way out of line for even asking that question. Maybe I am.

Maks shoots me a glare. "*What?* Fuck no. I'd never hurt—" He cuts himself off and I know why. He was going to say he'd never hurt Liam, but he already did. He tried to break up with him. Told him he'd never love him.

While I've ignored all the previous signals to leave the room, I decide this is my cue to give them some privacy. Grabbing Arianna's arm, I lead her away from them. Maks and Liam immediately start whispering on the sofa.

She spins into me in the hallway. "Did you know Maks is gay?"

"I've had my suspicions. It's not exactly something a man in our line of work admits to willingly." If his secret reached the wrong ears that could spell trouble for all of us.

"What are you going to do?" She studies me. "You're not going to hurt Maks because of who he is, are you?"

My gaze sharpens and I back her into the wall. "You still think I'm a monster, don't you?" The question's rhetorical. "No, I'm not going to do anything to either of them. I don't give a fuck who they love or want to screw." I brush my lips across hers. "And if anyone dares to paint a target on Maks's back, you know I'll fucking kill them."

Maks is family. All of the brotherhood is family, but Maks is even more so. We've been through so much together.

With a sigh, she melts into me. Pressing her mouth against mine, she drags my lower lip between her teeth, playfully biting down, and I moan. I fucking love it when she gets feisty. I slip my tongue into her mouth, tasting her, demanding more.

I'm about to lift her up and fuck her against the wall, when Maks enters the hallway.

The corners of his mouth twitch. "Get a fucking room, you two." Then his amused expression drops. "I'm taking Liam home, but I just want to be clear on one thing. All of this stays between us. No one else can know. Ever. Okay?"

I meet his gaze. "You have my word."

"Of course." Arianna nods.

"Good. I'll see you later."

I call after him, "Make sure Blake Baron knows we're not responsible for his brother's fucked up face."

"You got it, *Pakhan*."

Once Maks is out of sight, Arianna asks, "Do you think Blake knows about them?"

I shrug. "I don't know. But he's about to find out." My fingers slide into her hair. "Now where were we?"

CHAPTER 30
Arianna

"Not so fast." I glance down at Dimitri's blood speckled shirt. "What happened to you?"

"Nothing you need to worry about. It's not mine. We caught a Russian intruder this morning and he didn't want to talk, so I had to use my fists to loosen his tongue."

"You're a mess," I scold him.

"I know, *kisa*." He leans in for another breath-stealing kiss. "Come shower with me. Help clean me up."

I giggle as I let him lead me up the stairs to our ensuite bathroom. He's impossible to resist. I peel off my clothes, and he turns on the shower waiting for the water to steam. When I step under the spray, he follows me in, then leans close to murmur Russian sweet-nothings in my ear.

My knees grow weak. Held against his bare chest, his breath heats my skin, and his deep voice causes goose-bumps to prickle all over my flesh. My eyelids close as I listen to whatever filthy words he's saying in his native tongue.

I never realized Russian could sound so amazingly erotic. But when he murmurs in that deep, resonate voice, my brain short-circuits.

Dimitri caresses my curves, cupping my breasts in his massive palms. He teases my nipples until they ache, and I arch my back, silently begging for more.

"You're my perfect little slut, aren't you? Are you going to take your husband's cock in your tight pussy and let him fill you with cum?"

"*Yes*," I gasp.

Dimitri spins me around, then lifts me into his arms. My legs wrap around his hips as my backside hits the cold, stone wall. But the discomfort of the hard surface barely registers. Reaching between us, I grab his cock and give it a stroke. His eyelids flutter and he groans. I love that sound. I love the power my body has over him. How we make each other crazy. How we lose control.

I line him up at my entrance and rock my hips into him. He teased me plenty in the hallway, I'm ready for him. Now I want to feel him slide into me.

He chuckles, low and husky. "You're so needy for my cock, wife. Tell me what you want and I'll give it to you."

"Fuck me," I say, looking him straight in the eyes.

With a curse, he thrusts into my pussy, fucking me just like I demanded. Our gazes lock on each other, and the intensity and vulnerability in his always leads to my undoing. He looks at me like I mean everything to him, that I *am* everything to him. Like I'm the sun and he's a planet in my orbit.

Butterflies swarm in my stomach and my skin heats.

"You're taking my cock so good, *kisa*. Do you feel it stretching you? Fuck, you feel so good, so perfect. This sweet cunt was made for me and we both know it. Tell me I'm right."

All I can do is moan my agreement. His dirty words turn me on so much that I'm close. So close.

He dips a hand between us, circling my clit. "Come on my dick, *malyshka*."

My body trembles. With a low moan, I come apart, wave after wave of pleasure crashes through me as my pussy milks his cock.

"Good girl." Dimitri continues fucking me hard. He pinches my clit and I orgasm again. "That's my very good girl." He ducks his head, drawing my nipple into his mouth.

I shove my fingers into his wet hair, my grip tight, relentless. His teeth graze across my nipple. The pinch of pain sends me over the edge a third time and I cry out his name. A satisfied rumble vibrates from his chest.

His thrusts grow shorter, sporadic, until he buries his cock deep inside me and finds his release. A guttural moan vibrates in this throat.

He rests his forehead against mine. We're both breathing heavily, our wet skin flushed. Gazing deep into my eyes, he slowly pulls out. I feel a trickle of cum slide down my thigh. Dimitri catches it and slips his fingers into my pussy, pushing his cum back inside.

I shiver. Why is that so hot? Thank God I'm on birth control or I'd be pregnant a thousand times over by now.

I swear I read the same thought in his eyes. And a yearning. Maybe even a promise.

One day he's going to put a baby in my belly.

A future that's not meant to be ours flits through my mind's eye. Me, pregnant and wrapped in his protective arms, feeling so loved and safe. This intuitive knowing that he'll be the most wonderful father to our child.

I blink away that vision.

That future is impossible. Or is it?

Christmas is fast approaching and I want to give Dimitri a gift, but I have no idea what to get him. Why are men so difficult to shop for? I need to come up with something to give him because I'm going shopping with my sisters and cousin this weekend. It's the perfect opportunity.

I step into our shared closet. This is as good a place as any to find inspiration. Normally, I might buy a man a pair of cufflinks, or a silk tie, but he's not the type who generally wears those types of accessories.

I don't want to get him yet another pair of jeans or more black T-shirts. He has one leather jacket that he pretty much wears all the time.

Opening his dresser drawers, I find an array of expensive watches, and where he keeps his small stash of ties and pocket squares for those rare occasions when he does dress up. Another drawer holds boxers and socks. The bottom drawer is empty except for a wooden trinket box.

I pull out the box and set it on top of the dresser. Lifting the hinged lid, I expect to find men's jewelry, maybe some heirloom pieces. The box contains trinkets all right, just not the type I thought it would.

I stare down at a printed photo of myself. My heart stops. I grow still, blinking down at the box's contents. Beside the photo is a lock of hair—*my* hair.

With a shaky hand, I reach inside, discovering several more photographs. Who prints pictures in this day and age? My stomach drops when I find one of me sleeping in my own bed at my parents house.

Oh my god, he broke into my house, into my bedroom and took this photo. That must have been where he acquired my hair, too.

A chill rakes up my spine, my skin tingles. Candid pictures, taken from afar, is completely different than this.

He said his stalking was supposed to frighten me. He wanted me to pay for my father's decision to break the agreement. The threats, creepy texts, and candid shots were aimed to torment me, but this...

This is obsession.

This is collecting little pieces of my life and keeping them in a box.

This takes his stalking to a whole new level.

My heart lurches when I see a blue floral barrette at the bottom. The flower is outlined in gold. It's a Pontrelli family heirloom—and I lost it over two years ago at a Halloween party.

How the hell did this end up in Dimitri's possession? Unless...

I brush my fingers over the cool enamel and visions of that night bombard my consciousness. The details are hazy, I've never been able to clearly see the faces of the two men—one my attacker and the other my dark knight and savior.

What I do remember vividly is the stench of urine and stale booze in that alley. The sharp agony when my cheek hit that brick wall, whooshing the air from my lungs. His rough hands tore at my Halloween costume and kneaded my exposed flesh as I whimpered for him to stop.

Then he was pulled off me, and I ran. I have no idea how their altercation in that alley ended. I never saw the face of my savior either. And the features of the man who attacked me are blurry, all I remember is that he was tall, powerfully built, and had an accent of some kind.

What I know for sure is that's where I lost this barrette. In that dank alley outside a club. The man who attacked me tore it from my hair. Did he pocket it?

Suddenly dizzy, I reach for the dresser to steady myself. Dimitri was there that night, this is proof.

But which one of them was he? The man who tired to rape me or my rescuer? I wish my guess felt more certain.

He's given me the impression that he's been stalking me for a few months, not *years*. He swore he's not the kind of man to force himself on a woman, but can I believe that? This barrette places him in the alley that night. Has he been stalking me ever since, lurking in the shadows, playing a long game of cat and mouse until I was within reach? I shudder.

He has the ultimate power over me now, having forced me to become his wife. How long has he been planning this? *Months? Years?*

My stomach twists and I feel nauseated. Is this all some twisted game?

CHAPTER 31

Dimitri

"Arianna?" I peek into the library, but she's not there. Same when I look in the kitchen, living room, and the sunroom. Where could she be? I know she hasn't gone out. Maybe she's upstairs.

I'm home after a long day of hiring the new manager for Riot. Maks chose a couple of good candidates and I made the final decision. Hopefully the club will be back to running smoothly soon. We have another fight night scheduled for later this month at that venue.

I climb the stairs and enter our bedroom, where my steps falter.

Arianna's sitting on our bed, the wooden box I immediately recognize open in front of her, but it's the look in her eyes that punches me in the gut. *Fear.* Her gorgeous blue-green hazel eyes are wide with fear and suspicion.

I don't understand. Everything in that box is of her, and she knows about the stalking, the photos. Okay, maybe it's her hair and evidence that I snuck into her bedroom while she was sleeping that has her so afraid?

I'll admit that could come off as creepy even though I had no intention of harming her.

But that explanation doesn't settle quite right. Something's off.

I go to step toward her and she flinches, so I stay where I'm standing just inside the door. "What's wrong?"

She picks up the hair clip. "Wh-where did you get this?"

I sigh, raking my fingers through my hair. That's the first piece of her I collected, a couple of years ago in a grimy alley. I should have come clean about that sooner, but I was afraid about how she'd react. I guess now I know exactly how she'd react—like *this*.

"It was the first time I ever saw you, Halloween two years ago at Club Chrysalis. You were wearing a Little Bo-Peep costume, a white dress with blue flowers all over it. That was in your hair."

"But how did you get this?" Her voice wavers. She nudges the pillow beside her, revealing the gun—my gun that I keep in the nightstand—hidden beneath it.

Fucking hell, what did I do now? Is she going to shoot me because I've been keeping an eye on her for longer than she thought?

"Arianna, what the fuck is going on?" Acidic fear pools in my stomach. I can feel her slipping away like sand through my fingers.

"Answer the goddamn question." Her fingertips rest on the grey metal weapon. From this distance she could pick it up and get off a shot or two before I reached her. But why would she want to do that?

Then it dawns on me. There were two men in the

alley where she lost that barrette. But she can't possibly think... I breathe through the rage and hurt.

"I found it in that alley, where you had no business being." My tone is edged with anger. "If I hadn't followed you when I noticed that creepy motherfucker taking you through the side door, and then pulled him off you—I don't want to think about what would have happened."

Her features relax slightly and she searches my eyes. For what? Does she think I'm lying?

"I beat the shit out of him, then stabbed him to death." I take a step closer to the bed. "He bled out and died in the alley." Another step. "That was the first time I killed for you, *kisa*."

I reach the bed and drag her to me, my fingers wrap around her neck. How could she even suspect that I was the one who tried to rape her? Her suspicions fucking tear my heart out.

Softly, I squeeze her throat. "And I would do it all over again. Again and again. Anything for you. Anything to protect you."

Her features crumple, a sob tears from her throat, catching me off guard. "I'm so sorry," she says, her voice cracking. "I-I thought you might have been *him*. I can't clearly remember that night. It's all a blur. I'm so sorry."

I pull her into my embrace. "Shh, *malyshka*, it's all right. I've got you." Smoothing her hair, I pepper kisses on top of her head. She falls apart in my arms. Her sobs rip at my soul.

"It's the trauma," I tell her. "That's why you can't remember the details."

She nods against my chest. "I know. I'm still sorry that I thought the worst of you."

"So am I." My heart twists. Will she always think the worst of me? I hoped by now that she had some faith in me, at least a tiny bit. But today she confronted me, thinking that I tried to rape her in a dark alley.

I know I've done some fucked up shit, but that crosses a line that I never would. The fact she believes I could do something like that crushes me. It's fucking gut-wrenching.

At this point, I don't know how to be anything other than the villain in her story. She keeps painting me as one, and I'm afraid there's no going back.

She'll never trust me. Not really.

And I have only myself to blame.

CHAPTER 32

Arianna

The shopping plaza's packed this close to Christmas. People all around are either in a frenzied hurry or casually window shopping, there's very little in between. Sophia, Ginevra, Ravenna, and I are in the casual shopping category. Often in the way and a cause of annoyance to those on a mission to get from one store to the next in a rush.

Our security detail is having a hell of a day too, trying to assess whether any of the people who bump into us are threats.

Cian, Ravenna's Irish mafia husband, wanted to bar the public from shopping here for a day. Roman even went as far as to suggest buying the place so he could have full control of the venue's security. Dimitri thought that was an excellent idea.

But we talked them out of it on the basis that it would be unfair to the rest of the people trying to do their holiday shopping this weekend. After much back and forth, we finally settled on a five man security team on the ground and two snipers on the rooftops. Just in case anything were to happen.

With hot cocoas in hand, we make our way from store to store and it's reminiscent of the old days when we'd all hang out together more regularly. Gin sings along to the poppy holiday songs, while I tell her to keep her voice down. We don't want to get escorted out for causing a disturbance.

Sophia and Ravenna admire every shiny object like a pair of magpies. I run my fingers over the silks and satins, loving the smooth textures.

"Here's the men's section," Sophia announces, immediately going to the ties. "What do you think? Purple or blue? I already bought Roman a pair of diamond cufflinks, so this is just a little something extra."

Ravenna and Gin say, "Purple."

I point to the blue.

Sophia chuckles. "Sorry girls, when it comes to fashion sense Arianna knows best. Blue it is."

"Arianna knows best," Gin grumbles. "Why am I never the best at anything?"

"You're the best at having a good time," I point out.

"Says the event planner who doesn't know how to party," Gin shoots back.

I sigh. "Our definitions of *party* are entirely different."

"Will you two stop it?" Sophia purchases the tie, then we're on to the next store.

"Speaking of employment," Ravenna says. "I recently got a job."

I perk up. "Oh? Where are you working?"

"Well." She blushes, letting her deep auburn hair

shield her face. "It's nothing like what you and Sophia are doing. I don't have big goals like running an event planning business or becoming a museum curator."

"Spit it out." Gin elbows her.

"I'm a secretary. I'm working at a real estate development firm."

"That's nothing to be ashamed of, Rave. I'm so proud of you." I hug her to show that I really mean it.

Sophia smiles. "I'm happy for you. Do whatever makes you happy."

Gin nods. "Being a secretary is cool."

"I just had to get out of the house and be around normal people for a while. Cian is great, but he's busy all the time and I'm left to my own devices most days. I was going stir crazy. Not that finding a job was easy." Ravenna smirks. "Cian hated everyone I wanted to work for until I found this place. He denies that he's okay with this job because my boss is a woman instead of a man, but I know that's a lie. Have you noticed how feral they get when another man is around? It's insane."

Sophia and I exchange a knowing glance and say, "Yep."

"Boys, boys, boys, is that all you can ever talk about?" Ginevra pouts. Since she's the boy-crazy one her statement is cause for concern.

I whisper to Sophia, "What's wrong with her?"

"Papa won't let her go skydiving over the holidays with the smarmy investment banker she met at some club."

"What happened to that guy she was dating? Oliver."

Sophia shrugs. "You know how she is. It's the man of

the week club with her, a revolving door. Though she did date Oliver for several months. Now he's just gone. She won't even talk about him, so I don't know."

Hmm. For Gin that's actually not unusual behavior, though I do worry about her. She doesn't seem very happy these days.

"Speaking of men," I say, walking between Sophia and Ravenna. "I learned something wild about Dimitri the other day." They turn their heads toward me. "The first time he saw me was over two years ago at one of his high roller clubs. Remember that Halloween that we snuck out? I was Little Bo-Peep."

I leave out the rest of the details from that night. I've never told my sisters and cousin about what happened in the alley.

"Oh my god." Ravenna halts. "You mean he's been stalking you since then?"

"Not exactly. Well, sort of. He's been kind of like a creepy guardian angel always looking out for me."

After my meltdown in his arms, we talked. Dimitri is my dark knight. He did stop that purse snatcher in Times Square, and he's intervened in several other instances when some sleazy guy was making a beeline for me. I never knew about most of the instances.

Until now, and it puts a lot of things into perspective. It's why Dimitri looked at me like he really knew me when I woke up at his apartment. Though I thought we barely knew each other. This secret history between us, and his box of mementos, paints a rather vivid picture.

He's wanted me for years.

He's been in the shadows, looking out for me for years.

Is it only obsession, or could it be love? Do I want it to be love? Am I completely insane to feel *safer* around him now that I know the truth?

Sophia giggles, drawing my attention to her. "That explains why he looks at you the way he does."

"How's that?" I lick my suddenly dry lips.

"Like the world revolves around you, and so does he."

"Really?" I try not to sound too hopeful. I don't even know if I want Dimitri's heart. But I finally have a face to put to my dark knight.

"Yes, really." She cups my shoulders. "Arianna, your family is made up of some of the most powerful people in this city. Why do you think none of us have put a bullet in Dimitri? It's because of the way he looks at you. We all know he's madly in love."

My lips part. "No he's not. I mean... he's never said it."

"Maybe he's waiting for you to fall in love with him."

My mouth forms an O. I frown. Now I'm more confused about my feelings than before. Can I really see a life with Dimitri Kozlov as my husband? Warmth spreads through my chest and my stomach flutters, answering that question.

We start walking again to catch up with Ginevra.

"She's right," Ravenna says. "These men are ruthless and hard on the outside, but they're mush on the inside. Cian is *so* emotionally sensitive."

Sophia lets out a low chuckle. "Roman is too. And if either of you tell him I said that, I'll have to kill you."

"My lips are sealed." A glint of metal in the store

window we're passing catches my eye. "Wait. Let's stop in here."

Ravenna glances up at the sign. "An antiques shop?"

"Yeah." I pull the door open and head to the display. There, in a velvet lined box are a pair of beautifully engraved brass knuckles. They look heavy, like solid brass, and the fine filigree is stunning. It's the perfect gift.

"I'll take those," I tell the shopkeeper. When I turn around, Sophia and Ravenna are both smiling. "What?" My tone's defensive.

"Nothing." Sophia tries to suppress her grin and fails miserably.

"Whatever." I take my purchase and stride past them to where Gin is taking selfies with an enormous carved octopus. "Let's eat. I'm starving."

Over lunch at a nearby Thai restaurant our conversation flows from upcoming events, to Sophia's college life, to Gin almost getting caught stealing one of the auntie's scarves. I'm not surprised since those old women have hawk eyes.

As we're about to finish our meal, Ravenna leans in. "Do you know that man? He's been staring at you for the last ten minutes."

I follow her gaze to a tall, dark-haired man in a corner booth. Grey streaks his styled hair and short beard. Our gazes collide and my heartbeat pounds against my ribcage. There's something familiar about him, but I can't place what exactly. Apart from the familiarity, I swear I've never seen him before.

"No, I don't know him." I pull out my phone and text our security team, just in case.

When I glance back up the man is gone.

CHAPTER 33
Dimitri

My insides are tied up in knots as we walk up to the Pontrelli's front door. For the first time, I have to face all of my in-laws. On Christmas Eve. Without a brigade of my men as back up. Even Maks isn't here because he's with his boyfriend, Liam. Apparently they worked out their issues.

Color me surprised as fuck when Maks said Blake Baron was *completely cool* with them dating. I call bull-shit. Baron doesn't have a cool bone in his body. So either they haven't told him and they're hiding their relation-ship from him—which is a bad idea because that fucker has spies everywhere—or Baron is lying.

My bet's on Baron being a fucking liar. There's no way in hell he's fine with his baby brother in bed with my right-hand man.

Which means Baron is up to something. I just need to figure out what.

But that's a worry for another night. Right now I

have to survive Christmas Eve dinner with my in-laws—who loathe me.

Arianna squeezes my hand. "It'll be fine. Trust me."

I give her a tight smile.

Then the door opens and Mr. Pontrelli stares me down like I'm dog shit on the bottom of his shoe. Disgusted, and he can't wait to wipe me off. Maybe threatening his daughter's life, no matter how empty those threats were, wasn't the best idea in hindsight.

He lets us in, but only after Arianna pushes past him. "Papa," she chides his quietly aggressive behavior.

"Don't tell me you've fallen for this swine." He looks me up and down.

"I like him well enough," she says.

My gaze flies to Arianna. Coming from her that's practically a declaration of love. The corners of her mouth tip up. She certainly doesn't look abused, or in any way mistreated. If anything, there's a lightness about her that's new. She seems happy.

Her father grumbles as he leads us further into the house. I experience a moment of sympathy when I put myself in his shoes. If any man kidnapped and forced my daughter into marriage I'd fucking chop his dick off and gladly watch as he slowly bled out.

With that uncomfortable thought, I discreetly pat my cock. Maybe I should have worn armor.

We enter the living room and I'm greeted by a shriek. Ginevra, the youngest Pontrelli sister, throws her arms around me in a bear hug. I stiffen, unsure of what to do. This is not the welcome I expected from a family who despises my very existence.

"It's so nice to meet you!" She eases back with a big smile, and a devious glint in her light brown eyes.

"Gin, what are you doing?" Horror's written all over Arianna's face.

"Just welcoming him to the family." She smirks and turns away.

I watch her stroll across the room, my instincts telling me I've been scammed. But... I reach for my wallet, coming up empty-handed. Searching the rest of my pockets, I realize I've been pickpocketed. By Arianna's baby sister. Well, shit, I didn't see that coming.

Picking up on what just happened, Arianna glares at her sister. "Gin, give it back."

"Give what back?" She's the picture of innocence, blond curls framing her large eyes.

"His wallet," my wife grits out.

"Oh, you mean this one?" My wallet appears in her hand. Given that she's wearing a skin-tight dress, I'm not sure where she was concealing it. Having been a fucking thief and pickpocket when I was a child, I'm actually impressed by her skill. Not that I'd ever tell her that. She seems like enough of a hellion without any further encouragement.

"Ginevra!" Mrs. Pontrelli chastises her daughter. "I'm ashamed of you."

The girl rolls her eyes. "Oh come on, Mama, it was just a bit of fun." She tosses me my wallet. "Sorry," her tone is anything but apologetic.

Even so, I nod, putting my wallet safely away in my trousers pocket this time instead of my suit jacket.

The interactions with the rest of Arianna's family

goes more smoothly. Sophia is polite as always, and Roman claps me on the back in greeting.

I do a double-take when two redheads walk into the room with the scarred up man I recognize as Cian O'Rourke, head of the Irish mob. The women's features are so similar that I can't tell them apart. Identical twins.

Arianna introduces us. "These are my cousins, Ravenna and Elena. I'm sure you've met Ravenna's husband Cian."

He gives me a curt nod, which I return before murmuring a greeting to Arianna's cousins.

"Come now, dinner is served." Mrs. Pontrelli wraps her arm around mine, which earns her a scowl from Mr. Pontrelli. "You will sit next to me, young man. I want to know all about my new son-in-law."

I hold back a groan. Arianna warned me not to be fooled by her mother's sweet nature, beneath it she's a real battle axe. Whereas Mr. Pontrelli's bark is supposed to be worse than his bite. I haven't made up my mind about which of them is the real threat.

I sit between Mrs. Pontrelli and Arianna, with Roman and Sophia opposite of us. Christmas Eve dinner is a true feast, but casual, family style. Everyone passes around the dishes and helps serve each other. There's a quiet familiarity about it. The conversations focus on general life updates and news, flowing easily around the table.

Quietly eating the delicious food, I watch and listen, feeling like an outsider. They're so relaxed and easygoing with one another. Even Roman and Cian—two of the most intimidating men in the city.

Family.

It's practically a foreign word to me. My uncle brought me back to America with him, but by that time his wife had passed. He was never a warm family type man. Even to his own son, Nik, he kept a certain emotional distance. Which might be partly why Nik betrayed us all. Daddy issues? Though I'm the wrong person to be throwing that accusation around.

I don't remember my mother, and when I think of my father I see the lie he lived. Our home was a rundown apartment, so brutally cold in the winter months because we couldn't afford the heat. Yet my father wore expensive suits and always had money to bet at the tables, or the races, or on fights.

He was often around, but never really *present*. It was like he and I lived two completely separate lives. Mine consisted of threadbare clothes and gruel, while he brushed shoulders with powerful men every night.

Mrs. Pontrelli taps her wine glass and raises it in the air. "Thank you all for spending Christmas Eve with us. It's a pleasure to see you all together at least once a year. Here's to family."

"To family," everyone echoes, sipping from their glasses. I down the contents of my own in one go, which Mrs. Pontrelli promptly refills.

"Thank you," I say and she smiles warmly.

As the evening wears on, I can spot the differences more easily between the twins. Ravenna is outgoing and charming. She has a feisty side to her that reminds me of Arianna. Cian seems to enjoy that aspect of his wife, his eyes light with a pride every time Ravenna speaks passionately about a topic. She has a lot of opinions.

Elena is the opposite of her sister. She's as quiet as I

am. She keeps to herself, her shoulders slightly curved as if she's protecting herself from the entire outside world. *Troubled.* That's the word I'd use to describe her.

Troubled in a completely different way than Ginevra who continuously makes snarky comments. She's loud and boisterous. She seems to especially love goading Roman, of all people. Her attempts to get a rise out of him fail of course, but she's determined, only to simmer down when both Sophia and Arianna get on her case.

Their sibling squabble makes my lips twitch with amusement.

This is the kind of family that I've secretly dreamed of having all my life. I always wanted brothers and sisters. When I first met my cousin Nikolai, I thought I was going to gain a brother, but we never got on that well. Maks and I were always closer.

Holiday dinners with my uncle and cousin were somber affairs. I was always grateful for the food and comfortable home, but compared to this family, my own lacked warmth and that sense of really belonging.

I never really saw the stark contrast until this moment, surrounded by these people. Arianna's family—not mine. Though some day they might become mine too. *Yeah, when Hell freezes over.*

I've done absolutely nothing to earn my way into this family. I'm sure they all hate me, like Mr. Pontrelli does. He shoots me another glare as if to reinforce my thoughts.

Once dessert is served, I breathe a little easier. This ordeal will come to an end soon enough and we'll be on our way out of here. Then I'll no longer be intruding on their hospitality, and their home—where I don't belong.

Arianna takes my hand and squeezes it under the table. She's been a pillar of strength beside me all evening. I glance at her beautiful face and I'm hit in the chest with a feeling I often have—unworthiness. She's too fucking good for me and we both know it.

I try to shake off the dreadful sensation that gnaws at my stomach. She's mine for now. I want her so badly, but I don't know how to be worthy enough to keep her.

Mrs. Pontrelli shifts toward me, eyeing me over her port glass. "Mr. Kozlov, you are the newest addition to our family, and given the circumstances around your marriage to our daughter we're uncertain how long you'll be one of us. Understandably so, don't you think?"

"Yes, ma'am." I resist the urge to tug at my collar, suddenly feeling suffocated. "I suppose it was... unusual."

"Ah, so we're not going to hear a speech from you defending your decision to drug and force my daughter into marriage? Or how we owed you a debt, and it was your right to take her to get even?"

Fucking Christ, this woman has me by the balls.

"No, ma'am." I never had a mother, that I can remember. Are they all this intimidating?

"Well then, I guess I have one question for you." The table has grown awkwardly quiet, all eyes on us. "Are you in love with my daughter?"

Arianna groans. "Mama, you can't ask such things."

"This is my house, young lady, I can ask whatever questions I want." Mrs. Pontrelli pins me with her hazel gaze, obviously waiting for my answer. I'm not getting out of this.

I quickly glance around the table, which was a

mistake because fucking *everyone* is waiting for my reply. Except Roman, who smirks at me as he casually reaches for another slice of pie. Fucker.

"I am." My answer rings out loud and clear in the silent space. I peek at Arianna who looks mortified. "I've been in love with Arianna for longer than she'll ever know. I was a goner since I first laid eyes on her two years ago." My confession settles into the silent void.

Her gaze meets mine and her lips part. I can't tell if she's surprised or horrified at my admission. Either way, it's true. This is not the way I envisioned expressing my emotions to her, but now it's done. She can do whatever she wants with that information. I'm done hiding the depths of my feelings for her, and I'm certainly not going to let her nosey mother rattle me.

I face Mrs. Pontrelli. "I love your daughter."

Her eyes twinkle with delight. "I know."

The silent bubble around the table finally bursts when Mr. Pontrelli announces he's taking his wife to Italy for New Years. Everyone begins discussing their holiday plans.

Arianna leans toward me, keeping her voice low she says, "You didn't have to say that. I'm sorry, my mother can be such a bully at times. You could have spoken the truth and she wouldn't have punished you for it, I swear."

"That is the truth." I slide my fingers through hers and bring her hand to my lips. "I should have told you from the beginning, no matter how crazy I would've sounded."

Her gaze searches my face, seeking the truth perhaps? I open myself up to her, letting her see the sincerity in my eyes, the love and devotion I've carried for her for years that have recently crystalized. Beyond a shadow of a doubt, I adore this woman. This amazing woman who's always been so far out of reach, a part of my world, yet not.

When Mr. Pontrelli and my uncle originally agreed to an arranged marriage to join our families, I hoped Arianna was finally within my grasp. But then her father insisted that the eldest daughter marry first. I didn't want Sophia as my wife. When I refused the match, Nik stepped up. Uncle Vadim was fine with that arrangement, figuring he could marry me into an even more powerful family.

Considering how all of that could have turned out, had Roman not fucked it all up and broken Sophia's engagement to Nikolai, I think having Arianna as practically my sister-in-law would have been torture.

She would have been closer to me, yet so much further out of reach. There'd be no reason for me to also marry into the Pontrelli family.

An expression settles over her face that I can't quite read. Her face glows pink and drops her gaze.

But she doesn't say those three little words back to me.

In fact, she doesn't say anything at all.

CHAPTER 34
Arianna

My pussy clenches around Dimitri's thick cock—again. My head spins with a rush of endorphins and my breathing is ragged. He pounds into me, relentlessly, while I take him all and beg for more.

His breath is hot against my ear. "That's a good girl. Now give me another one, *kisa*, give me number five. It's Christmas, *malyshka*, you can do it. Come for me."

"Dima," I moan his name as another orgasm tenses my body.

He loves me.

"Fuck, yes. That's my good girl." He adjusts his angle and I gasp. "If you can stand up after this then we're not doing it right." This new position hits my g-spot just right and I'm right back at the edge.

He loves me.

"Oh, fuck yes, you want to come again for your husband, don't you?" He stares into my eyes with complete, open admiration.

"Yes," I breathe. "*Please.*"

His fingers squeeze my throat with just enough pressure that I orgasm again, a torrent of bliss sweeps through my body and drains the last bit of my strength. With a reverent curse, he follows me over the edge, into oblivion. Dimitri collapses on top of me, catching his weight on his forearms, and kisses me stupid.

He loves me.

My toes curl, my fingers dig into his thick hair, and I kiss him back, languidly. This is the best Christmas morning of my life.

After last night I feel like something has changed—like everything has altered. I want him with a desperation that wasn't there before. I no longer want this to be temporary. I want *him*. Forever.

He's so unlike the man I thought I'd marry one day, but he's better. He makes me feel alive, seen, adored. He's my dark knight, my guardian angel. I want him and I'm not ashamed to admit that now.

I want his passion, his vulnerability, and everything he's willing to share with me. He's an addiction I have no intention of kicking.

"*Kisa*, did I break you?" He gazes down at me, his brow pinched in concern.

A lazy smile spreads across my lips. "If you want to break me you'll have to try harder than that."

He chuckles. "Challenge accepted." Dimitri slips his softening dick out of me and sits up. "Do you want breakfast first or gifts?"

"Breakfast. I'm starving."

The smile he flashes is pure, wicked delight. "Then we should shower first."

Nodding, I go to stand and my knees wobble. "Oh my god, you *did* break me."

He sweeps me into his arms, carrying me bridal style into our bathroom. The caveman-like satisfaction radiating off of him amuses me to no end.

In the shower, I give him my first gift, on my knees, letting him fuck my face and come all over my tits. Afterwards, he punishes me with another orgasm for being a such a tease before I let him come. By the time we're finished, dried off, and dressed, two hot plates of breakfast wait for us in the kitchen oven.

"I thought you promised to give Nina and Kir the day off. It's Christmas."

He sets the food on the breakfast nook table. "I did. Nina prepared this last night and I snuck down here before waking you up and put them in the oven to warm."

"Oh. Thank you." Why do I always think the worst of him? Immediately, guilt slams into my chest.

He uncovers the trays piled high with waffles, three types of breakfast meats, and scrambled eggs. My stomach growls. We dig in, attempting to eat our body weight after this morning's sexcapade.

Dimitri slides a small box my way. "Merry Christmas, *malyshka*."

I lift off the top, unsure of what I expected but it's not this. I purse my lips. "What is it?"

"It's a butt plug." His eyes flash with unbridled lust.

My cheeks heat. "Yeah, I don't think so."

"Trust me, *kisa*. You're going to wear that around the house all day long while I play with you using that remote. Then when you're dripping wet, out of your mind with need, I'm going to fuck your sweet pussy and give you the best orgasm of your life. I promise."

I lick my lips, reconsidering. His promise sounds pretty enticing.

"Okay, maybe." I acquiesce.

"We both know that's a *yes*." He smirks.

I roll my eyes. He's probably right.

"But that's not your real Christmas gift. This is." He produces a long, narrow box from beneath the table. It's black with a gold design across the top.

I open it. My breath catches in my throat. "This is gorgeous, Dima. This is the one..." I caress the multiple stands of pearls. "The one from the charity auction. Isn't it?"

"Yes. I saw the way your eyes lit up when you looked at it. Here, let me put it on you." He lifts the pearl necklace from its box, his fingers caressing my neck as he works the clasp. "There. Beautiful."

I glance up at him, but he's not looking at the necklace, he's gazing at *me*. A blush heats my cheeks.

That look. That's the one that makes butterflies swarm in my stomach and my knees weak. My heart swoons.

He loves me.

"Thank you. It's stunning and I love it."

His smile lights up his handsome face, and he's simply breathtaking.

"I got you this." I push the gift box to him. "I hope you like it."

I'm overtaken by sudden anxiousness as he opens it, finding the antique brass knuckles inside. Does he like them? His fingers skim across the engraved filigree. They're gorgeous, and deadly, just like him.

"I love them." When his gaze meets mine it's filled with wonder. "This is perfect. You're perfect."

Relief washes through me. I reach for him, and he pulls me into his lap, our breakfast forgotten as we make out at the table.

We reluctantly draw apart when his phone pings twice, then three times. He retrieves it from his pocket and swipes the screen. A frown mars his handsome face.

"What is it?" I ask, remaining in his lap.

He hesitates, seeming conflicted. Maybe it's none of my business.

I open my mouth to tell him he doesn't have to answer, when he sets his phone on the table and sighs. His arm wraps around my waist.

"Katerina's adoption looks like it's going to go through." He rakes his free hand through his hair, his expression tormented. "I want what's best for her. I really do. She should have found a family years ago, but none of the ones we vetted were good enough. But this one seems to be perfect."

"You love her." It's an observation, not a question.

He glances up, surprised. "Yeah. As if she were my own daughter."

"Then why haven't you adopted her?"

"Because she needs a family—not a bachelor Bratva leader. I want her to grow up with two parents in a stable and loving household. But I don't know how to let her go."

"Why?"

His brow creases in thought. "I remember that night

so vividly. I was restless and finally gave up on sleep, deciding I'd head to the orphanage and see the children. The drive and their company always clears my head. When I got there I immediately noticed the bundle on the doorstep. She was wrapped in layers of blankets, so still and peaceful that I thought she was gone from this world."

He swallows hard, lost in his memories, and continues, "I picked her up and her eyes opened. She didn't cry or anything. She just looked at me—like she could see into my fucking soul. I can't describe what I felt, all I knew was that I lost a piece of my heart to that tiny face and those bright blue eyes. So I named her Katerina right then and there."

"Oh, Dima." I cup his strong jaw. "No wonder you can't let her go. Not after finding her that way."

"I know I shouldn't have named her. That's why she feels like my own flesh and blood when she's not."

"You can't close your heart off to everyone." I choose my next words wisely, my heart hammering against my ribs. "What if... What if we gave her a home?"

"With us?" His gaze bores into mine. Countless emotions and thoughts flicker in his eyes. "You'd be her mother?"

"I am your wife," I point out.

"My wife. You've never called yourself that before. Not like this." Raw possessiveness wars with uncertainty in his deep green gaze. He pulls me closer. "Will you really be my wife? Start a family with me?"

"Yes." I brush his lips with mine. "I want you. *Us.*"

"Fuck, *kisa*—"

An alert goes off on his phone.

"What now?"

"Your other gift has arrived." He kisses me. "We'll continue this conversation later."

I'm bewildered. What can possibly be more important than this conversation? We're talking about our lives —our future together. A family.

"Come." He lifts me from his lap, then takes my hand and leads us to the front door. We step through, standing on the covered porch. The blacked out SUV that's approaching has already passed through security at the gate. It parks in front of us.

The doors open and Sophia and Ginevra climb out. Why are my sisters visiting me today? I glance up at Dimitri, but his rigid expression gives away no clues.

"Dima—" I follow his gaze back to the vehicle just as a petite form emerges. Her long, wavy hair is so familiar. But it's when she lifts her turbulent grey eyes that my chest clenches and my stomach dips. "*Ilaria?*"

She nods. Tears spill down her sunken cheeks.

I rush to her, wrapping my arms around her thin frame. She hugs me so tightly I can't draw a single breath. Tears of joy and relief spring to my eyes. I've worried about her for *years* and fully expected to never see her again. This is a miracle. A Christmas miracle.

Drawing back, I ask her, "How? How is this possible?"

Sophia answers, a haunted expression crosses her features. "Dimitri's men found and rescued her. Roman and I have taken her in. She's under our protection now. No one can touch her ever again."

My gaze darts to Dimitri and my pulse stutters. This man continues to surprise me in the best of ways. He not only remembered our conversation about why I wanted out of this world, and my anguish over what happened to Ilaria, but he found her.

He did this for me—for both me and her.

In that moment, the remaining walls around my heart shatter, crumbling to dust. I feel light and floaty, unanchored. I'm in love.

In love with Dimitri Kozlov.

CHAPTER 35

Arianna

T he week between Christmas and New Years was a flurry of activity at Leonidas. Between my work, and Dimitri making sure his clubs were set to throw lavish New Year's Eve parties, we rarely saw each other. Maks drove me wherever I needed to go early each morning, and Dimitri wasn't home until well after midnight.

I'm honestly looking forward to this event's conclusion. Especially after I found out that since I'm working at Leonidas that night, instead of attending as a guest, I can't bring a plus one. It's not a social affair for the event planners and staff—it's work. And my boss's boss is a hard ass about it.

Thankfully, Roman agreed to bring Dimitri to the club on New Year's Eve as his guest. I'll be on call for the duration of the event, but I want to kiss my husband at midnight. Is that too much to ask?

New Year's Eve day I spend at the spa with Sophia, where we're massaged, scrubbed, and pampered until our muscles are relaxed and our skin glows. After this we'll move on to the salon for hair, nails, and finally makeup. Tonight we'll both be at Leonidas, along with the club's exclusive members, dressed to the nines.

"How is Ilaria doing?" I ask while lounging in the sauna. "She seemed... anxious the other day."

"You would be too if you'd recently been rescued from a sex trafficking ring. You have to remember that's the life she's known since she was sixteen. It's going to take a while for her to adjust to any sense of normalcy, safety, and for her to find herself again after such an ordeal."

Six years. She went through six years of hell. I'm impressed that she's as functional and capable as she is after all of that. Ilaria's in good hands with Sophia and Roman. I have no doubt they'll get her back on her feet. She'll be thriving in no time.

"Does her father know she's staying with you two?"

"That piece of shit?" Sophia angrily crosses her arms. "I don't know and I don't care either. He sold her and he's going to pay for that atrocity. Ilaria still hasn't told me her whole story, but my intuition tells me that a lot of what she's not saying has to do with her father. We'll deal with him once we know how long to make him suffer for what he put his daughter through."

I shake my head and smile. "You sound like a badass mafia queen."

"That's because I am a badass mafia queen—sort of. Roman has enough shady underworld connections that I feel like we can destroy pretty much anyone we want. Even Papa would back us on this one. If we don't want to get our hands dirty, there's always Blake Baron, he'll get it done."

I hum in agreement. "You sound happy," I note.

"I am happy." She relaxes against the wall. "School is great. Life's giving me more than I ever thought possible." Sophia eyes me. "What's on your mind?"

"I think I'm falling in love." I admit. Saying those words aloud gives them power. They flourish and grow in my heart, rooting deep.

"With Dimitri?"

A startled laugh leaves my throat. "Who else?"

She shrugs. "I don't know. Just checking."

"Yes, with Dimitri. The man who literally tattooed that I'm his property on my ring finger. Ugh, I hate him— or at least I used to hate him. He's not the man I wanted at all, but..."

"But maybe he's the right man for you. Maybe he's everything that you need. I mean, Roman had horrible intentions towards me in the beginning. I was his puppet for revenge. Look how that turned out?" Her expression takes on a dreamy quality.

I sigh. "Why is life so weird?"

"No clue. But you deserve to be happy, Arianna. If Dimitri makes you happy then take a chance on a life with him. It might prove to be worth it."

I'm already standing on that precipice. The other day I suggested adopting a daughter—that's a whole other level of commitment. What am I thinking? Are we moving forward too fast?

"You're going to drive Dimitri here later, right?" I ask Maks as we pull up in front of Leonidas. We're early, but I have work to do and guests will start arriving in the next couple of hours.

"That's right. Roman said his name's on the guest list, so he'll see you inside." Maks comes around and opens the door for me. "Have fun in there tonight."

I smile up at him. "See you later. Happy New Year."

"Happy New Year." He waits until I'm safely inside the club before driving away.

When I step through the doors my breath catches. I've seen all the decorations before, in bits and pieces during setup, but the final result is absolutely stunning.

Entering the club is like stepping into a winter wonderland. Enormous ice sculptures seem to grow out of the glassy marble, glittering in the chandelier glow. Overhead, a thousand crystals shimmer like icicles in the blue-tinted light, and the lobby floor is strewn with white and blue flower petals.

This is only the entrance, a moment unto itself, but the lavish decor continues through the many rooms, even flowing to the outdoors.

"I don't often hand out compliments, but... well done, Miss Pontrelli."

With a start, I turn around, coming face-to-face with the speaker and immediately struck speechless by a pair of steely grey-green eyes beneath styled jet black hair.

"My apologies, we haven't formally met." He extends his hand. "Grayson Hyde. I'm pleased to finally meet the new hire who Miss Ives has been raving about."

Politely, I shake his hand. Tarina has been raving about me? The thought makes me giddy.

"It's a pleasure to meet you, sir," I murmur. "And thank you for the compliment. Working for you and Tarina has been a wish come true."

He offers me a tight smile. "I'm not in the business of granting wishes, Miss Pontrelli, so whatever you've accomplished here has been earned."

"That's even better, sir."

Mr. Hyde's assessing gaze sweeps up and down my dress. While I've caught glimpses of him around the club, we've never stood in such close proximity before, and we've certainly never engaged in conversation.

"You're wearing a wedding band," he notes.

"Yes, sir. I'm recently married. It's Mrs. Kozlov now."

"I see. I'm guessing it's your husband you asked Miss Ives to add to this evening's guest list."

I blanch, knowing that he refused my request and I found another way to get what I wanted through Roman. Doing an end run around the boss doesn't seem like such a good idea anymore. "Yes, sir."

"He's now coming as Roman De Luca's special guest."

It isn't a question, but I answer anyway. "Yes, sir."

"Resourceful, aren't you?" he drawls.

I straighten my spine and lift my chin. If doing an end run is going to get me fired, then I'd rather go down with poise than cowering before this powerful man who most people wouldn't dare disobey.

I level my gaze on him. "I like to think so, sir."

Surprise and a hint of amusement flash in his eyes. His lips twitch, but that impassive mask remains firmly in place. I don't envy Tarina one bit for having to work directly with this man. Her boss. He's impossible to read. Any moment he could bust out laughing or fire me. I can't tell which he's leaning toward.

"We can use resourceful people around here. Just remember that you have a job to do tonight. Don't let Mr. Kozlov distract you from your work."

"I won't, sir." I sag a little with relief. He's not firing me.

"Good." With one last scrutinizing glance, he moves past me. "Miss Ives! I see you lurking in that doorway."

Tarina steps into the hall, exasperation and disdain stamped across her features. She looks amazing in a flowing blue dress that matches her eyes. Her blond curls piled high, expose her long, elegant neck. None of which Mr. Hyde seems to notice as he berates her over some insignificant detail—one she's already fixed from the look of things.

What a tyrant.

CHAPTER 36

Dimitri

"I'm not going to explain the club's capacity to you again," I tell the new manager at Riot over the phone, while unsuccessfully trying to tie my tuxedo bowtie in the mirror. "I don't give a fuck if there's a line around the block or halfway across the city. They can wait." I hang up.

Why is everyone so fucking incompetent tonight? All I want is to finish getting dressed and head to Leonidas so I can be with Arianna. It's already after ten at night. I meant to be there earlier. At that thought, I shoot off a text to my wife letting her know I'm running late but am on my way.

"Maks!" I bark. He steps into the room. "Fix this?" I gesture to the bowtie, wishing Arianna was here because she always knows how to do these fancy things.

"Sure thing, *Pakhan*." Maks straightens out the mess I made and has it tied correctly in seconds.

Glancing in the mirror, I study his handiwork. "Where the fuck did you learn to do that so well?"

He smirks. "Liam Baron."

Of course his fancy, billionaire heir boyfriend would teach him something like this. Arianna's tried to show me, but I haven't been able to get the hang of it yet. My attempts end up too loose and floppy.

"Looks good." I clap Maks on the back. "Let's go."

In the car, I'm restless, tapping my foot impatiently. "Turn on some music or something. I need a distraction."

Maks's eyes me from the driver's seat. "You know I can't hear over that shit."

"What is there to hear?"

"I don't know yet." He sighs. "Fine. Here." He tunes in to a local music station. Wailing opera pours from the speakers.

"What the fuck is this shit?" I catch his gaze in the rearview mirror.

"It's called culture."

I snort. "The fuck it is. You've been spending too much time around the hoity-toity. Don't get all fancy on me, Maks."

"Wouldn't dream of it—"

There's a flash of light, then a loud boom.

The car lifts off the ground.

Tilts. Turns.

Gravity's non-existent for a split second before the impact hits, jarring every bone in my body. My head smacks against the window. The seat belt is the only thing holding me in place.

We're upside down.

What the fuck just happened?

I release my seat belt and crawl out of the car. Adrenaline finally kicks in. My heart races. All of my senses heighten. A voice in the back of my mind screams *danger!*

Quickly looking around, I don't spot any threat nearby.

I find my phone and text my head of security. I need men here. Now.

Maks. Where the fuck is Maks?

There, in the driver's seat. He hangs limply, his arms dangling. I practically wrench the door off its hinges to get to him. He's heavy as fuck, but I manage to pull him from the wreckage and into the road's median strip. A layer of ice cracks beneath my shoes.

Headlights beam at our ruined car, and I'm temporarily blinded.

"Holy shit! Are you guys okay?" Some passerby has finally stopped. "I'm calling 911 now. Hold on."

Bang! Bang!

Shots ring out and the guy trying to help us crumples to the ground. His eyes stare lifelessly to the heavens.

I reach for my gun.

"Maks." I nudge him with my toe. "Wake the fuck up." It's no use. He's out cold. Hopefully still alive. I don't have time to check as three SUVs screech to a halt around us and men exit the vehicles.

Some of them I recognize. Boris. Anton. A couple of others from the old guard. They're all seasoned fighters.

Fucking traitors.

My gun raised, I point it at them, swiveling as they fan out and surround me. There are at least fifteen of them and I only have six shots. Why the fuck didn't I bring a bigger gun? Now I have to pick and choose which of these fuckers to kill.

One thing's for sure. Boris has to go.

I take aim at him, my finger applying pressure to the trigger. Once he's gone, I'll shoot them at random until someone takes me out. Damn, I'd hoped my life wouldn't end this way.

"Put the gun down, son."

I flinch. That voice... I haven't heard that voice in decades. This head injury must be worse than it feels because now I'm hallucinating. The man who belongs to that voice is dead. Long dead.

"I said, put it down. Now." A figure steps from the shadows and my heart stops. Dread encases me so swiftly it's like being plunged into freezing water. I can't breathe.

We stand eye-to-eye, though his frame is not as built as mine. But those dark green eyes are all too familiar—they stare back at me in the mirror every morning. Grey streaks his hair. He's older now, but there's no doubt it's him.

Father.

I'm frozen in place by a tsunami of emotions and thoughts. He's alive. He's been alive all this time.

He sold and abandoned me in Moscow.

He faked his own death.

He's a fucking piece of shit. Why is he here?

Something hard whacks me in the back of the head and my vision dims. My knees give out, hitting the ground as I lose my grip in the gun.

Boris's voice speaks in my ear. "It's payback time, you little shit."

Everything goes black.

CHAPTER 37
Arianna

I pretend to be walking the venue, checking in on everything, but in reality I'm pacing. Dimitri was supposed to be here an hour ago. He texted me when he left home, it's a half hour drive, and... I check the time on my phone. It's twenty to midnight. Where the hell is he?

"Good work tonight." Tarina smiles when I glance up. "You should go join your friends and have some fun. It's almost midnight. We'll talk next week about your permanent position here at Leonidas."

My heart soars. "Really? You'll hire me on full-time?"

"Like I said, we'll discuss the details later. But yes. You've put in a lot of hard work and you'll be rewarded for it. Just be sure to stick around here until after the midnight fireworks. Then you're free to go."

"I'll be here." I beam at her as she walks away. *I got the job!* Inwardly I do a happy dance and thank the stars above. This is my dream and it's finally come true.

I'm so excited. The first thing I want to do is tell Dimitri the news.

My elation washes away as I go in search of Sophia and Roman, finding them in the gaming room.

"Have you seen or heard from Dimitri?" I ask.

They glance at each other. Sophia answers. "No. Why?"

"He sent me a message an hour and a half ago that he was on his way. But he's not here."

"Maybe something came up?" Sophia says in a sympathetic tone.

"Maybe." I back away from their table and send Dimitri another text. He hasn't answered my last two. Then I message Maks as well.

Finding a quiet corner, I wait, my gaze locked on my screen. The minutes tick by, each one haunting me until a knot solidifies in my stomach. This isn't like them. Maks is especially quick to respond—it's his job. What could possibly have come up to keep them from replying?

My imagination summons all kinds of terrible events. But none of them—other than death or incapacitation—could result in them not having access to their phones.

Unless they're in a dead zone. For over an hour? Unlikely.

But even if something came up at work, Dimitri would have let me know. Right?

"You look stunning tonight." Connor's voice settles over me. "Though you also seem distressed. What's wrong, gorgeous?"

My gaze meets his bright blue eyes. There's concern in them, but I can't tell if it's real or not. He looks devastatingly handsome in that tuxedo, his hair perfectly styled, his cologne spicy and masculine. Yet his good looks do nothing for me. My heart and body don't respond to his presence at all.

There's only one man I want. Only one man who stirs my emotions.

"I'm waiting for Dimitri. He's late and not responding to my texts." My brow pinches with worry.

Connor studies me for a quiet moment. Rocking back on his heels, he sighs. "I don't have a chance with you do I?"

"No." My truth comes out in a whisper.

"You're in love with him, aren't you?"

Swallowing hard, I nod.

"I see." He briefly bows his head. "In that case, I wish you two much happiness."

He spins on his heel and disappears into the crowd. I release a relieved sigh. That encounter could have been much more awkward and difficult than it was. I'm glad whatever small thing we had between us is officially over.

Ten minutes have gone by and not a peep from Dimitri or Maks. Enough is enough.

"Sophia, something's wrong," I tell my sister as I approach their table again. "I need to head home and find out what's going on."

She takes in my anxious expression. "Of course. Roman?"

He's already up and out of his seat, phone in hand. "Let's go. I'm having the car pulled around right now."

"Thank you both. I'm so sorry to ruin your New Year's." I follow them toward the exit. Only once we're in the foyer do I remember Tarina's insistence that I stay until after the fireworks. But they could easily last twenty minutes.

Damn it. I'm already firing her off a text to let her know what's going on before I've consciously thought it through. I could lose my job over this. Tarina might understand a family emergency, but Mr. Hyde is not the understanding or forgiving type. Either way, I can't stay here a minute longer, or I'm going to go insane with worry.

"I smell trouble." Blake Baron rounds a column and quirks a brow at Roman.

Roman rolls his eyes. "The rumors are false, aren't they? You don't have an army of spies everywhere, you're simply at the right place at the right time. Admit it."

Blake shrugs, yet it comes off elegant and aristocratic rather than casual. "I'm not spilling my secrets. But you are. What's going on? May I be of assistance? This party is boring me near to death."

Roman glances at me, seeking my permission.

I face Blake. "Dimitri's missing. He's supposed to be here." I fill him in on the details and his eyes light with interest. It's the first time I've seen him look anything other than bored.

"I see. We should go." He inclines his head to the car that's just pulled up out front.

Roman ushers us inside and I give the driver the estate's address. That's the last place Dimitri and Maks were, so we'll start there.

On the way home, I keep glancing at the cars passing us going the opposite direction thinking I might spot Maks driving one of them. But I don't, and thirty minutes later we pull up to the massive iron gates.

Gates that are wide open. Not a guard is in sight.

"That's... not right," I murmur.

We roll slowly up the long driveway. No one stops us. There's not a soul anywhere on the grounds, and when we get to the house all the lights are out.

I start to exit the vehicle when Roman stops me with his hand on my shoulder. He and Blake Baron draw their weapons and get out first, doing a sweep of the front porch, then enter the mansion. Sophia and I follow after them.

Deeming the way clear, someone flicks on the foyer light. I'm struck by the sudden emptiness. The place has that eerie feel, like no one is home, not even the caretakers. But there's also no evidence of bloodshed or struggle. Every piece of art and furniture is where it belongs.

"Hello?" I call into the void. "Is anyone here? Dimitri? Maks? Kir? Nina?"

No one. They all left, including the guards. But why?

Roman appears at the top of the stairs just as Blake returns to the foyer.

"It's empty," Roman says, holstering his gun.

"What's that?" Sophia points to an envelope on the entry table. On top sits a folded piece of paper.

I reach for it. The writing's in Dimitri's familiar scrawl.

Arianna,

I can't go into the New Year like this. We come from two completely different backgrounds and we'll never be happy together.

*It's impossible. I know you tried to tell me
this from the beginning but I was too stubborn to understand.*

*But you've been right all along. So I'm
giving you what you've asked me for since
day one. Since I forced you into this, I've
taken the same liberty in ending our arrangement. You'll find the paperwork is all in
order.*

Have a happy life.

D.

My hands shake as I set down the note and open the large manilla envelope. The papers slide into my hand, and my gaze locks onto the bottom line, finding my own signature there, forged just like on our marriage documents.

"What is that?" Sophia asks.

"He's divorcing me."

I utter those words and my heart shatters in a billion tiny shards. What changed in the span of a couple of hours? Or is this how he's always felt and the idea of going into the new year with me is more than he can bear. I don't understand.

My knees tremble. I reach for the table to steady myself.

Yes, I told him numerous times this is what I want, but not recently. I thought we'd moved past this, that he knows I've changed my mind. I only want him.

I've given him my heart. Now he doesn't want it?

CHAPTER 38
Dimitri

My entire body screams in agony. Not in the way it does after a punishing fight in the cage, that I can handle, this feels worse. My vision swims in and out of focus. They must have given me some kind of sedative. Even so, I'm gradually becoming aware of my surroundings. Men's booming voices fill the space. Russian. They're speaking Russian.

I try to move my arms, but I'm met with resistance and the jangle of chains. That's when I notice I'm sitting slumped over, secured to a chair. I'm still wearing my tux, though it's torn and dirty. Somewhere I lost my bowtie.

I feel like I've been unceremoniously carried, dropped, and dragged multiple times.

Where the fuck am I?

I suck in a breath, my ribs shriek in protest. *Bruised.* I ignore them. The air smells different here—arctic.

"Are you awake, *mal'chik?*"

I glance up in time to see Boris's massive fist fly at my

face. My reflexes are total shit. The punch lands right across my cheekbone, my teeth rattle and eyes water. Just another bruise to add to all the rest.

"Enough!" Barks my father—Konstantin. He leans over me. "We have a lot to catch up on, son."

"Where am I?" My voice cracks, my throat scratchy and dry.

"Moscow." He straightens, slides a chair over and sits in front of me. "We flew in last night."

Moscow. I've come full circle, right back to the beginning.

"What do you want?" I croak.

"You. I've finally come for my son after all these years."

His son? Like hell I mean anything to him. He abandoned me on these very streets over twenty years ago. As far as I'm concerned my father died when I was nine years old, when Uncle Vadim took me to America and I left my past behind. This man seated before me is no parent of mine.

"I'm not your fucking son." I spit the words at him.

He backhands me across the cheek. The blow stings. Jagged memories that I'd forgotten about come flooding back. He likes to hit. What a piece of shit.

"I am your father and you'll keep a respectful tone with me, son." Like I remember from my childhood, he never raises his voice. His tone is calm, almost soothing so you never guess at what's coming. "What do you say to that, Dimitri?"

I grit my teeth. "Yes, sir."

"Good. Now I have some things to set straight. You

should know that I did what I had to do when you were a child."

I glare at him. "You fucking sold me."

Smack. He hits me again. "What did I say about that tone?"

My chin falls to my chest as I suddenly feel dizzy and nauseated. How long has it been since I ate? Or drank water?

Konstantin continues, "I sold you because I had no other option to pay off my debts. But that wasn't enough for those greedy bastards, so I had to fake my own death. Of course that is all ancient history. Those fuckers are gone. Now I own everything they once had. No one ever crosses a Kozlov and lives. But I digress." He settles back in his chair. "I was going to come for you as soon as I had the situation under control but my brother took you to America to live with him. He was unreasonable and wouldn't let me have you back. Vadim stole you from me. I waited years, but finally he had to pay the price."

Uncle Vadim knew my father was alive all this time? Why didn't he ever tell me?

"You killed my uncle?" I summon enough strength to lift my head.

Konstantin nods. "I did. He was never meant to be the Kozlov Bratva's *Pakhan* anyway. I was in charge before I left America and came back to our Motherland. But I only planned to be here temporarily."

Konstantin murdered his own brother, my uncle. Left to my own devices, I never would have found Uncle Vadim's killer. He's a ghost.

Now that my father has admitted to his crime I have someone to focus my rage on. The man who deserves it.

"Do you know why I came to Moscow all those years ago?" he asks, and I shake my head, silently plotting. "I came here to find a Russian woman. Not any Russian woman, but one from the old royal bloodlines. DNA tests make that so much easier these days. I found a woman of the right bloodline to give birth to my heir."

I stare at him. He's insane. Russian royal bloodlines? What the fuck is he talking about?

"There were actually two sisters that I could choose from. The older one had already spread her legs for a man so I took her younger virgin sister. She was delicious. Barely fifteen. You should have heard the way she screamed for me."

I cringe away from him. Sick fuck.

"You told me my mother was a prostitute." As much as I hate listening to him, I *need* to know more about my past, about my mother. The woman I don't remember at all.

"She was," he says. "All I needed from her was you. A son. My heir. After that I pimped her out to my men. She brought me good money while she lasted."

I charge at him, forgetting that I'm chained to this fucking chair. All he does is laugh as I struggle against the restraints.

"You've grown into such an impressive young man. Look at you. So strong and full of life." He crosses his arms, studying me while I seethe at him. This fucker is going to die. "Now it's your turn to carry on our family line, Dimitri. I've brought you here to marry a Russian woman with the right bloodline. I'm even giving you a choice between several. All virgins."

"I'm already married." I stop struggling against the

chains. I need to conserve my energy if I hope to kill this man and get the fuck out of here and home to my wife. She must be worried sick by now. And Maks, what happened to Maks? I hope he's alive.

A sly grin appears on Konstantin's face. "You'll be divorced soon. It turns out your soon to be ex-wife was quite vocal about wanting to divorce you. So I wrote a little note and left the divorce papers for her to sign."

A shiver of pure dread rushes through me. He left her a note? Saying what?

And the papers. Will she sign them?

Fuck, I wish I could talk to her right now. She hasn't told me she loves me, but I think she does. I've been open about my feelings for her. She must know that I'd never give her those papers.

Doubt gnaws at my insides. Does she love me enough to stay or is her freedom more important to her than I am?

Konstantin pulls out his phone and glances at the screen. "Ah, just in time. The divorce was pushed through this morning. Expedited." He pins me with his green gaze. "Congratulations, you're a free man."

I'm gutted. I can't breathe.

If those papers went through this quickly, that means she didn't even hesitate before signing them.

I have my answer. She doesn't love me at all.

CHAPTER 39

Arianna

All of us spent the night in the mansion. Sophia stays with me, while Roman and Blake each take a guest room. I let them borrow some of Dimitri's clothes—which he left in the closet along with all of his personal items. But I guess when you're rich you can afford to replace it all.

It's like he just up and left.

Then why did he text me that he was on his way to Leonidas last night? Why lure me along then dump me so abruptly? These questions and others have been whirling in my head all night and into the morning.

Sophia and I sit at the kitchen table. Roman's working out in the gym with Blake to pass the time.

What are we waiting for? Blake insists on finding Dimitri, but I'm not entirely sure why. He obviously left, cutting all ties. Roman and Blake both disagree with my conclusion. So they've hired someone to track him down. Which could take ages.

Sophia blows across her hot cappuccino. "I'm with the guys on this, Arianna. We all heard him say he loves you at Christmas Eve dinner. That was only a week ago, and he seemed damned sincere. Did something change in the span of a week?"

I've been asking myself that question too. "Not that I know about."

"Then let's figure this out, look at the alternatives. You said he forged your signature on those divorce papers. Could his have been forged too?"

"It hardly matters. He left that note. No one but him could have left that note, it was too personal." My heart breaks all over again when I think of what he wrote.

Sophia sets her cup down, spinning it in her hands as she thinks. "Could anyone else have known that you wanted a divorce in the beginning? I mean the rest of the note's contents are kind of generic. Anyone can see you two are quite opposite in a lot of ways and guess at there being friction in your relationship because of it."

"What about the fact it's his handwriting?" I don't understand why we're digging into this. He's gone. We're divorced. I should move to my parents place and try to get on with my life. Though every time I think about doing that, I choke on my own tears.

"An expert could have forged it." Sophia's so adamant that a tiny ray of hope shines in my heart.

I give her questions some real thought. Who could have known that Dimitri not only forced me into this marriage but also forged my signature? Only one name comes to mind. Maks. He was there in the church. Though so was the priest.

But Maks wouldn't do something this devious, would he? To what end? And the priest was probably paid to keep his mouth shut.

Coming between Dimitri and me benefits nobody. As far as I can see there's no motive for anyone to have forced us to divorce.

Unless Maks... Did he convince Dimitri to let me go? Ugh, I don't know. I'm so frustrated and heartsick. All I want to do is curl up in bed, hide under the comforter, and never come out again.

"Maks," I tell Sophia. "He's the only one who knows the details of our marriage. But he has no reason to do this."

"None that you know of anyway."

I shake my head and sigh. "He wouldn't."

Sophia eyes me. "You trust him that much?"

"I do." At least I think I do. Though he's also missing, just like Dimitri and it makes sense for them to be together.

"Okay, then—"

My phone rings and Maks's name shows on the screen. Speak of the Devil...

"Maks?" I answer right away.

"Thank fuck. Where are you?"

"I'm at the estate. Why? Where are *you*?" I'm jittery with nerves.

"We were ambushed on the way to the club last night."

I suck in a sharp breath.

"Hold on," he says, then I hear his muffled voice. "I don't have a fucking minor concussion. I'm checking myself out, now give me my clothes and get the fuck out of my room."

"Where are you?" I stand up, my heart racing.

"Hospital," he grunts. "Just leaving. Anyway, they must have grabbed Dimitri because he's not in here with me and I can't get ahold of him. I was afraid they might have taken you too."

They? Who is they?

"No. But everyone's gone. The caretakers, the guards, everyone at the estate. Who did this?"

There's silence on the other end of the line for a beat. I glance at the screen to make sure we're still connected.

"This is Bratva business, but I'd say it concerns you too at this point." Maks sounds hesitantly. "Everyone's been called in and reassigned. There's a big meeting at The Pit later today. Basically, Dimitri's not *Pakhan* anymore, and some guy named Igor has taken charge." Another moment of silence, then, "Word is that he's second in command to Konstantin."

I wait for him to elaborate. When he doesn't, I'm forced to ask, "Who's Konstantin? Did he take Dimitri?"

"Yeah. At least I'm pretty damn sure he did. Konstantin is Dimitri's father."

"But his father's dead." My head is beginning to pound.

"That's what I thought too. Until this morning and I get a call from one of my men who says he saw that fucker with his own eyes last night. I don't know what his father wants with him, or where they took him, but it can't be good. You keep your head down. I can't protect you right now, but your family can. Go to them."

"They're already here. I left the club last night with

Sophia, Roman, and Blake when you two didn't show up. And there's one more thing." I lick my dry lips. "Dimitri left me a copy of the divorce papers. Signed. They've already been filed."

"Bullshit. He didn't do any such thing." An engine starts wherever Maks is at. "They want you out of his life. I don't know why, but for now that's a good thing."

Relief hits me so hard that I sink into a chair. "They want us divorced?"

"That seems pretty clear. Since they didn't just kill you, they also don't want to piss off your family. So you're safe for now, but that could change at any time."

"Okay. I—"

"We've located him." Blake and Roman walk into the kitchen, both sweaty from their workout.

"Hold on a minute," I tell Maks before giving Blake my full attention. "Where?"

Blake's thumbing through his phone. "My source tracked him to Moscow, Russia. A private plane left last night with eight Russians onboard, one of them unconscious. One of the men on the fuel crew recognized Dimitri as the owner of Riot, where he apparently spends a lot of his free time."

Maks's voice comes through the phone. "They took him to Moscow? I guess that explains why this Igor guy was left in charge here."

"What do we do now?" I ask Blake.

"Go to Moscow. Obviously. If you want to rescue your Prince Charming." Blake shrugs. "Or you could leave him to his fate. It's your call."

I shake my head. "No. We're going after him. We

need to book a flight, but I don't think you can get a direct flight from here to Russia."

Blake sneers. "Who said anything about flying *commercial?* We'll take my jet."

Right. Of course he has a private jet.

"Then let's go." I speak to Maks, letting him know what's going on. "Are you coming with us?"

"I want to, but I can't." He quietly curses to himself. "Get Dimitri and bring him home. If I go with you, then the brotherhood will be gone by the time we return. I'm going to find each and every traitorous motherfucker here and wipe them the fuck out. Tell Dimitri there are still men loyal to him."

"I will."

It's a long flight to Moscow, but Blake Baron's jet is amazingly comfortable with every top of the line amenity a person could want. The inside is enormous. The main cabin's set up like a living room with swivel recliners, and a sofa in front of a flat screen television. In the back are two private suites with king beds and their own bathrooms.

Sophia and Roman claimed one suite for themselves and have hidden away in there for most of the flight. Leaving me with the broody billionaire who's been working on his laptop the entire time. Does this man ever sleep?

My sister insisted on coming for moral support. Her

husband told me it's his job to protect the Pontrelli girls, so he has to come along. Not to mention the fact that he'd never let his wife go anywhere potentially dangerous without him. As to why Blake is doing this, I have no idea. Roman insists that he didn't pressure him into it.

Finally, I decide to get that answer myself.

"Mr. Baron—" I start.

"At this point call me Blake," he drawls, not looking up from his laptop.

"Blake, thank you for doing all of this, it means the world to me."

He grunts.

"Why are you helping me and Dimitri?" I ask, folding my legs beneath me on the sofa.

"Out of boredom. So don't put me on a pedestal."

"I wouldn't dream of it." I keep my tone light and dry.

He finally lifts his gaze to mine. "Good. Since we're on the topic of motives, Dimitri Kozlov is going to owe me big for this one. Assuming everything goes to plan and I manage to keep you both alive."

"So you're really helping because you want a favor from my husband?" That figures.

"I don't know about the world you come from, but that's how it works in my sphere. Deals and favors." Blake continues working on his computer, ignoring me again.

I'm only half teasing him when I say, "Are you sure you're not doing it because you want to reunite two lost lovers?"

He grimaces. "Love is the most ridiculous reason to do anything. So, no, the fact that you two supposedly love each other has no bearing on my motivations. The potential for favors and information is the only reason I'm pursuing this adventure."

"And boredom." I remind him.

"And boredom," he agrees.

CHAPTER 40

Dimitri

Have I been here for days or weeks? I can't tell anymore. The minutes bleed into hours and time seems to have both slowed down and sped up. My reality has been reduced to this chair and these chains, an empty belly, and my father's fists pummeling my body. Even so, all I can think about is Arianna.

Konstantin's voice taunts me from somewhere nearby. "Agree to marry a woman of my choosing and this will all end. You'll be fed. How about a hot shower?"

I shake my head. Grabbing my hair, he lifts my face then slams his fist into my jaw. The pain spikes for a second before fading enough to blend in with the constant, miserable ache that's my body's normal state these days.

I was such a fucking coward with Arianna. I've been obsessed with her for so long that I was too afraid to give her a choice—terrified that she'd never choose me. And in the end she chose her freedom over me, so I guess I was correct the whole time. What is she doing with her newfound freedom? Did she start dating Connor fucking Bane again? Maybe she met someone new at Leonidas. I'm glad I'm a world away because seeing her with another man would be the end of me. I'd rather carve my own heart out than run the risk of bumping into her when she's with someone else—someone she *chose*.

She's moved on. I wish I could do the same. Except I left my heart in New York City with a woman who doesn't want it. Does it really matter what I do with the rest of my life?

My wife is gone. We're divorced. It's over.

Finally admitting that to myself, a hollow space opens up in my chest, right where my heart used to be. The agony is gone. In its place I feel nothing. Nothing but emptiness.

I raise my blurry gaze to Konstantin. "I'll do it," I croak.

The satisfaction and triumph that lights his features should have me worried about what I'm agreeing to—except I don't feel a thing, I don't care.

Fight night in a Moscow club is much the same as it is in America—the roaring crowd, the thirst for blood, the obscene amount of money that changes hands. But none of it holds the same appeal that it used to. I don't feel at home here. My head didn't clear as soon as the scent of blood and sweat reached my nose.

I'm not the man I used to be—and I'll never be that man again.

"Here they are," Konstantin says close to my ear. "Remember, they are all of the right bloodlines, so the choice is yours. Just choose a wife by the end of the night. We'll hold the ceremony tomorrow, then you can knock her up. Once you have an heir, a boy, you can keep your wife or get rid of her. Whichever's your preference."

I nod, watching the three women come into our VIP box that looks down on the fighter's cage. A blond, a brunette, and a redhead. They're wearing dresses that leave little to the imagination, and shoes that add at least five inches to their natural heights.

Soon I'll have to choose one, make her my wife, then fuck her. Honestly, I don't care which one it is. They come toward me, their hands all over my chest and stomach, touching, caressing. My muscles tense.

Konstantin was true to his word and released me from the restraints once I agreed to do this. Over the past few days, I've been fed and cleaned up, but I know I still look rough. The bruises and cuts on my face are going to take a while longer to heal. Even so, these women fawn all over me like I'm a real catch. Any one of them would spread their legs for me in a heartbeat. They've been instructed do so, maybe even paid.

I realize I hate that fact. Arianna made me work for it, earn it. Nothing with her was ever easy.

I mentally shake away that thought, only for my gaze to drop to the crowd below us where my imagination summons a woman who looks exactly like Arianna. Her dark hair is piled high on her head, exposing the smooth, gorgeous skin of her throat. A pearl necklace. The dress she's wearing has me clenching my fists. She shouldn't be in a place like this looking that fucking *edible*.

Then I remember, she's not mine anymore.

She's also not here. That would be impossible.

Arianna's in New York.

CHAPTER 41

Arianna

W hen we landed in Moscow, Blake paid off the customs officer and just like that we had our documents and could freely move about the city. Blake had a car bring us to a posh hotel where we stayed in a couple of their best suites. Personal shoppers delivered our new wardrobes and everything else we needed. I knew Blake Baron was wealthy, but the way he's been throwing money around the past few days has been eye-opening.

Money really can get you anything. Even information.

Within twenty-four hours of arriving, Blake's sources found Konstantin Kozlov and we figured out that he'd be attending a popular MMA event next weekend. Chances were good that Dimitri would be there too. It was our first solid lead.

As it turns out, Konstantin is a well-known figure in Moscow which made him relatively easy to track down— according to Blake.

That's why we're here on this Saturday night, among the masses, working our way through the crowd. The place stinks of testosterone, and I'm reminded of the fight Dimitri took me to in The Pit. That night seems like ages ago now. So much has changed since then.

Sophia taps my shoulder. "Roman and I are going to search that side. You stay with Blake, okay?"

"Okay." I glance at Blake. He nods, ushering me forward with his hand hovering near my lower back, but not quite touching me. We're looking for Dimitri on the other half of the venue.

He must be here. At the very least, we hope to get a good look at Konstantin and his security detail. One way or another we're getting Dimitri away from him.

If you told me a week ago that I'd be in Moscow right now with my sister and two billionaires on a rescue mission, I'd have called you crazy. A few months ago, the old me would have left Dimitri to his fate. But not now. I'm not leaving this country until I get my husband back.

Life really is full of twists and turns.

First, we search the front few rows because those are some of the best seats in the house. There's no sign of Dimitri, or Konstantin, or Boris. Where could they be?

A sudden prickle of awareness causes my skin to tingle. Someone's watching me. Intuition tells me exactly who it is...

My gaze lifts to the VIP boxes and collides with Dimitri's. For a moment my heart leaps with joy. Until I notice the three women hanging all over him, touching him, murmuring into his ear. They're all gorgeous and obviously eager to please him.

My pulse stutters. A jealous rage vibrates through

my entire body. They need to get their hands off of my husband. He's mine.

Then doubt and insecurity creeps in. He looks like a king holding court. Powerfully lording over his domain. He's not trying to fight off those women who are claiming him like they have every right to do so.

Did we get it all wrong? Maybe Dimitri did leave me, divorce me, and run off to Russia with his father for a fresh start. It's possible, right?

My thoughts and feelings are a jumbled mess as I watch Dimitri excuse himself and exit the VIP box. He comes down the stairs and I meet him at the bottom. Blake hovers nearby while also giving us space.

Hesitantly, I approach Dimitri. His face is painful to look at, partly because of the bruising, but mostly because of the coldness in his green eyes. There's no welcoming warmth in his expression either. This isn't the man I know. What's happened to him?

He breaks the heavy silence between us. "What the fuck are you doing here?"

I recoil. This is not the reunion I've been picturing. My heart plummets.

"I... I came to rescue you." My words fall flat, seeming pointless and rather pathetic given the situation.

His brow dips. "Rescue me? You divorced me, remember? Isn't that enough or are you here to rub that in?"

"*I* divorced you?" My temper flares. What the hell is he talking about? "You know damn well I didn't sign those papers."

He scowls, seemingly deep in thought.

Snapping out of whatever foul mood he's in, he grabs

my arms and hauls me into a short, quiet hallway. His body cages me against the wall, cloaking me in his familiar scent. I deeply inhale. God, I've missed him.

Just as I think he's going to kiss me, he takes a step back. Frigid air expands in the space between us. His expression's guarded, the look in his eyes unreadable.

"You have to leave," he says. "Go, and never come back."

My stomach drops. "What do you mean? What's happening, Dima?"

Anguish briefly flashes in his eyes before it's gone. "My father is alive and he came for me. He murdered my uncle, and if he sees you here he'll kill you too. He gave you an easy out—divorce. Take it and run. Walk away right now and never look back."

"No." I straighten my spine, defiantly lifting my chin. "Your father can't just swoop in and ruin us."

"He already has." Devastating heartache swims in his gaze, and I reach for him. "Don't," he commands in a strangled voice. "It's too late for us. I'm not worth risking your life over."

I poke his chest. "That's where you're wrong. You're worth everything I have."

He sighs, gazing skyward. "I won't let you do this. You were right all along, being with me puts your life in danger. I'm not willing to do this to you anymore. You're free. Go. Now."

"But I don't want anyone but you. Dimitri, I love you." I put all of my desperation to get through to him into my voice. He has to understand how much I need him, because we can't end like this.

His green eyes turn icy again. "I don't love you."

My lips part, shock and devastation rattle my entire body.

Dimitri turns away, disappearing back up the stairs to his private box. All I can do is stare after him. He doesn't mean that, does he?

I let everything he told me sink in and try to see it from his perspective. His father is holding something over him. He has to be. Dimitri wouldn't do this of his own free will. No matter how much he wants me to think that's what's happening here.

"How'd that go?" Blake steps into the hallway. "Is he coming?"

Slowly, I shake my head. "Not willingly." God, I hope I'm right about all of this. "He's afraid his father will kill me. So he's pushing me away in an effort to protect me."

Fortunately, I can see through his motives. He does love me. He loves me so much that he's willing to end our relationship in order to protect me, to sacrifice himself. He's trying to leave me because he loves me.

It's such bullshit.

He should know by now that I'm not the kind of person who goes down without a fight.

I purse my lips. "Tell Roman it's time for plan B."

"Gladly." Blake's eyes light with wicked excitement. It's the most emotion I've ever seen in him.

CHAPTER 42
Dimitri

She loves me. She came all the way here, still wearing the wedding band I gave her, to bring me home. She loves me. I wish with all my heart that I could leave with her, but I can't. Standing so close to her just now and holding back the overwhelming desire to kiss her, hug her, bury my nose in the crook of her neck and drink in her scent, was agony. Worse than anything Konstantin has dished out.

But I have to let her go. If I don't, I'm going to get us both killed. Konstantin wants me, not her, but if she interferes with his plans he won't hesitate to get rid of her. He won't stop at just her either, he'll murder her entire family. I can't let that happen.

That's how he's risen to this height of power in Moscow. Anyone who crosses him ends up dead—including their friends and relatives. Boris made a point one night of boasting about how Konstantin is a strong leader because there's no line he won't cross. That Uncle Vadim was killed because he was weak. If Konstantin can murder his own brother, use and discard his own wife, and treat me the way he does, he's capable of anything.

My wife will not be one of his victims. I'll keep her safe. Even if the cost is *us*.

I'm elated that she didn't sign those papers. In the end, she did choose me. I'm sorry I doubted her and there are a million things I want to tell her, but can't. At least I will die a happy man knowing she loves me. She *chose* me, even if we can't be together.

As soon as I enter the VIP box, Konstantin eyes me. He has a leggy blond in his lap who wasn't there before. He jerks his head toward the three women waiting for me, and grudgingly, I rejoin them. Sitting, the brunette settles in at my side, the blond at the other, and the redhead sinks to her knees between my legs. She starts fiddling with my zipper.

"Stop it," I bark at her, annoyed. Fuck, what have I gotten myself into?

"Let them please you, Dimitri. You may as well get a taste of them before you choose a wife." He stands, lifting the leggy young woman by her hair, then bends her over the back of his chair. "Watch and learn, son."

He starts fucking the woman right there in the middle of the room, in full sight of everyone, like he's untouchable. Which I guess he is.

The girl grunts and cries as he uses her hard. Disgusted, I excuse myself again, muttering about going to the restroom.

"You may go, but be a good boy." He continues to fuck the girl as he talks. "Remember that my reach is far. If you try to escape I'll hurt your brothers in New

York City. Especially that one you're so close to... Maks."

I still don't know what happened to Maks, but I won't risk his life any more than I'll put Arianna's in danger.

I give him a stiff nod, my fists curling and uncurling.

The two guards at our box's door step aside, but only after Konstantin gives them a signal to allow it.

This is my new life. Constantly under watch, my father in control of my every move. How can I bring a child into this? Konstantin is sure to treat his grandchildren as horribly as he treated me when I was young. To a man like him people are objects. I'm just a continuation of the Kozlov bloodline, that's why he wants me now. That's my worth to him. Family doesn't matter to him, but the bloodline does. For whatever insane reason.

Just as the fight starts, I step into the restroom to take a piss. A guy inside hurries out to catch the beginning of the action.

Sighing, I relieve myself in the urinal. My thoughts wander back to Arianna. I'm pretty sure I made her feel like an object, like a possession I own. I never meant to hurt her, but I am beginning to think that's the only way I know how to show love. It's fucked up. But given what I grew up with, I'm not all that surprised.

In the long run, if I really am that much like my despicable father, then Arianna's better off without me. Any child we might have had together is also safer without me as the father. The truth is, I don't know how to love properly. And I sure as shit don't deserve the kind of family I've always craved. I'm too fucked up for that. It took me having to reconnect with my father for me to see myself clearly. But I do now. I see who I am.

I'm washing my hands when the door swings open. Blake Baron and Roman De Luca enter the restroom. Their gazes zero in on me, their expressions guarded. They lean on either side of the doorway, blocking the exit.

"What the fuck do you two want?" I practically snarl at them, irritated that they won't leave me the fuck alone. They belong in my past with Arianna. Them being here puts all our lives in danger.

Roman casually strolls toward me, circling around to the other sink so that I have to turn to face him. I glance over my shoulder at Baron, uneasy about having him at my back. But I can't keep an eye on both of them at the same time.

"Do you love her?" Roman folds up his sleeves, gazing at me in the mirror.

"What the fuck to do you think?" I snap.

"That's not an answer. What I think is irrelevant." He so damn calm it sets me on edge.

I glance back at Baron, who's leaning against the wall, bored.

"Of course I fucking love her, why else would I be doing this?" I step closer to Roman, getting in his face. "You don't know Konstantin and what he's capable of doing. If you care about all the Pontrelli girls as much as you say you do, then get Arianna out of here, as far away from him as possible. Do you hear me?"

He levels those yellow-hazel eyes on me. "That's exactly what I hoped to hear. Welcome to the family, Kozlov."

He punches me and I stumble back, stunned. What the actual fuck is wrong with him?

That moment of distraction costs me big time. Blake fucking Baron hits me on the back of the head—hard enough that my knees buckle. Then a hood is tugged over my head. A slight pinch in my arm is the last thing I feel before everything goes dark.

M y entire face pounds with a splitting headache. I feel like I've been carried, dragged, and dropped—again, numerous times. But as far as I can tell I'm not bound to a chair. Instead, I'm lying horizontally on a soft surface, the hum of engines all around. Taking a chance, I peel my eyelids open and find out I'm in an airplane cabin, on a bed. Movement to my right catches my attention.

Arianna. I blink, once, twice.

No, she can't be here. This can't be right.

I start to sit up, but she rushes toward me. "Don't move. Lie down."

"Did you fucking kidnap me?" I glance around in horror. Roman and Blake jumped me in that restroom and somehow got me out of that place and onto a plane. Konstantin is going to lose his shit. He's going to come after us.

"We need to turn around," I tell her. "You don't

understand the kind of danger we're in. Konstantin will—"

"Have some faith in me, Mr. Kozlov." She elegantly folds her arms. "I know exactly what kind of danger we're in. Which is why I had to go to these extremes to extract you from the situation."

I shake my head. She's not getting it. "No. Arianna, he'll *kill* you, your family, Maks. Everyone."

"Shh." She climbs onto the bed. "Maks is fine. He's been kept up to date on what's happening. My family is taking precautions, too. Everything is going to be fine."

"Maks is alive? He's okay?" I hoped he made it after the car crash.

"He was a little banged up, but he's fine. I'll let him fill you in on everything once we land."

Panic soars through me. My palms grow clammy and I can't draw in a full breath of air. "We need to turn the plane around. Right now." My vice squeezes my chest.

Arianna straddles my lap and cups my face. "God, what did that man do to you, Dima? You're terrified. I've never seen you like this before. This isn't you."

I close my eyes, taking comfort in her touch. She's right. I've never been this afraid before. Though that's not exactly true. Flashes of long forgotten memories keep bombarding my mind. I'm not even sure if they're all real, but the sensations are. Panic, dread, and horror struggle for dominance. So much *pain*.

"It's because of him." I reach for her, burying my nose in her hair as I hug her close. "I remember things... Awful things."

I thought my time living on the streets was rough, but that turned out to be a blessing, an escape from my vile father. His fists pummeling my small child's body I've never forgotten about, but the other things...

He'd lock me in the chest freezer until I passed out. The scar across my eyebrow is from when he beat me so badly I couldn't get off the floor for days. Twice, when he thought I'd talked back to him, he'd waterboarded me in the bathtub.

These and other snippets from my childhood keep flickering through my mind and it's only getting worse.

"Dimitri," Arianna says in a firm tone. "Look at me. Whatever he did to you, you're not that helpless little boy anymore. You're not alone either."

I gaze at her beautiful face, wishing I felt stronger. "If he can get to my uncle, he can get to anyone."

"Your uncle didn't know Konstantin was alive. We do, and we're ready for him. Trust me, Dima, please."

"He did know," I correct her. "He knew all along and never told me. I can't let Konstantin hurt you, *kisa.*"

She leans forward, capturing my mouth with hers, and nips at my bottom lip. She does it again, harder this time. The pinch of pain helps to clear my thoughts.

Arianna's here, with me, saving me from not only my father, but from myself. I fucking love this woman.

She starts to strip off her clothes. I run my hands over her body, familiarizing myself with the feel of her, her scent, her taste. She takes off my shirt, then opens my fly to release my growing cock. Fuck, I've missed her.

She wraps her small palm around my dick. "How does it feel to be kidnapped, Mr. Kozlov?" She's breathless, her skin flushed. This is payback. "There's no escape from this jet, and you're completely at my mercy."

I groan. She feels so fucking good. I'm torn between

trying to make her understand how dangerous Konstantin is and just submitting to the pleasure she's giving me.

"This isn't a game, *kisa*. He'll hunt us all—"

She sinks onto my cock causing my words to falter. I grab her waist, guiding her all the way down, until I'm buried inside her sweet, warm pussy. *Home.* If this isn't heaven I don't know what is.

"This is a game, Dima." She starts to ride me. "It's a game of life and death. He's going to pay for everything he's done to you. I'll make sure of it."

"You're fucking crazy, *malyshka*. You know that?" I slip my thumb between us to draw circles around her sensitive bundle of nerves. She moans my name and rides my cock faster.

"I'm crazy for you." She swivels her hips in a way that just about undoes me. "We can't keep doubting each other. I never should have believed that you left me, not even for an instance. I'll never let anyone get between us like that again. I promise. I love you. I'm sorry I didn't tell you sooner."

"I love you, too. I'm sorry for pushing you away." I suck a nipple into my mouth.

"You can't get rid of me," she pants, arching her back.

"Never again." I hold her as she climaxes in my arms. Then I flip us over and drive into her until I come. I may never be worthy of her, but she's my fucking home. From this day forward, I'll try my best to be the man she deserves.

Maks and a crew of men meet us on the tarmac. I embrace him, clapping him on the back, so fucking thankful that he's alive.

"*Pakhan*, it's good to have you back. Here's your phone. I found it on the ground when I woke up." He walks us to one of three cars, where Arianna and I scoot into the back seat. Roman and his wife get into a different car, and Blake Baron's in the third.

"Catch me up," I tell Maks as we start to roll.

"I'll start from the beginning. Boris and a handful of the old guard decided to follow Konstantin when he came here to murder Vadim. They joined with Konstantin's men to infiltrate our Bratva. Igor, Konstantin's second, was put in command here, but those of us loyal to you took him out. I've been leading the Bratva while we've been preparing for your return."

Maks. He's so damn competent. I don't know why I didn't see it before, but he should have always been my number one choice as second. I'll make it official soon.

Maks continues, "Thanks to your lovely wife, we have the Italians and the Irish on our side too. As soon as Konstantin and his men set foot in this country we'll know about it. We'll be ready for them."

I squeeze Arianna's hand. She's told me countless times that she wants out of this dangerous world we live in. But right now she's thriving in it. She was born to be a mafia queen. With her by my side, I'm beginning to believe that we can overcome anything.

She smiles at me and my heart sings. I love this woman.

Maybe I have let my fears and trauma get the best of me lately. It was hard being held captive by Konstantin. He's a sick bastard who relishes breaking me down until I'm nothing more than that cowering seven year old boy again. But that's not who I am anymore. And he's no longer the undefeatable monster lurking in the darkness. I can, and will, stand up to him.

Arianna's right. I'm a grown man, and seeing myself through her eyes, I can find my strength. Konstantin is going to pay for not only what he put me through, but also for what he did to my mother and my uncle. I'm going to make him beg for death. I want him on his knees, to see the terror in his eyes, before I give him the mercy of a bullet in his head. Or perhaps I'll watch as he slowly bleeds out.

Either way will be too merciful for a man like him.

CHAPTER 44
Arianna

W e've temporarily moved into the safest place in the city. The Manor in Manhattan is the one place where we're untouchable. The building is teeming with criminals of all types but beneath this roof the members have all agreed to the no violence policy. It's the most secure, ritzy safe house on the East Coast.

Dimitri kisses my bare shoulder. "I have to go out. But I'll be back as soon as possible."

"Why?" I roll over in bed and sit up. "Why do you have to go?"

"It's okay, *kisa*. I'm just meeting up with Maks for some important Bratva business that can't wait. Today he officially becomes my second in command. He'll have the authority he needs to do what has to be done."

I know this is important to both of them, but I still don't like that he's going outside of The Manor. It's not safe out there. Not until Konstantin and his men are dealt with, but so far no one has seen them.

"Hurry back," I tell him.

He kisses me, then disappears out the door that auto locks.

Stretching, I reach for my phone. It's past nine in the morning, so I decide to get up and shower, then put some proper clothing on.

The shower sprays water on me from multiple directions. The entire apartment is like living in a five star hotel, no expense was spared in constructing this place. There's even a small walk-in closet off the bedroom. I had some of my things brought over. Today I choose a knee length wool dress with long sleeves. It's comfortable enough to lounge in, but put together enough to make me feel somewhat in control of my life. A touch of makeup and blow drying my hair completes the look.

I grab my phone and open the messages app. Tarina texted me days ago with a quick note to call her when my family emergency was solved. The situation hasn't resolved yet, but I can't put off speaking to my boss much longer.

Hell, I don't even know if I have a job anymore or not. There's one way to find out. I press the call button and listen to the ringtone.

"Hello, Arianna," she answers.

"Hi, Tarina."

Silence follows our greetings.

"I understand you had a family emergency," she says. "However, it's too bad it interfered with the most important night of your job. Mr. Hyde wants me to point out that you were supposed to be on call until after midnight."

"Yes, I know, and I'm sorry. But I couldn't stay."

"I realize that, and Mr. Hyde has agreed to hiring you on in a full-time position at Leonidas."

"Really?" I squeeze my phone tighter.

Tarina softly chuckles. "Really. You're excellent at your job, so you'll be my personal assistant. Can you come by the club today for the paperwork?"

"I... No, not today." Crap, now I'm going to have to disappoint her some more. "I'm still dealing with this family crisis, but I'll hopefully be available next week. Does that work for you?"

"That's fine. In fact, why don't you just shoot me a text when your schedule's open."

"I will. Thank you, I appreciate your flexibility."

"Chat soon. Take care." She ends the call.

I heave a relieved sigh. Not only did I get the job, but I have a wonderfully understanding boss. That personal assistant position puts me as her right-hand employee. I couldn't have asked for more.

Practically giddy, and starving, I order breakfast from a nearby coffee shop that delivers. My order arrives via a member of The Manor's staff, since for security reasons they don't let anyone in from the outside—especially delivery people. I tip and thank them, then settle by the window to devour my black tea and pastry.

My phone pings and I glance at the message.

DIMITRI

Meet me downstairs. Side door. Red
SUV. See you soon.

That Bratva business didn't take long at all. Not surprising as Maks has been leading the brotherhood since Dimitri was abducted. I'm so happy that he decided to elevate Maks's position from bodyguard and driver to underboss. Maks deserves it.

I text him that I'm on my way down. Slipping on a pair of sensible heels, I grab my trench coat, wondering where we're going. Dimitri didn't say anything about us going out after he's done with work, but he does like surprising me. I guess I'll find out.

Is it really safe to go out? It must be, or he wouldn't be picking me up outside. Plus, given the lengths that he was willing to go to keep me safe, I fully trust him.

I take the elevator down to the lobby and head toward the side exit. It's a pick-up and drop-off zone. The sky outside's overcast, dense clouds roll in, blotting out the sun. A threat of snow hangs heavy in the January air.

I immediately spot the red SUV and walk toward it. The windows are tinted, same with all of Dimitri's vehicles, though I don't recall this cherry red one in any of his garages. He's more of a black SUV kind of guy.

My steps slow as a chill runs up my spine and over my scalp. Something feels... off, but I can't pinpoint what. All I know is that my instincts are telling me to run.

I come to a complete stop just as the SUV's doors open and men dressed in long charcoal coats step out. I'm about to bolt, when two men appear at my sides and catch me. I scream, but one of them roughly covers my mouth.

Kicking and trying to bite down on his gloved hand, I'm hauled into the back seat of the vehicle.

The doors audibly click as they lock.

Tires screech and we lurch forward.

Panic spikes through me, my heart thunders. This

can't be happening. Where's Dimitri? He told me to come down here.

What the hell is going on?

The man in the passenger seat turns around and gives me a smile that doesn't reach his cold, mossy green eyes.

Konstantin. I recognize him instantly.

No, no, no. This can't be happening.

"Shh, little bird," Konstantin says in a voice that's too calm. "You've caused me so many headaches. Now you've brought this upon yourself because you won't stay out of my way." His gaze slithers down my body, undressing me with his eyes, and I shiver with disgust and fear. "You'll fetch a nice price."

My heartbeat kicks up. Cold terror settles in the pit of my stomach.

"Wh-what are you going to do with me?" Mindlessly, I clutch the pearls at my neck.

Wrathful delight shines in his eyes. "Have you ever heard of the skin trade? Human trafficking? I'm going to sell you. You'll disappear, no trace left behind, you'll never be heard from again."

Fear lodges in my throat, choking me. Konstantin laughs in my stricken face.

As if to drive home his point, he takes my purse from one of his men and empties its contents out the window. My phone, ID, and everything is gone. My life's being stripped away before my very eyes, replaced with my worst nightmare.

By the time we pull up at the docks, I'm paralyzed from fear.

The vehicle glides onto a ship and I don't even try to

fight back when these men haul me out of the SUV.
They practically drag me through narrow corridors and
flights of stairs to the ship's belly. A metal door creaks
open, revealing a cargo space lit by bare bulbs. The room
is full of large dog cages that aren't quite tall enough to
stand up in. My kidnappers shove me into one of the
kennels and padlock the door.

I fall to my knees, shaking. *This can't be happening.* I
repeat that phrase over and over in my head. *This can't
be happening.*

Denial is the only thing keeping me from completely
losing my shit right now. Long forgotten nightmares,
from when Ilaria disappeared, threaten to invade my
mind.

But the layers of avoidance begin to shed when I look
to my left and right. Those cages are occupied too. A
young woman in each, cowering in the corner, terror in
their eyes. We all know there's no escape. This is just the
beginning of the horror to come.

The ship sways. Rumbling motors come to life. It's
leaving port soon with all of us trapped in here.

I open my mouth and scream.

CHAPTER 45

Dimitri

The initiation ceremony for Maks wraps up and I thump him on the back, then step away so that the others can welcome him in his new position among the brotherhood. Not a single one of them contested that he should step into the role of my second in command, so proceedings went smoothly.

Now that the Kozlov Bratva has a solid line of succession we can continue our business with a sense of stability and structure that's been missing for too long.

For the couple of weeks that I was held prisoner in Moscow, Maks led the brotherhood through a massive cleansing. Igor and those loyal to my father died in a blood bath that will not soon be forgotten. Order and loyalty has been restored, all thanks to Maks. He's the best right-hand man I can ask for.

My cell vibrates, a reminder of the text that I received during the ceremony. I pull it from my pocket.

ARIANNA
I'll be down in a minute.

I stare at the screen. Confusion mingles with apprehension. Down? Down where? She sounds like she's meeting me somewhere, but the last text I sent her was a photo of herself sleeping.

Did someone spoof my fucking phone number and message her?

Immediately, I call her phone. The call goes straight to voicemail. I try again and get the same thing.

Shoving my hand through my hair, I dial Blake Baron who answers on the first ring.

"Yes?" he drawls.

"Where's *my wife*?" I demand. "Activate the tracker I put in her necklace."

"On it." He sounds like he's typing in the background. "She's at the docks. GPS puts her on a cargo ship."

"Konstantin must have grabbed her." White hot fury momentarily blinds me. "We need to get there. *Now*."

"I'm sending you the location. We'll meet you there." Baron hangs up.

I don't have time to wonder who *we* is, so I turn to Maks. "Konstantin took Arianna. Follow me."

Maks starts barking orders. The men immediately spring into action.

I jump onto my Harley and speed toward Arianna's location. Maks and the rest of our men aren't far behind.

That was too easy for Konstantin to get to her, but he's a sly bastard. I've seen the forged letter that I supposedly left to break up with Arianna. That was some professional shit right there. Even I believed I'd written it for a second. The signatures on the divorce papers were a pro job. Of course Konstantin has a hacker working for him too. I'm sure that fucker has all his bases covered.

Except he doesn't know about the tracking device I put in Arianna's pearls. She wears those everywhere, all the time. That necklace is guaranteed to be on her even more than her wedding band. That's why I chose it.

I'm already planning to make Konstantin suffer before I end him, but if he's hurt one hair on my wife's head...

At the docks I ditch my bike and move on foot toward the location pin on my phone. My gun in my free hand. I'm almost to the ship when Blake Baron steps out of the shadows and motions me to him. Movement catches my eye behind him. Roman De Luca and Cian O'Rourke are with him. I guess that's who he meant by *we*.

"Their engines are warming up," Baron says in a hushed tone. "They're readying to leave port soon. We need to sneak on board. The element of surprise can work in our favor as long as we're quiet. Put away that gun."

I scowl at him, but do as I'm told. He's right. Our best option is to storm the ship as quickly and quietly as possible.

Maks jogs up with ten men at his back. We briefly go over the plan from our hiding place between two walls of containers. The light's growing fainter by the minute as snow flurries begin to fall. Dense white flecks quickly

326 • CASSIA QUINN

hinder our line of sight. We need to get on that ship, now.

Stealthily we creep toward the cargo ship. The towering bridge sits in the middle surrounded by colorful cargo containers. On the side of the hull, we climb the narrow steel ladders and emerge onto a perimeter walkway.

The ship groans and gradually moves forward on its way out of port.

Roman clasps my shoulder. "Don't worry, this ship's not going far. Port authorities are going to be all over this once I signal them. Let's find your girl."

I nod, grateful for his influence over the docks. He's basically the king of the shipping business up and down the East Coast.

We make our way to the stairs that lead to the crews private quarters. I'm sure Konstantin paid off the captain to allow him, his men, and their cargo onboard. If we'll find them anywhere it'll be in the passenger cabins. Hopefully Arianna's with them.

On silent footsteps we advance along the hallway. A door opens and a Russian steps out. I recognize him as one of Konstantin's men. Before the door closes, I catch snippets of conversation in my native tongue. My fist strikes with his throat. His eyes bulge, but not a sound escapes. Another jab and he slides to the floor. I step over him, encouraged, knowing that we've found them.

When I step into the room, seven Russians turn their heads my way, guns in hand. My gaze latches onto Konstantin. But Arianna is nowhere to be seen.

My fingers ball into fists and flex. "Where the fuck is *my wife?*"

K onstantin's grin is so smug it makes my teeth clench. "That Italian whore is currently getting her fill of Boris. He couldn't wait to get his dick wet. I'm sure you know how much he likes a nice piece of Italian ass."

All I see is red as I stare down the guns trained on me. After I kill each and every one of them, I'm going to skin Boris alive.

Konstantin stands, coming to eye level with me, radiating confident dominance. Not that long ago I would have backed down, feeling small in his presence. Unable to shake the cowering child version of myself, and the past trauma. But the past stays where it belongs this time, and I face this monster as a grown man. One who will do anything to rescue his wife.

Anything at all.

I stare back at him. We have him outnumbered and cornered. This confrontation is nearly at its end. All I need them to do is lower their weapons.

"Tell me where to find my wife." Command booms in my voice. Konstantin's eye twitches as if he's not used to being spoken to in such a tone.

"Be a good boy and tell your friends to leave. This is over. I have your *ex*-wife and now I have you as well." He spreads his arms wide. "Don't you see I've won?"

I snort. "So this is a trap set up to catch me?"

"Of course. I knew you'd come for that Italian slut, though I don't understand why. She's nothing."

She's everything, but I'm not going to tell him that and give him any more power over me.

"You're wrong. You're the one who's nothing." I spit on the floor. "Go fuck yourself."

Crimson rage travels up his neck, across his face, and into his hairline. "Don't you dare use that tone with me, boy. You ungrateful wretch. One day you'll understand what I've done for this family. When we can come out of hiding, openly reclaim our true surname, and once again sit on the Russian throne, then you'll *thank* me."

What the fuck is he talking about? The man's psychotic.

"I don't give a shit about your delusional schemes. You're nothing but a crazy old man."

"What did I tell you about showing respect, boy?" He lurches toward me, his fists swinging.

I pull the brass knuckles from my pocket and punch him square in the face. He stumbles back. The shock written across his features is almost comical.

Wasting no time, I drop into a crouch and pull my gun. The first shot rings out in the confined space. A symphony follows as Konstantin's men and mine exchange fire. Maks leads the charge.

In a matter of seconds I'm kneeling in a growing pool of blood. Konstantin's men slump all around the room, either bleeding out or already dead.

I walk right up to their dazed leader and punch him again. He drops to the floor in an unconscious heap. Arrogant fucker really thought he'd won. He'll learn soon enough that I'm the victor, and an avenging angel as I make him pay for his crimes against my loved ones.

"Take him to a holding cell at Riot," I order Maks. "I'm going to find my wife."

Pivoting, I exit the room and continue along the corridor, where I run into Blake. He motions me to a door at our left.

"We've searched this floor. Nothing. The crew's cooperating with us, so no need to worry about them. Let's go down a level." He leads and I follow. Judging by the way he moves I'd think he had military training, then I remember that he's a billionaire trust fund baby. Maybe he's spent too much time playing virtual reality first person shooter games.

Or, he has enough money, maybe he pays people to play war-camp with him on the weekends for fun.

I shake away the irrelevant thoughts and focus on my surroundings. This level is storage and general cargo hold. We search two rooms that both hold generic supplies including food, water, and dry goods.

Frustration makes my jaw work. The primal *need* to get to Arianna grows stronger by the second. Konstantin delayed me for too long already. In that time, what has Boris done to her? My gut hollows out at just the vaguest notion.

I have to find them.

I have to find *her*.

A shrill scream pierces my ears when Blake pushes open another cargo hold door. That sound wraps around my insides and squeezes tight.

Rushing into the room, I find row after row of dog kennels, all containing women. Halfway down one row I hear them before I see them.

"Get back here, you little bitch," Boris roars. "You're going to take my dick. One way or another."

He has my wife on her hands and knees, her dress pushed up around her hips to expose her bare ass. He's kneeling behind her with is dick in hand. She's struggling to get away from him.

Blind fury like I've never experienced before overtakes my body. I charge.

CHAPTER 47

Arianna

Boris's meaty hands keep reaching for me, tearing at my clothes and trying to hold my hips still so he can force himself on me. Rape me. I scream, for all the good that does, and struggle against his hold. My desperation drives me, giving me a strength I didn't know I had.

But it's not enough. I'm shut into a barred cage with this man. There's no escape. My fate is sealed.

And if Konstantin's telling the truth about selling me, then this will only be the first of many assaults to come. Pure terror twists in my stomach. I feel like a caged animal fighting for a hopeless chance at freedom. All reason has fled, leaving only my instincts intact.

Fight, run, or freeze. Those are my only options. All of them are pointless.

This happened to Ilaria six years ago. I've always known it would happen to me, too. Deep down, I knew we'd share the same fate, we were so close, inseparable.

I'll never be safe. No matter what. Not unless I can

get far, far away from this brutal world. Away from men who use and discard women as easily as a condom. Away from the darkness that overtakes us all in the end.

But, it's too late now.

Boris grabs my hips and pulls me against him. My ass smacks against his balls. Another soul-splitting scream crawls up my throat. He curses at me.

Then cool air sweeps across my backside. Suddenly, he's gone. I'm free.

I pull my skirt down and scoot away until my back hits a corner. I need to get out of here. I need to—

My panicked gaze finds Boris lying on the floor right outside of the cage. Dimitri's on top of him, pummeling his face. Finally, I tune into the *thwacking* sounds of pounding flesh and the crunch of bone.

This isn't a fight, it's an execution. It's punishment.

Dimitri doesn't slow until Boris has no face left. All that remains is a mass of sunken gore and blood.

When my eyes meet Dimitri's I see his rage burning bright. But there's more too. I see the monster that lurks within him. The violence that feeds a part of his twisted soul. Here, right now, he's in his element. This is the darkness where he thrives.

How did I never see it before?

Was I so blinded by his handsome face? Or was I in denial?

It doesn't matter. I see him for his true self now.

He's just like the rest of them.

"*Kisa?*" He reaches for me with a gore smeared hand. "It's okay, *malyshka*, I've got you."

Vehemently, I shake my head, cowering into the corner. "No!" I shriek. "Get away from me!"

The monster within him recedes enough that his gaze softens with concern. I screw my eyes shut, unwilling to witness him transform from a murderous brute into the semi-civilized man who fogs my brain with pretty words and sinful touches.

I won't be duped again.

Right now I have clarity. No one can take that away from me. I see everyone around me for who they truly are. They can't hide any longer.

I was right all along. They're all monsters. I'm a monster too.

Monsters.

Monsters.

Monsters.

Dimitri touches me and I scream. I feel, rather than see, him recoil.

"Roman, take her to her parents house," he says from a little further away. "I need to deal with Konstantin."

Konstantin's still alive? *No, no, no.*

He'll come after me. I know he will.

"Arianna," Roman says, his voice calming. Peeking through my lashes, I gaze at Roman. He's squatting right outside of the cage. "We're going to get you and all of these other women off this ship. I'm going to take you home to your parents. Do you understand? Sophia will be there for you, too. And Gin and Ravenna, even Ilaria if you want her with you."

I stare at him. I'm sure he's a monster too, but suddenly I'm too exhausted to care. My single nod is all he needs. He enters the cage and drapes his jacket around my quaking shoulders. Scooping me up, he steps over Boris's mutilated body and carries me away from this hell.

Zoning out, I barely remember the boat ride to shore, or the car taking me to my parents home. Roman busies himself on his phone the entire time, frequently glancing over to check on me. By the time we arrive it's evening.

Did all of that just happen in the span of one day?

It feels like a dream—a nightmare—instead of reality.

The front door opens and I'm immediately encircled in my mama's arms. The last bit of strength I've been holding onto drains away and I finally break down. A sob tears from my raw throat.

I cry for what feels like an eternity. Only to fall asleep and be plagued by nightmares. Men with caved in faces, blood leaking down their bodies, pin me to a concrete floor and tear off my clothes.

I wake up to my own screams.

H e broke her. He broke *my wife*. My split and bleeding knuckles crash into his jaw again, but it's not enough. The woman who looked back at me from inside that cage with terror in her wide eyes, who screamed when I reached for her, that wasn't Arianna. That was a broken fragment of her soul.

And he's to blame for all of it. He's going to pay for it, too. Over and over until his mind and body gives out. Hell, I might even take his soul.

He spits a mouthful of blood and a couple of teeth onto the floor. "You can't break me, son. You don't have it in you. You're soft—too much like your mother. She only lasted a couple years after your were born because she was weak."

I slam my fist into him again. "Don't you even fucking think about my mother, you worthless piece of shit."

"See? I'm still in your head and under your skin. You can't shake me." He laughs, revealing a bloody smile. "I'll always be with you. You'll think about me when you're alone, you'll hate me, but you'll never be rid of me. I shaped you into who you are today."

"Shut the fuck up!" This time I knock him out.

Fury rushes through my veins. He's right, he is in my head, fucking with my mind. The fact that I'm here, punishing him, instead of going to my wife says it all.

I glance at Maks. "Torture him all you want, but keep him alive." I scrub his blood from my hands in the wall-mounted sink. "I'll be back later."

"You got it, *Pakhan*. I'll take care of him."

Konstantin stirs and Maks takes over.

"You'll never be rid of me!" Konstantin hollers at my retreating back. Clenching my teeth, I ignore him. He's not nearly as important to me as Arianna. I have to get my wife back.

"She doesn't want to see you. Now get the fuck out of my sight." Mr. Pontrelli bars the door, his glacial stare pinned on me. "There's no way you're getting into my house. Leave my daughter alone."

Holding my hands up, I back off. We've been around and around about this for the last ten minutes. He's not letting me in. End of story.

"Tell her I stopped by," I say, stepping backward to my motorcycle.

Mr. Pontrelli sneers and slams the door.

I'm not getting to her through the front door, but I do

need to see her, to talk to her. She's suffering, all because of my deranged father, and I need to make it right. My palms tingle with the urge to hold her and sooth away all of her fears. I shouldn't have stayed away this long.

Hold on, I'm coming for you, malyshka.

My motorcycle revs to life and I drive away from the Pontrelli's house, only to kill the engine around the corner and park. Dusk will be settling over the city in a couple of hours. I check in with Maks, then walk the neighborhood until my feet bring me back to the Pontrelli's front gate.

Half hidden behind a bush, I wait for the cover of night, then sneak onto the grounds. Having spied on the place before, I expertly avoid their security cameras and quickly make my way to the back of the mansion, where I scale the climbing rose trellis up to Arianna's bedroom window. It's unlocked—I'm going to have to speak with her about safety. Sliding it open, I duck inside.

The room's dark and quiet. An untouched dinner tray grows cold on her bedside table. She hasn't eaten tonight. That very thought has my blood roiling with anger. Arianna loves food. She'd only go without if she was in extreme distress.

I type out a quick text to Maks reminding him to keep Konstantin alive. That man hasn't suffered nearly enough yet.

As I move toward the bed, which is a jumble of comforters and pillows, I finally spot her angelic face resting on the pillow. Even in sleep her features are twisted with misery. Which is so unlike her.

Oh, my sweet *kisa*. I'm here.

Settling on the bed, I scoot toward her and she stirs.

Her eyes open wide with terror. Her lips part. I clamp my hand over her mouth before she can scream and tug her body against mine.

"Shh, *kisa*, it's me. I've got you. Everything's all right." I hold her close, sweeping her hair from her face. "Don't scream, *malyshka*."

Once I feel her nod, I remove my hand from her mouth and switch on the bedside lamp.

Her eyes are red and puffy like she's been crying for hours. Her silky hair's a knotted mess, hovering around her face in wild waves. But it's the gut-wrenching wariness in her eyes that undoes me. She'll barely meet my gaze.

I tighten my hold on her stiff body. "What's going on? Tell me what you're thinking."

The silence stretches for so long that I'm beginning to think she won't answer. I continue to stroke her hair, even though she refuses to relax against me. What did I do wrong?

"I... I can't do this," she whispers.

My heart twists. "Do what?"

"This. Us." She pushes my hands away and slides across the bed, putting too much distance between us. My chest feels like it's in a vice. I can barely draw breath.

"No. Please." I reach for her before dropping my hand, curling it into a fist. "Tell me how to make this right. I'll do anything for you. You know I will."

Her bloodshot eyes glisten with tears. She shakes her head. "There's nothing you can do." A sob tears from her throat and it takes all of my will power to stay where I am, to give her space. "I thought I was stronger than this, but I'm not. I knew the dangers, the risks, of this lifestyle and I ignored them. I can't do that anymore. I want out. I *need* out."

Her declaration guts me. I can't live without Arianna in my life. The idea of being without her is too bleak to even consider.

"Listen, life is dangerous. It doesn't matter where you go or how you live." Desperate, I run my hand through my hair to keep from touching her. "Stay with me. I will protect you, I will come for you, always. No one will ever take you away from me like that again. I promise."

She looks at me with so much hopelessness that my heart sinks further. "You can't promise me that." Slowly, she shakes her head. "I always knew one day I'd disappear like Ilaria did. We were so close growing up, I knew our destinies had to be entwined. No one can protect women like us. We'll always be used, as either prizes or leverage. It's the world we're born into and the men who rule it that control our fate. I can't stay here any longer."

She doesn't believe that. She can't. Where is her fight, her determination? Has that really been stripped from her in a single night?

I don't believe it for a second. Her stubborn perseverance isn't just on the surface, it's soul deep. But I have a feeling that she needs to rediscover that for herself. All I can do is support and encourage her until she finds her inner strength. Just like she brought me back to mine when my father got inside my head, exploiting my every fear and weakness.

"You are strong," I tell her. "You're the strongest woman I've ever met. Don't let anyone take that away from you. Don't take it away from yourself either."

Silent tears stream down her cheeks. I can't hold myself back any longer, I reach for her, but she raises her hand to make me stop.

"Don't," she says.

I retract my hand. The rejection stings. Why won't she let me comfort her?

Reaching for her left hand, she twists off her wedding band and holds it out to me. I stare at it, unwilling to hear what her actions and words are telling me. This can't be over between us. Not like this. When I don't take the ring, she drops it on the blanket. The soft *plop* echoes in my ears.

She frowns down at her ring finger, the black ink tattoo crisp and glaring in the lamp light.

All at once, everything she's said sinks in.

Born into this world.

Used for a prize.

Men who control women's fate.

She's talking about *me*. The reason she thinks my promise to protect her is an empty one is because I can't protect her from myself.

I did this to her.

Konstantin and his men took her over the edge, highlighting in bright neon marker that's been there all along. But I did this to her when I took her for myself. When I permanently stamped my name and claim of ownership on her flesh is when all of her fears came to life.

She doesn't want me. She never has. I forced her into this, and I've been too fucking delusional to see the truth. Until now.

Clearing my throat, I stand. "I'll make you an appointment to have that removed."

"It's fine. I can do it myself."

"I put it there, I should pay for its removal."

She shrugs like she really doesn't care so long as it's gone.

"I never meant to hurt you, *kisa*." My voice is barely above a whisper. "I'm sorry."

Her gaze snaps up to meet mine. *I'm sorry.* Those are words I should have said to her a long time before tonight. But I refused to admit I'd done anything wrong. I'd been too arrogant to see that I was hurting the woman I love. Now it's all quite clear.

Those two words, *I'm sorry*, have come too late.

Backing away from her, I rub at my chest where it aches. We're done.

I can't, and won't, force her to be mine anymore.

All I ever wanted was a chance with her and she gave me that. It's my own damn fault that I royally fucked it up. I held onto her too tightly, so determined to make her love me. I put her life in danger, manifested her worst fears, and broke her beautiful soul.

I've done enough damage to last a lifetime.

Slipping back out the window, I glance at her one final time. She stares at her lap. Shoulders slumped, cheeks wet with tears, head bowed. She looks like a shell of her former self.

Guilt slithers through me, eating away at my insides.

I vanish into the night—disappear from her life. Only to wind up at a pub in upstate New York, drinking my body weight in vodka ten times over.

CHAPTER 49
Arianna

Ilaria wrinkles her nose at the sight of me, but her eyes are full of compassion. "Have you been out of bed at all this week? Like... maybe to shower?" There's genuine concern in her voice.

I feel terrible wallowing in front of her when the ordeal I went through for a single day is nothing compared to what she suffered for six years. *Six years.* How is she even functioning?

I voice my thoughts. "How do you live day to day after... everything."

Her laugh is edged with a hint of hysteria. "Oh, I'm *not* okay. If that's what you're thinking. Sophia found me a really good therapist and that's helping a lot. As for the day to day... determination. I survived so much. I'm a survivor and I won't let anyone take that away from me. I function daily, mostly normally, because I want my life back." Her stormy grey eyes briefly flash with rage. "Survival is a choice. But you either do or you don't. That decision is entirely up to you."

A chill sweeps through me as I listen to her speak. She's right, of course. The world and people around us throw crap our way, but it's up to us how we deal with it.

I'm still figuring out how I want to deal with everything. At this point I've lost my job, my sense of self, and... Dimitri. The anguished look in his eyes when I tried to hand him my wedding band filled me with so much self-doubt. I almost snatched it back.

But I didn't. I let the ring fall in the space empty between us because more than anything, I need a clean break.

I couldn't stand one more second of my choices not being my own. He forced me to marry him. His father forced me to divorce him. Then everything I fought for was ripped away from me in that cage. From that point on, I was nothing but property to be bought and sold, used and tossed aside. Over and over again.

I need a fresh start. Severing all ties, even distancing myself from my family, has given me room to breathe, to gain perspective.

Yes, I'm in my parents home, but I've locked myself in my room for the past week. After that first night, I've barely seen anyone. Mama and Papa still loiter, but they don't bug me. Gin spends most of her time in her own room, she's in some sort of funk that I don't have the energy to figure out right now. Sophia's attending college and lives with Roman. Ravenna checks in every day through the door, spends an hour in the hall, then leaves.

Ilaria is the first person I've let in. A conscious choice I made because I want to see her.

She sits on the bench at the foot of my bed. "So, have you decided if you want to survive or not yet?"

With a shaky inhale, I bob my head. "I want my own life."

"That's good. And when are you going to start living it?" She casually glances around my bedroom, but her tone is serious. "Life is short, Arianna. When you have it all stripped away, even for a single minute, you realize how precious it is. Don't waste your time hiding in the shadows. Figure out what you want and dive headlong into it."

"What is it you want?" I ask her.

She thinks for a few seconds. "I'm trying to figure that out. Mostly, I'm trying to discover myself. I was taken away at sixteen, I don't know who I am as an adult yet. But I'm slowly finding out." Her gaze lands on me. "But you already know what you want."

"I do?" My brows pinch together. "How do you know that?"

"You were always the decisive, headstrong one growing up. You had a million plans. Sophia told me all about your event planning and how good you are at it. How hard you've worked to make that your career. Don't give up on yourself."

I lick my parched lips, considering what she's saying. "But I've made some bad choices in the past. Ones that led me here. I don't know if I trust myself to make safer choices going forward."

"Safer choices?" She shrugs. "All we can ever do is our best. The world is full of danger no matter who you are or where you go. Sure you can try to play it safe, but then you miss out on life." Ilaria drops her gaze to her folded hands. "When my father sold me I was playing it safe. I should have run, or fought, but I didn't because that would have gotten me into more trouble. I didn't fight back because it was *safer* that way. Even at the worst times, I didn't want to die, so I played it safe. You can see where that got me."

I stare at her, speechless. I never would have thought about it like that.

"Anyway," she says. "What do I know about life? I'm just a traumatized twenty-two year old trying to start living again. I'll never be able to repay Dimitri for what he did for me. Without him, and you, I'd still be... Well, you know. Thank you for never giving up on finding me."

"I did," I admit. "After a few years, I did give up. I told Dimitri about you one time and he put the effort in to find you. I didn't even know he was doing it. He..." He rescued Ilaria as a gesture to me. To show that he listened, that he cared about me and would do anything within his power to make me happy.

How can the man who found Ilaria, who shines with fatherly love when he sees Katerina, who practically worships at my feet, be the same man who drugged and forced me to marry him? Who tattooed that I'm his *property* on my skin.

I consider everything I know about him now. How his mother died when he was so young, his father selling and abandoning him, his cousin's betrayal followed by his uncle's death.

Dimitri has abandonment issues written all over him. Is that why he's held on to me so tightly, staked his claim? He's terrified that I'll leave him?

Walking away, letting me go, must have been so difficult. But he did it. I haven't heard from him in over a week. He's not trying to force me to be with him, or choose him, or anything.

And he apologized. I never thought I'd hear those two words from his mouth. *I'm sorry.*

All this time I thought it was arrogance and an over-inflated ego that made him claim me like he did. But that's not true. It was fear. Fear drove him to possess me in every way possible. Fear of loss.

A fear he faced and let go of the night he climbed out my window. I'd fully expected him to kidnap me from my own bedroom, to beg and plead, but he didn't. For the first time, he stepped back and let me make my own choices. He didn't like my choice but he respected it by leaving.

You're the strongest woman I've ever met. His voice rings clearly in my memory. *Don't let anyone take that away from you. Don't take that away from yourself.*

My heartbeat pounds in my ears, drowning out all other sounds. I need more time to think, to figure out what I really want my life to look like.

"Thank you," I say to Ilaria. "I'm so glad you're back."

She smiles sweetly. "I'm glad to be back too."

A knock sounds on my door. "Come in."

My mother peeks her head in before fully stepping into the room. Shooting Ilaria a welcoming grin, she hovers over my bed.

"You know I love you and want what's best for you." Mama rubs my shoulder. "Don't you, *mio tesoro?*"

I nod. "Yes, Mama."

"Good. So that's why you're going to get up, shower, and come out with me tonight."

I open my mouth to protest, but she keeps talking.

"Mrs. De Luca is having a small gathering at her house. It will be safe and intimate. I don't want any argument from you, young lady, you will get dressed and come to dinner. You've been hulled up in this room for too long."

I glance at Ilaria for support but she just says, "It's time."

I'm out numbered. With a groan, I haul myself out of bed.

The gathering at Mrs. De Luca's house is relatively small, only about thirty or so people. As soon as we enter, though after the required niceties, Mrs. De Luca sweeps Mama away for herself. They became fast friends as soon as they met and have been inseparable ever since. I know Mrs. De Luca likes me fine, but we don't have a friendship like her and Mama, more of a professional relationship.

The moment I'm left alone, Connor Bane appears at my side. I stifle a groan. I'm pretty sure we've already had whatever conversation he has in mind—on New Year's Eve. Can't he leave me alone?

I pick up a flute of champagne and drain it in two swallows—very unladylike. Connor takes my empty glass and hands me a full one.

I lift a brow, finally meeting his gaze. His striking blue eyes swim with concern, making me uncomfortable.

How much does everyone know about what happened? God, I really don't want to be the center of gossip. Not tonight, and not ever.

When I try to move past him, Connor places his hands on my shoulders and steps in front of me. His body language is clear. There's no escaping him.

"I'm so sorry." His voice is low, for my ears only. "I never meant to put you in harms way. I didn't think—" he cuts himself off.

My narrowed gaze snaps up to his. "What are you apologizing for exactly?" My heart's galloping so hard that I have to strain my ears to hear his reply.

"I didn't think they'd hurt you. That man told me he would free you from Kozlov, that's all he wanted. I know that's what you wanted too, so I told them..."

"You told them what?" I'm pretty sure Connor's grip is the only thing holding me up right now. "Who?"

He features twist. Remorse blazes in his brilliant eyes. "Konstantin. That was the man's name. He came sniffing around for information on Dimitri. I heard about it, confronted him, and he told me what he was up to. So I told him everything you said to me about being forced into marriage, your signature forged, and how you wanted a divorce." His thumbs skim up and down my bare arms. "I thought if I could free you from him then you'd give me another chance. I never thought they'd hurt you. I'm so sorry."

"You..." I breathe the word on an exhale. My mind reels. I do remember him confronting me at Leonidas that one time. I'd been so flustered that I'd told Connor the highlights. I never thought that quick conversation would come back to bite me.

I'd never figured out how Konstantin knew the details about what went on between me and Dimitri. Maks was the only one who knew. And Connor. How had I overlooked Connor?

He's the snake. The one who gave Konstantin the information he needed to set this all in motion. And it's my fault for giving Connor those private details in the first place. I feel sick.

I clear my throat, trying to find my voice. "You did this?"

"I had to get you away from him. The opportunity presented itself and I took it."

"You have no idea what you've done." I yank free from his grip. "You have no idea what you put us through."

"Us?" He sneers. "You're divorced."

"Because of *you*."

"Don't tell me you're actually in love with that Russian piece of trash. I heard his mother was a whore and—"

I deck him. People around us gasp. Jarring pain shoots across my knuckles and up my arm. Damn that *hurts*.

Connor rubs his jaw. "I guess that answers that question."

"Go to hell." I gulp down my champagne and shove the empty glass in his chest. "Don't ever speak to me again."

I spin on my heel, going straight for the exit. I'm not even entirely sure where I'm headed until I hail a cab and give the driver Dimitri's penthouse address at Riot.

My rage slowly fades as it's replaced with nerves. I'm

on my way to see Dimitri and, what..? Apologize? Beg him to take me back?

I'm still reeling from the knowledge that I'm in love with him.

I want him.

I choose him.

My fresh start includes him and I'm more than okay with that choice.

We pull up in front of Riot and I pay the cabbie. Weaving my way through the club, I press my thumb to the biometric scanner at the elevator, somewhat surprised when it works. He hasn't removed me from the system.

Hope springs free in my chest as I ride the elevator up, then knock on Dimitri's door. I don't want to barge in on him. Waiting for him to answer, I smooth down my dress and fidget with my hair, hoping I look okay.

The door opens and Maks stands at the threshold. "It's about fucking time," he grumbles.

"It's good to see you, too." I shoot him a curious frown and step into the penthouse. "What..." the word dies on my tongue. This gorgeous place is completely trashed. Takeout containers cover every horizontal surface, empty vodka bottles are lined up on the counter-top, some furniture is toppled over. Dead flowers have withered in their vases. What happened here?

I glance up at Maks who exasperatedly shakes his head.

"He's passed out over there." Maks points to a corner where the floor to ceiling windows meet. There's a bare mattress on the floor, Dimitri's prone form on top of it.

Oh my god. "Did you just find him like this?" I ask, moving further into the living room.

"Yeah. He stopped checking in with me a few days ago and I finally tracked him down. What a fucking mess." He grabs a plastic bag and starts cleaning up.

Unsure of exactly what to do, I hesitantly approach Dimitri. He's wearing black jeans and a stained T-shirt. Several days worth of growth darkens his jawline. His relaxed fingers circle the neck of a vodka bottle. I crouch down, taking the drink away, and notice the puffy dark circles under his eyes, fresh bruises on his face, and hair matted with what can only be blood.

God, what's happened to him? He looks like he came from a bar fight.

"Maks, will you help me with him? Let's get him in the shower."

CHAPTER 50
Dimitri

The first time I regain consciousness must be a dream because I'm drenched in hot water with the most gorgeous sight before my eyes. Arianna's soaked through, wearing a cream dress that clings to her curves, leaving little to the imagination. Her hands are all over me as she peels my clothes off. When she shoves my jeans down, my raging wood springs free.

A deep chuckle sounds to my left, but I can't tear my eyes from my *kisa*.

"He must know you're here because that boner sure as fuck isn't for me."

"*Maks*," Arianna chides. "Just hold him up so I can get his jeans off. That's one foot. Now the other." She stands, looking up at me. "Dima?"

"*Kisa*." My vision darkens and fades away.

The second time I wake my head hurts so badly that I groan and roll over, letting sleep take away the pain.

"Kisa, please. *Please.* No, don't go away." I wake myself up, the nightmare fresh in my mind. A devastating sense of loss settles deep in my bones. My empty stomach twists and heaves. Squeezing my eyes shut against the raging late morning, or maybe afternoon, light, I reach for the vodka that must be here somewhere. Only my fingers don't scrape against cool glass, they find warm skin instead.

I freeze.

Did I bring someone home last night? Did I cheat on my wife? *Fucking hell.*

That annoying voice in the back of my head reminds me that she's not my wife anymore. She took off her ring and dumped my ass. One heart-wrenching conversation and we were done.

Over.

Finished.

Where's my fucking booze? I know from experience that I have to drown out that little voice, those reminders of what happened before they take hold or I'd spend the day spiraling into despair so deep that it smothered out all possible reasons for living. But no matter how many fights I've gotten into, not one of those fuckers did me the mercy of finishing me off.

Life is just cruel.

I can't find my fucking vodka bottle anywhere. Rubbing my eyes, I mentally prepare myself for whatever poor woman I brought home last night. She must be desperate to have wanted to jump in bed with me. Yeah, no, I have no memory of a woman or anything we probably did.

Jesus Christ. This is a new low.

I thought I'd hit bottom, but I guess not yet. Have I finally arrived?

Squinting, I glance at the woman lying beside me in bed. In... my bedroom. Not on the mattress on the living room floor. What the fuck is going on?

All I can see of her is half her face, but she looks so much like Arianna, with her dark hair, that my heart begins to race.

Now I'm picking up women who look like *her*? This is a form of self-punishment that even I didn't think I was capable of inflicting. That's just harsh. I'm a fucking masochist.

"You need to leave," I tell the woman.

She startles awake. Fuck, I'm such an asshole, but I can't deal with this right now. It's too shameful. I never fucked another woman after the first time I saw Arianna and followed her into that alley. Every time I even thought about having sex with someone all I could see was her gorgeous face. I waited years for her, only her, and now in the span of a week I've...

"Dimitri?" Her voice drags my gaze to her. She sits up, wearing one of my T-shirts, her hair disheveled. "I'm so, so sorry."

I stare at her, unbelieving.

Now I'm fucking hallucinating? How much vodka did I drink?

"You're not real," I tell this illusion. "There's no fucking way you went from dumping me to being in my bed. That's some crazy shit right there."

Her low chuckle startles me. "I had to get you cleaned and patched up with Maks's help. I wasn't going to strip in front of Maks and then get in the shower. My dress is at the dry cleaners. As for being in your bed this morning, after we tucked you in you wouldn't let me go. So I had to stay." When all I do is stare, she continues, "I'm sorry, Dima. I freaked out and needed time and space to think things through."

As soon as she called me *Dima*, my denial rushed away. Arianna. She's here, in my bed, talking to me. I sit up and my head spins. But I ignore it as I focus on the woman I can't live without.

"And?" I prompt. "Did you think things through?"

She reaches for me and I stay completely still, afraid to move and break this spell. "I want a fresh start. With you." She cups my cheek, then her palm falls away. "If you'll have me, that is."

I frown at her. "You choose me?"

"I choose you." Her gaze is so full of hope and uncertainty that it crushes me.

I launch myself at her, pin her beneath my body and

kiss her. This kiss conveys all the anguish, desperation, and love that I feel. She gives as good as she gets. Her fingers thread into my hair, holding me to her like she's afraid I'll float away.

Easing up for a second, I strip my T-shirt from her body, then devour her mouth. She wraps her legs around my hips. My rock hard cock slides against her pussy, becoming slick with her wetness.

"Is this what you want, *kisa?*" I ask, pressing the head of my dick into her tight hole.

"I want all of you." She pants. "Give me all of you."

I ease into her, inch by inch. It's both excruciating and intoxicating. "You have all of me. I've always been, and always will be, yours."

"I love you." Her words are a salve to my tattered soul.

I bury myself in her, drinking in her floral scent. "I love you more."

CHAPTER 51
Dimitri

"Are you sure she'll like it?" I ask Sophia, fussing with the diamond ring as it catches the light. The impressive twenty carat, princess cut rock is set in a simple but elegant band. Maçon Jewelers followed my instructions perfectly. But I wanted to make sure it was ideal for Arianna, which is why I asked her sisters and cousin here today.

Three faces beam up at me. Ginevra is practically bouncing with excitement, unable to take her eyes off the diamond. Ravenna gives me that reassuring smile that sets me at ease.

"It's just right. She'll love it," Sophia confirms. "Good luck tonight."

"Thanks." Nerves rattle through me. Tonight's a big night.

They let themselves out of our newly renovated penthouse. Thank fuck the ring is perfect. Now for the rest of it...

I get dressed in the tailored suit I ordered. Fastening

the tie, I admire my handiwork in the mirror before slipping on my shoes. Arianna will be home from work any moment now.

As if on cue, the front door opens.

"Dimitri, are you—" She stops in her tracks, her hungry gaze travels down and back up my body. She licks her lips, and I seriously consider staying in tonight. "Are we going out?"

"Yes. There's a dress for you on the bed. Put it on." I kiss her, then point her toward our bedroom.

"Are we celebrating something?" Her brow furrows as if she's trying to remember an important date she may have forgotten. "You're wearing a suit."

I chuckle as she states the obvious. "We're celebrating your new job." The white lie slides off my tongue. Okay, maybe it's more of a half-truth than a lie. Her boss did hire her back at Leonidas and today was her first day at work. Which is worthy of celebration. "Now go get dressed." I slap her lightly on the ass.

Half an hour later we're ready to leave. We take the limo across town to Arianna's favorite Lebanese restaurant, Al-Amir. She perks up as I help her out of the car and we head for the door. Her expression falls when she notices the dark curtain drawn across the windows.

"I think they're closed," she says. "That's too bad."

I can barely hide my smirk. "Let's just try the door. Oh look, it's unlocked."

Guiding her inside, we slip through the curtain. My smirk blooms into a smile when Arianna gasps.

A trail of flower petals leads to a single, candle-lit table in the middle of the restaurant. All around us is a sea of floral arrangements, glowing candles, and soft music. The scent of cardamom, cumin, and garlic drifts through the air. Arianna is stunned, taking it all in.

I move in front of her and drop to one knee, pulling the ring box from my pocket. Her eyes widen. Nerves spike through me from what I'm about to ask.

"First I was drawn to your innocence and beauty. I thought I fell in love with you when I was an outsider looking in, observing your life from afar. But I was wrong." I clear my throat, gathering my thoughts. "I fell in love with you when I discovered your intelligence, your stubborn determination, and your compassion. Every time you fought me, I fell a little more. Every time you showed me compassion when you had every reason not to, I fell a little harder.

"You are the bravest, strongest, most driven woman I've ever met. Being with you makes me strive to be worthy of you each and every day. We come from different cultures and backgrounds, but I have no doubt in my mind that you're my soulmate and I want to spend the rest of my life with you." I open the box. "Arianna Pontrelli, will you be my wife?"

Her lips part as she gazes at the massive sparkling diamond. Then she focuses on me, and without warning, throws herself into my arms. I catch her with a startled laugh.

"Yes." She cups my face and kisses me. "A million times, yes."

My chest floods with warmth as I slide the engagement ring on her finger. She's mine. And I'm hers. Forever and always.

Three Months Later

"No. *No.*" Arianna whimpers in her sleep. She thrashes against an invisible attacker and I reach out to calm her. She's having another nightmare about the cage. It's always about being taken and put in that kennel.

"Shh. Wake up, *kisa*. Come here. I've got you." I pull her against my side, stroking her hair to gently wake her up.

Her eyelids flutter open and she focuses on me. "Dima." She sighs, plastering herself against my body.

Minutes later, she's fallen asleep again, but this time she'll have peaceful dreams. As long as I'm holding her, she sleeps soundly. After how she pushed me away when she went through that traumatizing experience, I'm glad she now seeks refuge and comfort in my presence. I bury my nose in her hair, inhaling her sweet scent.

The hour is still early so I drift off again for a while. When her alarm goes off, we spend the morning making love, showering, then grabbing a bite to eat before she heads to work. I kiss her good-bye before she leaves the penthouse.

Something about today feels different than other mornings. I'm finally ready to fully let go of the past.

With that in mind, I take the elevator to the garage and take my Harley out for a ride. Not just anywhere though, I head out of town to a remote, secure warehouse where I've stashed the remainder of my haunted past.

Inside, I take the stairs down to the dank basement. The only thing on this level is the holding cell and its occupant. Quietly, I step inside and close the door behind me.

The naked man sitting in the corner is not Konstantin Kozlov—not anymore. He's a broken, frail thing that's been stripped of not only his name, wealth, and power, but also his identity. The man who used to hold so much power over me, who gave Arianna night terrors, I've reduced to nothing over the last few months.

Now that there's nothing left to break in him, enough is enough. I'm done holding onto the past, the rage, and my need for vengeance.

Next month I'll marry the woman I love. I want a fresh, clean start.

Grabbing my gun, I point it at the shell of a man who's barely registered my presence with his one remaining eye.

"This is for what you did to my mother." I pull the trigger. He howls in pain, clutching his thigh. "This is for Uncle Vadim." I shoot him in the shoulder. "And this is for *my wife*."

A bullet to the heart shuts him up for good.

All I feel is relief as I walk away, toward a much brighter future.

Epilogue - Arianna

"You look perfect, sweetheart. Are you about ready?" I ask Katerina and she nods. She looks adorable in her pink and white flower girl dress, basket of rose petals clutched in her tiny hands. Dimitri and I adopted her as soon as we were officially engaged and it's been the best decision. She's ours now, a part of our family.

My father clears his throat and offers his arm. "The real question is are *you* ready?"

"Yes, Papa, I am." I take his arm, my heartbeat picking up speed. "I'm ready."

We leave the bridal preparation suite in the old cathedral and walk toward the chapel where all of our guests have gathered. This is the wedding of my dreams. I'm wearing a one-of-a-kind gown created by Skye Adair. A plethora of flowers bring a romantic quality to the venue, and beyond the sea of people who've come to witness our nuptials stands the man I love.

Live music starts up and the procession begins. I

chose Sophia as my maid of honor, and Ginevra and Ilaria as my bridesmaids. Standing beside Dimitri are Maks, Roman, and Blake.

As soon as my gaze falls on my soon-to-be husband it doesn't waver. He's ridiculously handsome in that tuxedo. His shoulders relaxed, his olive green eyes full of wonder as he stares back at me. He's the last man on earth I thought I'd marry, but now the only man I want. Forever.

Papa shakes Dimitri's hand, his grip stronger than it needs to be. When I move toward my fiancé, Papa tightens his hold, forcing me to glance at him. He frowns, his expression grim.

Papa ducks his head to whisper in my ear. "Are you sure about this? I can find a way to have him eliminated. You don't have to marry him."

"Papa," I gently chide. "I'm marrying him. I love him."

His frown deepens, but he gives a curt nod. Releasing me, he shoots Dimitri a death glare. I'm beginning to doubt they'll ever warm to each other.

Dimitri barely seems to register my father's wrath. His gaze remains locked on mine, taking in all of me while the priest performs the ceremony. It all goes by so quickly and then it's time to say our vows.

Dimitri takes my hand in his, a serious expression on his handsome face. "I, Dimitri Kozlov, take you, Arianna Pontrelli, to be my lawfully wedded wife, to have and to hold, for better, for worse, for richer, for poorer, in sickness and in health. I promise to be the best man for you each and every day. I will strive to be worthy of you, to protect you, and to always give you a choice. I shall love and cherish you, till death do us part. This is my solemn vow."

I swallow past the tears clogging my throat as he slides the diamond studded gold ring on my tattooed finger. I never made that appointment to have it removed.

"I, Arianna Pontrelli take you, Dimitri Kozlov, to be my lawfully wedded husband, to have and to hold, for better, for worse, for richer, for poorer, in sickness and in health. I will strive to love you as you deserve to be loved each and every day. I shall cherish you, till death do us part. This is my solemn vow."

I take his hand, lowering my gaze to the wedding band as I slip it on his finger, and freeze. The dark ink encircling his ring finger is new. My heart floats up to my throat, rendering me speechless.

The words he had tattooed, I can clearly read. *Property of Arianna Kozlov.*

I settle his wedding band over those words. Sealing them forever.

"I now pronounce you husband and wife, you may kiss—"

Dimitri sweeps me up in his arms, his mouth crashing down on mine and I open for him. The priest grumbles something about patience being a virtue, but I can barely hear him over the roar of applause.

Our kiss becomes languid and I suck in a breath of air. "*Ti amo,*" I whisper.

"*YA lyublyu tebya,*" he murmurs against my lips.

After receiving an overwhelming number of congratulations, we make our way out of the church and to the reception venue. For the next several hours we dance, eat and drink, and mingle with our friends and family. The celebratory atmosphere buzzes all around us. I relax against Dimitri's side and he loops his arm around my waist. He feels like home.

He and Maks are deep in conversation, so I let my gaze travel the room. Ginevra's loud giggle draws my attention to where she's dancing with one of Dimitri's men. She keeps glancing over his shoulder and I turn slightly to follow her gaze.

Blake Baron stands against the wall with a murderous expression. His knuckles are white from how hard he clutches his champagne glass. Any moment now it's going to crack. His stare bores into Gin. I glance back and forth at them just to be sure. There's certainly something going on with them.

My guess is confirmed when Blake downs his drink, drops the empty glass on a tray, and storms over to Ginevra. He grabs her by the arm, yanking her away from her dance partner. The man backs off immediately.

Blake drags my sister to the stage and taps on the mic. The band falls silent and everyone turns to gawk at them.

"Sorry to interrupt," Black says, sounding anything but apologetic. "We have an announcement on this happy occasion." He hauls Ginevra close to him. "Let me introduce you to my future wife Ginevra Pontrelli."

Gin's eyes widen with shock and horror. Her lips part, but for the first time in her life no sound comes out. Stunned silence fills the ballroom.

The smile that twists Blake Baron's lips is that of a satiated predator who just devoured his favorite prey.

Oh, Gin, what have you done?

Are you excited for Blake and Ginevra's book next? It's a grumpy/sunshine, age gap, fake fiancée/fake marriage, billionaire romance.

In order to access his inheritance, Blake Baron must marry. When he catches Ginevra Pontrelli stealing a priceless possession, he gives her two choices: Either face criminal charges or temporarily become his fake wife.

Pre-order *FOREVER FAKE.*

Do you want more of Dimitri and Arianna? Grab their bonus epilogue here: subscribepage.io/uVuYMo

XX,
Cassia

Newsletter Signup

For works in progress updates and new release announcements, as well as giveaways, author life snippets, and more, sign up for Cassia Quinn's newsletter: www.CassiaQuinn.com

Acknowledgments

I'd like to thank my husband and alpha reader for suffering through this book. No, I'm not going to give Dimitri a mullet. LMAO.

Andra Kapule, your encouragement, feedback, and support means the world to me. Thank you!

To my friend, and fellow romance author, Luna Pierce, thanks for letting me include your brainchild The Manor Manhattan in this book from your *Sinners and Angels Universe*.

Geissa Cecilia with GP Author Services, thanks for dealing with my insane timelines. I appreciate you!

Thank you to all of my readers! I wouldn't be able to create these stories and live this author dream without so. XO.

About the Author

Cassia Quinn writes billionaire romance with steam and angst. She currently resides in the Pacific Northwest with her husband and kitty fur babies. Her favorite activity is reading on rainy days with a glass of wine.

Keep In Touch With Cassia Quinn

Facebook Reader Group:
https://www.facebook.com/groups/cassiaquinnromance

Website:
www.CassiaQuinn.com

Instagram:
https://www.instagram.com/cassiaquinnauthor/

TikTok:
https://www.tiktok.com/@cassiaquinnauthor

BookBub:
https://www.bookbub.com/profile/cassia-quinn

GoodReads:
https://www.goodreads.com/cassiaquinn